NEW HAVEN PUBLIC LIBRARY

W9-CMN-569

3 5000 09341 4539

DATE DUE

SEP 1 1 2004

OFFICIALLY WITHDRAWN
NEW HAVEN FREE PUBLIC LIBRARY

MAR 0 4 2024

Under the Manhattan Bridge

Irene Marcuse

A Tom Doherty Associates Book • New York

FREE PUBLIC LIBRARY
133 ELM STREET
NEW HAVEN, CT 06510

Under the Manhattan Bridge

This is a work of fiction. All the characters and events portrayed in this novel are either fictitious or are used fictitiously.

UNDER THE MANHATTAN BRIDGE

Copyright © 2004 by Irene Marcuse

All rights reserved, including the right to reproduce this book, or portions thereof, in any form.

This book is printed on acid-free paper.

A Forge Book
Published by Tom Doherty Associates, LLC
175 Fifth Avenue
New York, NY 10010

www.tor.com

Forge® is a registered trademark of Tom Doherty Associates, LLC.

Library of Congress Cataloging-in-Publication Data

Marcuse, Irene, 1953–
    Under the Manhattan bridge / Irene Marcuse.—1st ed.
        p. cm.
    "A Tom Doherty Associates book."
    ISBN 0-765-30804-5
    EAN 978-0765-30804-7
    1. Servi, Anita (Fictitious character)—Fiction. 2. Brooklyn (New York, N.Y.)—Fiction. 3. Seventh-Day Adventists—Fiction. 4. Women social workers—Fiction. 5. Artists—Fiction. 6. Jews—Fiction. I. Title.

PS3563.A6433U53 2004
813'.6—dc22

                                                            2003071104

First Edition: July 2004

Printed in the United States of America

0 9 8 7 6 5 4 3 2 1

For Philip,
again and always

Acknowledgments

Thanks to my readers, who gave up hours of their time for no more than a free book, the rare opportunity to give me solicited advice, and this fragment of glory: Philip Silver, prince among men; Janet Jaffe, sister by choice, opinionated by nature; Peter Marcuse, dad, etc.; and R. M. Peluso, soon-to-be-published protégé. Also to the writing group—Gordon Cotler, Eleanor Hyde, Beatrice Selden Rosen, Leah Ruth Robinson, and Timothy Sheard—for shorter chapters and keeping me on track, and to Ellen Pall for moral support.

Several people helped with technical information: Darryl Keil and Dan at Vacuum Pressing Systems told me how not to use their machines; Cathy Schechter and Rob Mandel provided deep background; David Edelstein led me on an insider's tour of Williamsburg; Deborah Karpatkin and Bruce Trauner handled the legal niceties.

Although it may seem out of place in this book, I need to give a shout-out to adoptive parents, especially Carol Gross, Ann and Tim Lacy, Susan Livermore and Christopher Thomson, Ellen Pall and Richard Deckerd, and Roslyn Weinstein. You all know why.

Oh yeah—thanks also to *One Life to Live,* for inadvertent, environmentally correct assistance.

And Tabitha, here's to the future.

Under the Manhattan Bridge

One

IT ALL SEEMED TO COME AT ONCE. I BROUGHT MY BEST FRIEND,
Barbara, to the hospital the night before the planes hit the
Trade Center Towers. Her funeral was on September twenti-
eth. Eleven days later, I found the body in the vacuum press.

Benno was the one who made the 911 call.

I was alone in the finishing room when I found it. I think I
went into some kind of shock. I walked up the stairs to tell my
husband. When I got to him, I seemed not to have any words
whatsoever at my disposal. I tugged at his arm until he followed me down to see what was wrong.

If it had happened a week earlier, my husband could've sum-
moned a cop by opening a window and hollering down to the
street. Since September thirteenth, the cross streets between his
woodshop and a Con Edison generating plant that occupies a
quarter-mile stretch of Brooklyn waterfront have been blocked
off by hulking green sanitation trucks. At each intersection, a
squad car and two uniformed officers kept watch.

The trucks were still there on October first, but the human
presence had been reduced to a command post three blocks up-
river. Security, I know, but it didn't make me feel any more
protected. What were those barricades going to do? Prevent a
truck bomb from blowing up Con Ed—sure, by allowing it to
explode right in front of our door.

And where were the police when the body got itself into our
vacuum press?

For two decades, Benno's cabinetry shop was located on Canal Street. Courtesy of a building owner eager to convert the light-industrial loft spaces to residential units, he was forced east across the river this past January. Linearly, it was less than three miles from Tribeca to Dumbo—Down Under the Manhattan Bridge Overpass—in Brooklyn. Financially, by the time the new space was fixed up with machines, lights, outlets, and a dust-collection system, well, you don't want to know.

When I first started working with Benno, he treated me like any apprentice, and I sanded my little hands off. What I'd wanted was a respite from social work, a chance to use my hands rather than my heart; learning the fine art of woodworking from the basics up wasn't what I had in mind. Eventually the boss let me try spraying, his least-favorite part of the job. Turned out I could keep up a steady flow and lay a light, wet coat of lacquer on even the largest cabinet door. It's an art, finishing, and I was surprisingly good at it.

Apart from the toxic fumes that meant I had to wear a heavy-duty vapor mask and filter apparatus, I liked the work. It was rhythmic, peaceful, challenging enough that my mind was occupied with what I was doing but not so demanding that I lay awake at night worrying over how to approach the next set of cabinet parts. A relief from the sometimes insoluble problems of my former clients.

After September 11, we were extremely grateful to have moved when we did. The building where Benno's shop had been, although structurally intact, was off-limits inside the frozen zone for several long weeks. Thanks to our former landlord, we watched the disaster from the safety of Brooklyn, our main worry being how to get back onto the island where Clea, our twelve-year-old daughter, was in school.

All the bridges and tunnels into Manhattan were sealed off. Stunned pedestrians flowed steadily out of the city, but no one was allowed in, not even on foot. In the end, it was the subway that got us home. God bless the MTA; by three they had trains back up and running.

I'm drifting away from the other thing, the body in the vacuum press.

The main shop occupied the entire three-thousand-square-foot fourth floor of the former Peerless Paint building on Plymouth Street. We also rented half of the third floor—my domain, otherwise known as the spray room. When I first noticed the odor, I attributed it to the air blowing in through the open windows from lower Manhattan.

Even though I was working with lacquer, I closed them. The chemical fumes smelled better than what was outside. After the weekend, however, the stench of organic decay was unmistakable—sweet and rotten. I figured there was a poisoned rat decomposing in the walls somewhere.

I only uncovered the vacuum press because I thought I heard the motor cycle on. Just a faint hum, easy to miss if you weren't standing right next to it.

A vacuum press is exactly what it sounds like, a machine that sucks the air out of a bag and presses down on the bag's contents. Benno kept his downstairs in the spray room because of its size. Basically, the thing is a sheet of plywood inside a heavy-duty, clear plastic bag with a sort of reverse-vacuum-cleaner motor attached by a hose. You insert whatever you're gluing, seal the bag at both ends, flip the switch, and the motor sucks all the air out. It's a wonderful tool. Exerts a steady, even pressure, two thousand pounds per square foot.

The press was covered, first by a blue wool electric blanket that regulated the temperature while Benno was gluing, then with a stack of thick, quilted furniture blankets. I'd thrown a piece of plastic sheeting over the top to protect it from random drifts of sprayed lacquer. Mostly I ignored the thing. It took up half the far wall, tucked into a corner, a rarely used object. The suction could have been cycling on for weeks without me noticing.

I bent down to switch the motor off, and noticed a fan-shaped mark on the wall. When I touched it, the tip of my finger came away stained dark red. Rather than hitting the button to stop the suction, I rocked back on my heels and tried to figure out what was going on.

The hose from the bag was equipped with an exhaust filter to prevent the motor from being fouled by any dust and moisture that might be sucked out. The filter spits what it can't handle through a small vent. Thus, the splatter on the wall.

But what was it? Red, damp. And the smell—I already knew what came next would be bad.

The vacuum maintained, the machine cycled off. I let it be and stood to pull the blankets off the table. For the longest minute, my brain refused to process what lay in front of me.

The shape of the thing was recognizably human yet subtly distorted. The bag of the press had followed the contours of the body even as it flattened them. The feet had been forced straight down, unnaturally elongating the silhouette. The nose, held in place from the sides as well as above, retained more of its shape.

Apart from a sleeveless white undershirt the body was

naked, and clearly male. His skin was the mottled purplish blue of a bruise. Streaks of vivid red drained from the face and filled the creases between plastic, table, and flesh.

That'll teach you to uncover things, I thought.

I had the sensation of my own bodily fluids being compelled toward the surface of my skin, capillaries rupturing from the pressure of liquid seeking exit from every opening. Mouth, nose, ears, eyes, orifices leaking life. I reached to wipe my cheek. Looking at my hand, I expected blood but saw only tears.

For how long had I not known about this presence in my space? How long had I been inhaling his spirit with the very air I breathed?

But then, there were so many lost spirits floating around us.

After the planes hit, when people on fire fell from above; when the people inside were crushed by pancaking floors; when the whole of lower Manhattan was obscured, what we heard and felt in Brooklyn was the silent, searing aloneness of those souls set wrenchingly free, drifting across the river in a constant plume of smoke and ash.

In the aftermath of skies with no planes, streets with no trucks, car horns not honking, the great exodus of people on foot not speaking, I was still spooked. In that silence, I heard a roar. Like standing on the rim of the Grand Canyon, all that vast silent emptiness ringing in your ears, except in this absence of sound there was no peace.

The body in the press put me as close as I've ever come to falling apart. Not another death, I couldn't bear another death. Maybe without everything else, I'd've been able to pull myself together. Maybe.

TWO

WE WAITED ON THE STEPS IN FRONT OF THE BUILDING FOR THE police to arrive. It was another in a string of gorgeous blue days. When I closed my eyes to the sun, the color inside my lids went red, and I had to open them again.

"Did you recognize him?" Benno asked me.

"No, did you?" I turned to study my husband. Handsomer than ever, his face with the character lines of maturity, hair still black and thick as the proverbial sheep's.

"No."

I settled back against his side. That's marriage for you, the ability to let your thoughts drift off and know the other will still be there when they land.

It would've helped to know who the dead man was.

Exactly what the Brooklyn cops thought.

Not that any of them said so much as a word to either Benno or me. We were made to hover in the hall outside the spray room, guarded by a uniform with muscle-bound arms.

"So do they have any idea who this guy is?" Benno tried to make conversation and got a beefy-shouldered shrug in non-answer.

We gleaned a bit of information by listening while the people in white jumpsuits with "Crime Scene Officer" on their backs did their jobs. The pair of them pretty much filled the room, taking pictures, putting things in plastic bags, dusting other things with little brushes.

Like tea to China, I thought, adding dust to a woodshop. Although my area was relatively dust-free, what with the need to— Shut up with the jokes, Anita, I told myself.

What I gathered was that due to the unusual condition of being hermetically sealed in plastic, no one had a fast answer about when the owner of the body had died, or how long it had been in the press. More than a day, less than two weeks, was the consensus on the scene.

As to identification, pending a lengthy process with missing persons and/or the long shot of fingerprints or DNA matching anyone they had on file, all they knew about the guy was that he appeared to be in his late teens. One of the techs noticed that the white undershirt had knotted fringes in the corners, meaning it could be tzitzis, the undergarment worn by Orthodox Jews, so there was a probable on his religion as well.

After much discussion, they decided to take the entire vacuum press with them—motor, table, bag, macabre occupant, all in one piece. Better to unseal it in the morgue, they thought, let the mess spill out there.

Much better, Benno agreed.

Then the detective showed up, and her familiar face prompted my first smile since I'd uncovered the boy in the press.

"Inez!" Detective Collazo used to be on foot patrol in the Manhattan precinct where we live. Promoted, now she was out of uniform and in a moss-green pantsuit with jacket cut loose enough to drape nicely over the gun under her left arm.

I hadn't seen her in years. This would be the third time we'd met at the scene of an unnatural death.

After a look at the spray room and the body, she asked if there was someplace else we could talk.

"Upstairs," Benno answered. We settled into the office in

the main shop, a raised room he built over a storage area for unused lumber. I sat in the swivel chair. Benno brought stools for himself and Inez.

"Start at the beginning, Anita. What made you uncover the—vacuum press?" She looked to Benno for confirmation that she'd gotten the name right.

For Inez, I began to speak. "I heard this whirring noise, like the motor, so I went over to check if it was on." I stopped, remembering what I'd seen then.

"And was it?" Inez prompted.

"Yes. Then I saw the bloodstain on the wall, only I didn't know it was blood. I couldn't figure it out. I mean, I knew it was something from the filter—the filter keeps the motor from getting fouled up by spraying out gunk."

"What did you do then?"

"The motor cycled off. The vacuum shouldn't have been on if nothing was in the press, so I dumped the blankets on the floor to see what it was."

Remembering what the body looked like shocked me into silence again.

Inez kept asking things like *Did you recognize . . . When was the last time . . . How often do you . . . When did you notice . . . How does . . .*

Benno answered as best he could. It was all so vague. The press hadn't been used in months. I wanted to help him but I found nothing to say. My teeth made little clicking sounds when I tried to open my mouth.

That seemed to mean something to Inez, and she stopped the questions.

"She's in shock. Is there something we can use to keep her warm?"

Benno found a stray furniture blanket and wrapped it around my shoulders. The smell of wood dust was lovely in my nostrils. I smiled at my husband. That got me an icy liquid shot of fire: vodka kept in the freezer for the end of a long day.

It did the trick almost too well.

"How are your kids?" I asked Inez. If I remembered right, she had two; one Clea's age, the other a few years older.

"They're fine, Anita." To Benno she said, "I just have a few more questions. First, who knew about the vacuum press? Not just what it was, but how to work it."

That was the question, wasn't it. Smart woman, Inez, I thought.

"Who knows?" Benno said. "I mean, people are in and out of here. I get deliveries, garbage pickup, the landlord's guys. There's not quite so much traffic downstairs, though—Anita?"

"It's hard to say. We've only been here since February, but remembering everyone who came in and out, I don't know . . ."

"You keep a calendar?" Inez pointed to the desk.

"That might help." Benno flipped back to the beginning of the year and started paging through the days.

I got my own date book out of my bag, although I didn't think it would do much good. Now that I didn't have a regular job, I kept it mostly for doctor's appointments and the various social doings of Clea, the family member with the most active schedule. I also kept sporadic track of hours worked, which ranged from day-long stints of spraying lacquer to occasional bill paying or lending Benno a hand.

We both got to the month of June at the same time. Benno had been tying up the loose ends of a big project, starting to plot out delivery and installation. I'm not big enough for the physical work of lifting and holding cabinets, so he'd been looking to hire someone.

"June fourth," Benno said. "I talked to a couple of guys about working with me for a few days. Anita, do you remember if I brought them downstairs?"

"I've got their names in my book, too, so you probably did. Roger Madison and Ricardo Padilla, but you didn't hire them, did you?" The names conjured up no images of the men they belonged to, although I had some memory of Benno and a couple of guys standing around the finished pieces in the spray room. What I recollected was wishing they'd get on with it and leave so I could get back to work.

"No, because Grant finally returned my calls. Grant Farrell," he explained to Inez. "He's a sculptor I've known for a few years—in fact, he helped me locate this space—and he's done installations with me before."

"I'll need contact information for all of them," Inez said.

"Roger and Ricardo, all I have is phone numbers." Benno read them off. "Grant has a studio in the building on Front and Jay, but I don't think he was ever in the spray room. I had the cabinets delivered to the job site, and Grant met me there—oh, yeah, I suppose the two guys who loaded the truck would've seen the press. We used all the furniture blankets to wrap the cabinets, so it would've been exposed."

Inez took down the name of Benno's trucking company, and the date.

"Do any of these people have keys to the space?" Inez, right on top of things.

"No," Benno said.

I shook my head in negative agreement. "We're the only ones with keys."

"And the landlord," Benno added.

"Who would be?"

Benno provided that information, too.

"And after June, was there anyone else?"

We went back to our respective calendars. I came up with nothing of interest. Benno paused in August.

"Carlos Sanchez." He said it reluctantly. "He's an artist, just had a one-man show. I made some curved frames for him, and we worked out the design together. He lives across the street, and he was here when I glued them up."

"I don't expect much to come of it, but I do need to talk to these people. It's simply a matter of routine," Inez soothed. "Did Mr. Sanchez have a key? Was there anyone else?"

No, and no. I pulled the furniture blanket closer around my shoulders. My teeth were chattering again.

Inez stood up and put a hand on my shoulders. "That's enough for now. Thank you both. Anita, it's good to see you. I'll be in touch later, maybe tomorrow when we know more."

Three

TUESDAY I TOOK A MENTAL HEALTH DAY AND STAYED HOME. I did a few loads of laundry and fussed with the houseplants, but I couldn't really focus on anything. I kept wondering about the young person I'd been sharing my space with. Who he was and how long he'd been there were questions for the police to answer, as was the issue of how he got there in the first place. I knew there was nothing I could do, but I fretted about all the unknowns.

Finally I got up and called Benno, hoping for answers.

Not that he had any, but he did have a story.

"One of the landlord's minions was on the doorstep when I got in this morning," Benno told me. "He wanted me to chip in to a collection so they could, quote, 'give the poor unfortunate a religious funeral and a proper burial,' unquote."

"Someone identified him already?"

"No, that's the thing. I asked, and the guy said, quote, 'A Jew is a Jew even if you don't know his name,' unquote. So I asked when the funeral would be, and he gave me some complicated answer about the public administrator and getting an unidentified body released sooner than thirty days. God knows. These guys—he said they had the plot covered, you'll pardon the pun, he was just looking for help toward the coffin. Plain pine box, how much could it cost? Anyway, I forked over a twenty."

"At least he wasn't asking you to build it for them."

"There is that." I could hear the smile in Benno's voice. "I will say, they take care of their own."

"Will you go to the funeral, whenever it is?"

Even over the phone, Benno read my subtext perfectly.

"Don't even think about it, Anita of my heart," he said, knowing I was tempted by the opportunity to experience a Jewish burial. "Just put your feminism aside for a minute and realize that as a woman unrelated to the deceased, you'd be particularly unwelcome in the cemetery."

"I could pretend I was visiting someone else's grave."

"Right, Anita, and how would you get out there?"

"Subway?"

Benno just laughed. Both his parents are buried in a big Jewish cemetery in the wilds of farthest Queens, where the E train extends a single tentacle that terminates in a spaghetti of bus routes. It's a two-hour trip, easy, by public transportation.

The truth was, I wouldn't go even if they invited me. I'd watched Barbara's coffin lowered into the ground too recently to have any desire to bear witness to another interment.

"Do you think he was Hasidic?" I asked.

Many of the aspiring young businessmen who work for Benno's landlord are. Dovid Fine himself, however, is an Israeli immigrant, the kind of Orthodox Jew known as a black-hatter.

It can be confusing. They all wear black hats, but the Orthodox go in for fedoras, while the Hasidim invariably wear *kippahs*, black velvet skullcaps, and add high-crowned, flat-brimmed hats over them on the street. The other thing that differentiates them is that Orthodox men are usually clean-shaven, while the Hasidim have full beards and long, curled locks of hair in front of their ears. It took me quite a while to get all that straight.

"He didn't have a beard or *payess*, did he?" Benno asked.

"No." I didn't want to remember the details of the boy's face.

"Then all I can tell you is that wearing tzitzis means he was an observant Jew."

"Funny that's all the clothes they left on him."

"Anita." Oh, yes, he knew me, my husband. "Don't start now."

But I was already off and speculating. Plenty of Jewish men worked in our neighborhood, Hasidim and Orthodox both, and most of them probably lived in Williamsburg, a short bus ride north of Dumbo.

"In a tight-knit community like Williamsburg, wouldn't you think they'd notice if someone went missing?"

"Assuming that's where he was from." I heard the seat of Benno's office chair squeak, and I knew he'd turned to stare out the window at the Con Ed plant. "There are Jewish neighborhoods all over Brooklyn—Borough Park, Crown Heights, Brighton Beach. He could be from anywhere."

It was true. Unattached young men are a large and fluid segment of the population. They come from all over to study in the yeshivas of New York. Some earn room and board by working in family businesses; others live in rooming houses. Dovid Fine played host to several of them.

Around the first of every month, a man in sober clothing, his face pale under black velvet *kippah*, jacket buttoned over white shirt, grubby fringes from the tzitzis sticking out below, stops by to collect the rent. It took Benno and me a few months to realize that we never saw the same man twice. I was embarrassed to admit it, but their faces all blurred together.

Any ethnic group you're not a part of, they all look alike, no matter how much you think you're paying attention.

Besides, every one of them made a stab at proselytizing. It always started the same way. First the check tucked into a vest pocket, then: "You're Jewish, aren't you?" A man is polite to his landlord, and also to his landlord's minions. Yes, Benno is Jewish.

That pretty much let me out. Although I do have a Jewish father, I didn't know it until a few years ago; I was raised by an extremely lapsed Catholic mother. Benno, on the other hand, grew up in a kosher home.

The admission of Jewishness was enough for theological discussions to ensue. Benno considers himself a spiritual atheist. As he sees it, just because there's no God doesn't mean there's nothing. Not an argument that gave pause to the devout.

Second month we were there, Benno got talked into buying *schmura matzoh* for Passover. Not that he's at all observant, but we do attend seders—more political than religious, mind you—at my newfound father's. It's the only Judeo-Christian holiday I feel wholeheartedly behind, because it celebrates freedom from slavery. None of this birth/death/atonement business, just a relevant reason for joy.

Anyway, Benno shelled out twenty dollars for what was essentially flour and water, albeit flour and water hand-ground and hand-shaped in Israel. It tasted like library paste, and we wound up throwing the rest of the box away. About that time, Benno stopped trying to debate religion with them. Forget winning; no way any of them would ever acknowledge Benno was even entitled to his point of view.

"Hey! Earth to Anita!" Benno's voice reminded me I was still holding the phone.

"I'm here. I was just thinking . . ."

"Well, don't. The police are taking care of what needs to be done, and there's nothing for you to do."

"Okay, okay. Gotta go now, my soap is on."

That did the trick. "Yeah, you watch *As the Voild Toins Ovah.*" Benno hung up, reassured that I was back to normal.

But after Aunt Rose's favorite show was over, I didn't feel any better.

I paced six steps, back and forth, all that our small living room permitted. There was nothing I could do. I wasn't Inez; I couldn't question the bouquet of possible suspects we'd handed her yesterday. Nor was I a forensic scientist, able to read and interpret the physical evidence.

I couldn't leave it alone, either. That boy's dead body had lain hidden in the room where I'd worked for too many days while I went about my business unaware of its presence. The situation was creepy, distressing, unbearably sad. I felt like an absolute idiot, to have been so oblivious.

Yes, part of it was a self-induced numbness. It had only been two weeks since Barbara's death, I didn't discount that. The truth was, I'd had enough of death, really enough, by last December. That was why I'd quit doing social work.

My entire career, I'd worked with the elderly. Old people die, that was a fact I could live with, but the deaths that had occurred in my orbit in the past few years were not limited to people who'd lived long lives. I needed a break, that was all. Now the respite of woodworking seemed to be over.

In the first days after September 11, I did make an effort to volunteer my dormant professional skills. I made calls, left messages, but never heard back. I figured so many people offered assistance that my name still hadn't swum to the surface of any lists. Frankly, I was relieved. I didn't have enough to sustain my own self, let alone anyone else.

Grief counseling. What I learned after Barbara died was that the bereaved don't want counseling; they want to howl.

I took my second shower of the day and wept while I washed my hair.

By the time I was towel-dry, I had an idea. The technicalities of determining *Who* and *How* might be out of my league, but there were aspects of the story behind an unnatural death that an amateur could unravel. Employed or not, I was still a mental health professional, and *Why* fell smack-dab in my area of expertise. That was the question I'd found an answer to in several of the deaths that had presented themselves to me over the years. I could do it again for the boy in the vacuum press.

Because if I didn't, his body would spend the month, unclaimed and unmourned, in the Kings County morgue.

Four

I RAN INTO INEZ ON THE STREET IN FRONT OF THE TWO-STORY building where Dovid Fine had his office.

"Good morning, Anita. Are you feeling better today?"

I was, better enough to notice how beautiful Inez had gotten. Now that she was out of uniform, she wore her thick hair, a shade darker than her caramel skin, pulled back in a French braid that let a few delicate tendrils escape around the nape of her neck. I was about to get personal and ask about her kids again, but Inez was all business.

"I'm looking for your landlord's office. I interviewed him by telephone Monday afternoon and he gave me the address, but—"

"You've got the right building," I told her.

Although the place didn't look much like it housed an office. The street-level space was occupied by a Chinese-run automotive place, a full-service operation: body work on one side, mechanics on the other. One of those new cars that all look alike, in one of those indistinguishable colors with names like Smoke and Mirrors, rose into the air on a lift. Someone started up an air gun and began taking the lug nuts off its wheels.

I raised my voice over the noise. "I'm on my way to see him myself. I don't suppose you know when the crime-scene seal will come off the spray room? Not that I'll be able to work in there—I'm hoping that having a dead body as a cotenant is reason enough to void the lease."

Inez just laughed.

New York: everyone's obsessed with real estate; no one has a clue what the next hot neighborhood will be. Dumbo was below the radar when we first moved over here, but it's suddenly come to the attention of the *Times*'s Real Estate section. It's an up-and-coming area, getting quite profitable for those converting industrial spaces to residential. Mr. Fine wasn't into that yet, at least not in our building, but there was no way to predict whether he'd let us go without a fuss or insist that we keep paying for the space.

"Have you identified the boy yet?" I asked.

"No." Inez reached into her shoulder bag. "But I have a picture. Here, take a look at your friend."

She handed me a five-by-seven-inch photo in a laminated sleeve.

Preserved, like the boy himself had been preserved in the plastic bag of the press. A gust of wind off the East River made its way under my leather jacket, up my spine.

"The medical examiner took a digital photograph, then a sketch artist enhanced the features to get them closer to what his actual face would have been. All the soft tissue was so smushed, he looked like—" Inez stopped when she noticed the expression on my face. "I'm sorry, Anita. Have you ever seen him before?"

It was amazing how real the boy in the picture seemed. Brown hair cut close to his skull, brown eyes, and a softness to his cheeks where he hadn't yet lost the puppy fat of adolescence. As good a job of restoring his features as they'd done, to me he still seemed like a generic type: young Orthodox male. Not Hasidic, though—no *payess*. I could have passed him every day in the neighborhood, bought my wedding ring from him, sat across from him on the subway, and I still wouldn't have been able to distinguish him from his cousins.

There's a kid's song about pairing up, and how only a clam can tell whether another clam is male or female. New York, you see all types all the time. They don't all look alike, but the casual eye gets adept at categorizing. Differentiating black, white, Asian, or Hispanic is child's play. Haitian, Ethiopian, Alabamian? Irish, Polish, Russian? Chinese, Japanese, Korean? Puerto Rican, Mexican, Colombian? Those are distinctions for the pros.

"He's not someone I saw regularly, I'm sure of that, but I don't have much to do with the people who work for the landlord, if he did. Do you know how old he was?"

"In his late teens. Seventeen to twenty is their best guess."

"I'm sorry, Inez."

"We've had flyers made up." She put the laminated photo back in her shoulder bag and took out a sheet of paper. It was a photocopy of the picture, with a headline that read *Do You Know This Man?* Underneath was the information that he'd been found in a building on Plymouth Street, and how to contact the police.

"They'll be posted around the neighborhood today. I wanted to show the photo to Mr. Fine in person. His office is upstairs?" Inez stepped back and scanned the front of the building, looking for an entrance that wasn't through the auto shop.

"Around the corner." Dovid Fine had construction techniques that drove Benno wild. Wherever he wanted something, he just put it in. In our building, that meant one day without warning we couldn't use the front door to get to the freight elevator; the minions had walled off a hallway on the ground floor and put in metal stairs to the basement, thereby making it another rentable space.

In typical fashion, Mr. Fine had added an exterior iron staircase to the side of this building, and expanded a window into a door in the brick facade. Building permits? Inspected and approved? You must be joking.

Inez followed me up the rickety metal steps. The one thing Mr. Fine spent money on was security. We buzzed and were scanned by a wall-mounted camera before the door was opened by a young man who, on first glance, could have been the brother of the boy in the press, except that he had curls of hair hanging in front of his ears and the wispy beginnings of a mustache on his upper lip. As far as I could tell, I'd never seen him before.

Not very communicative, either. Inez showed her badge and asked for Mr. Fine. The young man studied us for a moment before he stepped back to let us enter.

We were in a large, open room lit by a double row of hanging fluorescent fixtures. All noise stopped at the sight of us. Half of the space was partitioned off by a wall of four-drawer gray metal filing cabinets. I caught a glimpse of a woman's face peering over at us before she ducked back down. In the area where we waited, two men who kept their gazes carefully averted sat behind desks piled with papers, yellow invoices, receipts, work orders. A third person, with his back to us, tapped away at a computer. A phone rang, and seconds later a fax machine started spitting paper.

The man at the computer turned to look at the faxed sheets. He had a wide face, hazel eyes, and a nice-Jewish-boy nose. Him I recognized—Sroeli, the minion who'd recently been making the most effort to win Benno over. In his late teens,

Orthodox, wearing a suede yarmulke along with a blue work shirt and jeans. He gave no sign of noticing me. The two men at the desks were clearly Hasidim.

While the youth who'd let us in made up his mind what to do with us, I drifted toward the filing cabinets. Behind them was another work area, this one occupied by two women with long light brown braids down their backs. Uncovered hair meant unmarried, but that was all I could tell. Whether they were Orthodox or Hasidic, well, distinctions among observant women were not so obvious as with the men. They were doing time in the workforce before settling down to husband and children. One answered a ringing telephone; the other bent over an adding machine spewing tape.

The young Hasid came to a decision. "Over here."

Five

HE JERKED HIS HEAD FOR US TO FOLLOW HIM ALONG A SHORT corridor lit only by a filtered gloom from the frosted-glass transoms above the closed doors on either side.

The boy knocked on one of them. Dovid Fine himself opened it. He was a tall, barrel-shaped man in his fifties, a little older than Benno, clean-shaven, the hair under his black velvet yarmulke dark and closely trimmed. He wore the regulation outfit—black suit and white shirt, size large. You wouldn't want to be a cockroach when those shoes came stepping around.

"Vos iz mit dir? Gey avek!"

The response was also in Yiddish.

I knew enough German to extrapolate that Mr. Fine had said something to the effect of *What's up with you? Beat it!* but the young man's explanation was too long and too fast for me to make sense of. Whatever he said, it got us into the office.

"Ladies." Dovid Fine said it with a faint tone of displeasure, like you might say "rats" or "head lice."

Inez offered him the laminated picture. Mr. Fine gave it a quick glance. "I never seen him in my life."

"He didn't work for you?"

"If I tell you I never seen him, how could he work for me?"

"How many people are in your employ?" Inez asked.

"In my employ. Eight, ten—depends what needs to be done. Regular, I have four. And two girls for the office. This unfortunate I do not know."

"I'll need the names and addresses of everyone who works for you, please."

Mr. Fine's distaste for parting with the information showed in the near-illegible script he wrote it down with. Inez made him enunciate each name, repeating them so she could get the pronunciations right.

I was intrigued by the guttural, musical sounds of the names, and I scribbled them down on the manila envelope with the lease that I'd brought with me. Jacob Liebtag, his son-in-law, managed the residential properties; Yitzchak Zaskin handled the commercial spaces. They were the two older men in the office. The others were Heschel Kirsch, who'd let us in, and Sroeli Kohn, the computer expert. Both were from Israel, and both boarded in the Fine household.

"How long have they lived with you, Mr. Fine?" Inez asked.

"Those two?" The beard got a thoughtful stroking. "Six months, Sroeli. The other came just before the Towers."

"And do you have other boarders?"

"Only these. Three daughters, I have. All married now, *kanehore*. Would I take a young man into my house when I had unmarried girls? No. Some do. I am not one of them."

I was in the room while this went on simply because no one had stopped me. I'd followed Inez in, sat down in the second chair across from the desk, and kept my mouth shut. It's a technique I learned as a child, when my mother had people over for dinner. If I stayed quiet, the grown-ups overlooked me. Call attention to myself, however, like if I couldn't resist a question, and I'd be sent up to bed.

"Excuse me, Mr. Fine, but what about Eliezer?" The name of the man who'd sold Benno the matzoh swam into my memory, and I had to ask.

The look Fine turned on me was scarier than any of my mother's go-to-bed-right-now faces. "Eliezer? A *landsman* I hired as a favor. From Tel Aviv. One month only he worked for me."

"I'll need his name and current address." Inez at least was grateful for my question. "Is there anyone else you did favors for, Mr. Fine?"

"Favors, sure. These boys come to New York, they need a place to stay, a few days, a few weeks, whatever it takes to find their feet. So, they need a little money, I have a little work. They don't stay long." He brushed Inez off, now that I'd drawn his attention. "What are you doing here, Mrs. Servi?"

It didn't seem like the best moment to talk about voiding a lease. Inez helped me out. "Just a few more questions, please, Mr. Fine. Do you have keys to the space where the body was found?"

"Keys, yes. I have keys to all my properties. Tenant moves out? I change the lock. New tenant moves in? He gets a key, I keep a key. Sometimes people change the lock again themselves. It's in the lease, no new locks permitted unless I have a key. There's a problem? I need a locksmith to get in? Tenant pays for everything. Believe me, they put their own locks anyway and don't tell me." He glared in my direction.

Inez joined him. "Have you or Benno changed your locks?"

"No, of course not. We didn't see the need for anything more secure than what was already there." Both spaces, upstairs and down, had come with police locks, the kind with a metal bar across their middles. When locked, the bar shoots into the brick wall. They're called police locks because they're intended to keep the cops from breaking down your door. You know, like on TV, when two cops swing that battering-ram

thing, and the door just flattens? Not with one of these de-
vices. Police locks show how much faith we put in our Fourth
Amendment protections here in New York.

"Where are the duplicate sets of keys kept?" Inez asked,
very thorough.

Dovid Fine jerked his thumb at the side wall of the office, in-
dicating a tall gray metal box, easily three feet across, mounted
on the wall. Its door was held closed by a layered steel padlock.
"In there."

"Does anyone else have access to that?"

He stood and reached into his pocket. "Only I."

He withdrew a ring of keys on a long chain that was attached to a belt loop of his pants and jangled them at Inez.

She didn't blink. "And if there's an emergency in the middle
of the night . . ." Inez smiled at him.

"They call me." Fine showed his teeth, large and startlingly
white. "Like a doctor or a detective, I am on call as you say
'twenty-four/seven.' "

He was, too, always quick to respond when the elevator
wasn't working or a pipe burst in the building—although his
solution to any problem was to send one of the not-necessarily-
competent young men from his entourage to deal with the
problem. This time I held my tongue.

Inez considered Mr. Fine. If she was thinking what I was,
it was that he was the kind of man who would never tell anyone all of what was going on in his business, let alone in
his thoughts. Dovid Fine had real estate holdings all around
Dumbo, a little empire that needed many hands to run. He
wouldn't be giving out the names of anyone who worked for
him on an as-needed basis because he most likely paid them

under the table. No payroll taxes, no W-2s or 1099s at the end of the year.

"What? What else can I tell you? This is a tragedy, a *shande und a kharpe*. The poor unfortunate, whoever he is, may he rest in peace. You want to talk to my boys? I give you permission."

Inez straightened in her chair, preparing to stand. "Mr. Fine, do you have any idea who might have done this?"

"You want to know that, you ask the *artists*." He said it with a sneer. "They say they want studios to work? Sure! And to use drugs and to live, this they do also. The city inspector comes, he tells me this is not code, to have people living in these buildings. You think I don't know that? The city tells me I should evict them? In New York, everyone has rights, everyone except the owner. I tell the artists, get out, you are violating your lease. But if they don't move, what can I do?"

Inez raised her eyebrows.

"Ekh, you think I should take them to court? Where they tell lies? No, *they* take *me* to court! The judge looks at me, and he thinks always the landlord is the bad guy. So, they pay the rent, I let them stay."

"Are there people who use the building on Plymouth Street as a residence?" Inez looked to me for an answer this time.

"No, I'm sure there aren't."

"In that building, no one lives. It's too small, I would know about it." Mr. Fine backed me up. "This other one, across the street, I got people living where they shouldn't be."

I returned the favor. "I see lights on in the evening on the top floor, and a window full of plants."

"Orchids!" He snorted. "A greenhouse I didn't rent them."

"What about the other space on the third floor?" Inez asked. "We haven't gotten any response from whoever is there."

Dovid Fine said nothing, so I answered.

"There was a woman, an artist who did something with spray-painted umbrellas, renting it when we moved in. She left a couple months ago. I thought there might have been someone around over the summer, but I never saw them."

"Mr. Fine?" Inez asked him directly. "Was the space occupied during the summer months?"

"No. Maybe you heard my boys cleaning. Umbrellas! A mess is what she made."

Inez stood. Now that she was leaving, Dovid Fine had more to say.

"You want more suspects? Ask the ones with the green windows, those Witnesses. People of the Book, they call themselves!" Another snort. "They noodge my boys all the time with their pamphlets."

"Jehovah's Witnesses," I amplified. "They have buildings all over the neighborhood—all the ones with the window trim painted green."

I found the Jehovahs harmless but annoying, a bit overzealous in their neat suits and dresses, offering religious tracts to everyone they passed on the street. I was surprised they tried it with the Orthodox, though. Converting them would seem like a lost cause right from the gate.

"Thank you, Mr. Fine." Inez offered him her hand.

He ignored it and opened the door. "Heshie!"

The young man appeared. Dovid Fine spoke to him in rapid Yiddish, then turned to Inez. "He will look at your photograph, and so will the others. I told them to answer your questions."

Inez thanked him again. Dovid Fine watched her walk down the corridor before he turned to me, leaving the door open.

"Mrs. Servi."

He didn't sit back down, either, so I stood to face him. No point in subtlety; I told him we wanted out of the lease on the third-floor space.

To my total astonishment, all I had to do was ask, and the agreement was voided. We'd paid up through the end of the month, and I offered to forfeit the last month's deposit as well.

But no, Mr. Fine didn't need to keep the deposit. He trusted us to leave everything in good condition.

It felt like I was getting the bum's rush. I didn't mind, but I did wonder whether Dovid Fine was willing to tear up our lease with so little fuss because he knew more than he'd admitted— either about the dead boy, or the summer activity in the supposedly empty next-door space. I was also curious about that stream of Yiddish, and exactly how cooperative he'd instructed Heschel Kirsch to be.

Inez was just coming out from the women's work space behind the filing cabinets, with a frustrated expression on her face, when I left Mr. Fine's office.

"Lady." Sroeli stood up from the computer and addressed Inez. "Give me some of those papers. I'll put them around in Williamsburg. Maybe somebody knows him."

"That would be a big help." Inez smiled and held out a stack of flyers. Rather than taking them from her hand, Sroeli nodded at his desk.

"Thank you," Inez said. She walked over to the other desks and deposited her card with each man. Then she raised her voice to address all of them. "If anyone thinks of anything else that might help, please call me. This boy deserves a name, and a proper burial."

I took a few flyers myself, just to hold on to the boy's face. Over the next week, I nodded to him whenever I walked by one of the telephone poles where he was sharing space with the ghosts of September 11.

Six

AND THAT WAS WHERE THE MATTER STAYED. THE POLICE RAN stories in various Yiddish papers, talked to the artists across the street from our building, knocked on doors in the green-windowed buildings, learned nothing. They're insular worlds: the Orthodox community, the artists with lofts in Dumbo, and the Jehovah's Witnesses. There aren't many points of overlap among them, let alone cross-cultural friendships. In retrospect, it struck me as odd that Dovid Fine had even suggested there might be.

For all how incomprehensible his building methods were to me, I could understand the logic behind them, the rationale for optimizing the available space. When it came to a connection between the boy in the vacuum press and the Jehovahs, however—*go know*, as Benno's Aunt Rose would say.

Thursday, I helped Benno clear a corner of the main shop where he planned to frame up a room to use for finishing. Until the police unsealed the spray room, there was nothing else to do; we couldn't even get the equipment moved out. Friday morning, I didn't bother going in to work with him.

Not that staying home was any better. Given the choice between vacuuming and defrosting the freezer, I opted for a field trip. Know the victim—isn't that one of the principles of investigation? Seemed like a good place to start.

Getting to Williamsburg was complicated. When I first came to New York, I felt like a tourist, relying on maps to get around the city. I've since learned that even the natives do it. I keep a laminated street map in my purse, and consult it frequently. The subway insert told me that the best route involved the 1 train to Fourteenth Street, transfer to the F to Delancey Street, then hop a J or Z one stop to Marcy.

That's right, Z. The MTA was sprouting some odd routes even before a handful of IRT stations got buried under the rubble of the Towers. W, Z—why not π? The system's become as arcane as solid geometry.

When the train rose from the depths to cross the Williamsburg Bridge, all heads in the car turned to the windows on the south side. There was the Manhattan Bridge with one square pillar of the Brooklyn Bridge visible through its arched belly. What everyone strained to see was the view of nothing, yet another vantage to take in the shocking absence of the city's tallest towers. I looked away, north to the sun-glittered deco spire of the Chrysler Building, the solid reassurance of the Empire State.

On Marcy Street, with the train rumbling off overhead and traffic curving from the bridge to the BQE—Brooklyn-Queens Expressway, one of Robert Moses's infamous neighborhood-splitting arteries—it was instantly obvious that I was in one of the city's other boroughs. Shorter buildings, narrower streets, more cars, fewer yellow cabs.

On the other side of the tracks, the neighborhood is being colonized by artists and adventurous young families, but the area below Broadway is still largely Jewish. Immigrants crowded out of the Lower East Side moved here in the early years of the last century, after the Williamsburg Bridge was built, then were joined by an influx of European refugees in the forties. The more recent settlers are Latin American, Dominican, Puerto Rican.

I meandered over to Lee Avenue, the main shopping drag of Jewish Williamsburg. I felt like a tourist in a foreign country. Or a different century. Two old men with grizzled beards, long black coats, and flat-brimmed black hats stood talking on a corner. Boys with long silky earlocks hurried past. Women in navy-blue coats and thick ecru stockings held the hands of neatly dressed little girls.

The people spoke to each other in unfamiliar languages; the shop windows displayed signs in a script I couldn't read. Well-scrubbed teenage girls in below-the-knee pleated wool skirts wore their shoulder-length hair held back by black velvet bands.

They were all in a hurry. I can do the New York walk as well as anyone, but in this neighborhood I was trying to maintain a sightseer's pace. It wasn't possible. Although no one looked directly at me, I was obviously an obstacle to the smooth flow of sidewalk traffic. Every woman who avoided me did so with a muttered *tsk* or a hissed *sha*.

It dawned on me that it was the morning before Shabbos, and there were special meals to prepare. The aroma from a bakery pulled me in to join a small mob emptying the shelves of challah. It was a mixed crowd, a few men in full Hasidic dress, women of all ages with scarves over their heads, a sprinkling of children. The man on line ahead of me, in a workman's plaid wool shirt and dusty jeans with a red knit cap on his head, hefted two brown paper shopping bags packed with fat loaves up on the counter. The transaction was conducted in English and concluded with a *Gut Shabbes* from the saleswoman. They were all buying for that night's meal; I intended mine for Sunday morning French toast.

When I left the bakery, I was almost engulfed by a cluster of black-hatted young men with beards and *payess*.

"Nu, tsatskele, vuhin gehst du?" one of them called.

In German, he'd've been asking where I was going. I suspected the first word was an insult. *Tsatskele,* I repeated it to myself so I could ask Benno what it meant.

The line spilling outside a check cashing place included a pair of elderly Hispanic women and several Hasidic men; money, the universal language. A girl about Clea's age, pushing a fancy baby carriage bigger than she was, ran over my foot with a white-tired wheel. I gave up on gawking and quickened my pace.

Three blocks later I hit Flushing Avenue, and a bus stop with a handy little map that showed me the B57 would take me to Dumbo, at just about the right time to catch up with my husband on his lunch break.

It was a ten-minute wait and a free transfer with my Metro-Card. Boarding the bus was culture shock all over again. Mixed as Manhattan is, white is still a common color. Here, every face except mine was a shade of brown. And one other—a clean-cut young man in the kind of jacket high school jocks wear, navy-blue wool with cream-colored vinyl sleeves, hung on to a pole in the back.

I sat next to an ample woman reading a Bible in Spanish who got off at the same stop I did, in front of the projects on Sands Street.

The white kid left the bus there, too. He passed me on Gold and hung a left. I followed him, heading for Los Papis, our luncheonette of choice.

Between the storefronts on York, there were stretches of stone wall that were dotted with the flyers of the missing. The boy slowed his steps as he went by them, as if studying the faces. Then he paused and tore one of them away.

It was almost shocking, that someone would interfere with the forlorn hopes of those who refused to believe their loved ones weren't still out there, somewhere, lost. I hustled to catch up to him.

Several light poles were also decorated with the flyers. The kid scanned those, too. He seemed to be after one in particular. When he found it, he ripped it down. I followed him along York to Jay. At the entrance to the subway station, a cluster of teenagers seemed to be waiting for him.

All of them were white. Three boys in jackets and ties, neat short hair, slacks and loafers; two girls in wool jackets and skirts that were not quite as long as the style au courant in Williamsburg but still well below the knee. Their straight hair was pulled back and held by simple barrettes. From the way they were dressed, I figured the kids were Jehovah's Witnesses. A Christian version of the Orthodox, I thought.

This part of Brooklyn is home to the Jehovah's Witnesses' world headquarters. They own at least two dozen old factory buildings; the *Watchtower* and *Awake!* are printed here. There's a brand-new residential hotel for the mostly young, mostly single people who come to do a year of service. They work long hours in the printing and shipping plants, doing other maintenance work for the organization, and proselytizing in exchange for room, board, a small salary, and glory.

They are hard workers. Every one of the green-trimmed buildings is immaculate. Loading docks clear, garbage neatly bagged and tied, sidewalks swept, windows washed. From what I understand, serving in the Brooklyn community is considered a great honor.

These were not the kind of delinquent youths you'd expect to be interfering with public postings.

I slowed my stride as I came closer and entered the station. The one in the varsity jacket held out his handful of torn-down flyers to show the others. I got enough of a look at the photo to realize it was the boy from the vacuum press. What the—?

I was about to say something to the kids—in their straight outfits, I thought they might be more receptive to a voice of adult authority than the average gaggle of teens—when they scattered. Two of the boys went north, toward the residence. The girls circled around me and slid through the turnstiles. I caught a glimpse of what one of them was carrying—a stack of *Watchtowers*, confirming my assessment of them as Witnesses. The boy from the bus folded the flyers and stuck them in his pocket, then headed across Jay. I watched him scan the next two light poles he came to and pass on without tearing anything from them.

I tried to remember what his face looked like so I'd recognize him if I saw him again, but as with the Hasidic youth, I found it hard to pick out distinguishing features. From their sandy hair to their khaki pants, the three boys could have been each other. Even the letter jacket was anonymous—it should have had at least a school name on the back, but there was nothing so easily identifiable: no numbers, writing, logo, insignia.

What was that all about, I wondered—Jehovah's Witnesses, a flyer with the picture of a Jewish boy—was Dovid Fine's remark about the Witnesses having something to do with the death on the mark?

On the surface, it still didn't seem likely. As insular a community as the Hasidim are, the Jehovahs stick just as tightly together. The main difference is that the Witnesses are given to proselytizing in a way the Jews aren't. Sure, sects like the Lubavitchers might reach out to bring a stray lamb like Benno back into the fold, but they're not interested in converts from Christianity. In Judaism, you're either born one or you're not, which is why our landlord's minions have left me alone. I may have a Jewish father, but in the matter of religious inheritance, it's the mother's blood that counts.

Besides, if Varsity Jacket knew the dead boy, why was he pulling down the flyers instead of coming forward to identify him?

I felt the subterranean wind from the tunnel that meant a train was about to pull in. I forgot all about my plan to join Benno for lunch at Papis, and ran for it. It was a purely Pavlovian response—rushing to catch an incoming train is as automatic as it gets.

I closed my eyes and let the F jolt me along while I replayed the images from Williamsburg. I can't say I gained any insight into the community the boy may or may not have come from other than an impression that if he had lived there, he'd've been missed. Any area where kids as young as six or seven walked the streets unaccompanied by adults was a neighborhood where people knew each other.

As I went back over the sights of Lee Avenue, I remembered that the light poles there too had been papered with the ubiquitous missing posters. I opened my eyes and sat up. In spite of Sroeli's offer to post them in his neighborhood, I couldn't recollect seeing a single picture of the boy in the vacuum press among the others.

Seven

IN ONE OF THOSE ODD NEW YORK COINCIDENCES, THE BREAK IN making an identification came the following Wednesday, from a sort of acquaintance of mine.

Friendships in the city are built largely on proximity. People move out of the neighborhood, and they might as well be in Poughkeepsie for all how often you see each other. Then there are the subsets, people you know from work, or who have season tickets next to yours at the Met or the Mets. That's how I knew Helen Baum, from years of visits to the Russian baths on East Tenth Street.

One thing I missed when I came to New York was hot baths. I was practically weaned on late-night drives to the mineral baths at Esalen, on the Big Sur coast. Don't even get me started on Berkeley hot tubs, circles of redwood echoed by New York's water towers, or pilgrimages to Ojo Caliente, in New Mexico—Saratoga Springs, upstate, is a faint fizzy pretender by comparison.

The Russian baths, while satisfying, are an entirely different breed. No soaking here; the Tenth Street experience is all about sweat. The radiant heat room is the hot heart of the place, where you park yourself on a narrow bench and *shvitz*. Only the Yiddish word does justice to the amount of fluid produced by a body in a room where the ambient temperature hovers around 250 degrees.

Benno took me there on our second date, after learning on

our first what a bath-rat I was. He'd been observing guys' night at the baths for decades, the second Tuesday of the month, with six or seven friends. The baths used to be men-only five days a week, with Wednesdays and Sundays reserved for women. The owners went co-ed ten years ago; times for single-sex, read "nude," bathing were reduced to Wednesdays for women, Thursdays for men.

You ask me, it's a shame. I'm as modest as the next person, but when it comes to water, the experience is best without the interference of clothing. Swimming is as close to elemental beings as we get. Green lake, moving river, salty ocean—immerse me in any of them, I prefer to be unclothed.

Anyway.

The week after I found the boy's body, I was in sore need of a sweat. Now that I'm not working a regular job, I make it about every other month, usually in the morning, with my friend Janis.

Like half of New York, Janis works temp jobs to support her less profitable, more artistic endeavors. She makes jewelry: spidery multistrand necklaces and wrap bracelets that she sells at the craft shows on Columbus Avenue. The rest of the time, she hires herself out to big companies in temporary need of extra staff, and devotes her nights to directing avant-garde theater.

On women's days, we're part of an eclectic mix. Janis and I are both in our mid-forties, me a few pounds overweight and Janis a few pounds heavier. While I've let my hair go nicely silver, Janis dyes hers New York black. It's straight and cut in a wedge shape, the points meeting under her chin when she swings her head forward.

Other regulars include a group of African-American women, also in their middle years, who slather themselves with clay masks; a contingent of young gay women, complete with exotic tattoos, piercings, and shorn heads; and an older woman, slight, shriveled, silent, always alone.

I used to think she was a cancer survivor, there for medicinal purposes. After several years with no change in her appearance, I asked Vera, the owner, about her. Her name was Helen; she was a painter who still lived in the Lower East Side tenement where she'd been born; she'd been coming to the baths every week for at least the thirty-odd years Vera had been behind the counter. In spite of her long history, I worried about Helen. She looked so fragile, I was sure each time we went to the baths she wouldn't be there.

But she was, every time. Never got older or healthier-looking. Rarely said a word to anyone. Janis, gregarious, used to try to draw her out, without response. I was more successful—mostly, I think, because I didn't try to start conversations. A few times when we happened to be sitting near each other on the bench downstairs, or dressing in front of adjacent lockers, I was on the receiving end of an abrupt, non sequitur of a question.

Six months ago, out of the blue, Helen asked me, "Do you have children?"

"Yes, one daughter."

"Daughters!" It was the beginning of a muttered monologue, more to herself than me, about the perfidy of girl-children, how you thought you were as close as sisters, taught your daughter everything you knew about men, and still she found unsuitable ones and married them, not once but twice.

Another time, maybe a month later, the question was: "Are you Jewish?"

"My father is, but I wasn't raised that way." I gave her the literal truth, not bothering to explain that I'd known neither my father's name nor his religion until I was well over forty.

Not so easy to keep Janis quiet, however. We were all by our lockers, getting dressed, and she butted right on in to the conversation. Not that my father is all that well known, but he does have a certain level of name recognition in the city. Janis couldn't resist.

"Anita's father is famous," she stage-whispered to Helen. "You've heard of Aaron Wertheim, right? He's the lawyer who defended—"

I kicked Janis in the shin with my bare foot, hard enough to make her sit down and shut up.

I swear, Helen looked at me with actual concern. "I know who Mr. Wertheim is. You're not trying to 'reconnect with your Jewish identity,' are you?" Sharp as a bayonet.

"Well, I have started learning more about the holidays. My husband is Jewish, too, and—"

It was enough to launch a diatribe. "Never mind that. You live how you were brought up. These Jews they have now, with their invitations to dinner and their matchmaking, they're no different than any other cult. I brought my daughter up to have faith in herself, not this God who needs to be praised every day by men who give thanks for not being female."

Helen paced back and forth on the warped floor, in dingy maroon sweatpants and a once-white, little-girl undershirt with a satin bow at the neckline. She could have been a macabre windup toy.

Condensed, the gist of what she was complaining about was that her daughter had been "brainwashed"—her word—by some ultra-Orthodox rabbi's wife who'd set up shop in the Village and was intent on—her words again—"rekindling the flame of religious awe in every wayward Jewish breast." Helen, to say the least, disapproved.

"All my daughter wanted was to learn Hebrew. God knows why." A rueful chuckle at her inadvertent joke. "Yes, God knows. Ruthie claims it was *bashert,* meant to be. That woman drew her in, always with the invitations, a meal here, a party there, until they've got her keeping a kosher house and they find her a husband. A real *nebbish,* if you ask me, but they tell her it's not easy to find a man for someone in her situation, a divorced woman almost thirty, with a son already."

Helen put her hands on her hips and glared at me. "If I wanted my daughter to spend her days cooking and washing four sets of dishes and kowtowing to a husband, I would have brought her up the way my mother did. In her eyes, too, any husband was better than no husband. Well let me tell you, it's easier to have children than to raise them."

It's a common enough pattern: repressive parent breeds free-spirited child whose offspring revert to a more conservative path. Look at my own family—my mother got as far away from her German parents as she could, choosing to raise me on my own in California. In response to a childhood where my mother's erratic employment status determined whether we dined on salmon steaks or rice and beans, I opted for a professional career and a husband with a steady income. Not that I by any stretch turned away from the free-thinking values I was raised with, which Helen's daughter evidently had.

"How many grandchildren do you have?" I asked, hoping to turn the tide in a more pleasant direction.

Stupid, not to have thought that if the daughter had religion, so did the children.

"Three." Helen rummaged in her locker and came up with

a battered leather purse. She withdrew a small photo album and handed it over. It was an ornate thing, with a dark blue velvet cover and silver corners. I opened the book at the beginning and held it out, inviting her to show me. Inside were plastic sleeves to hold the photographs. Helen nodded permission for me to turn pages as she spoke.

"That's Simon. The child of my daughter's first marriage. He was five when she remarried." Helen stroked the boy's face. His full lips were curved into a tentative smile, and he wore a black yarmulke on his little head. "It might have been all right for him, but then Ruthie gave the husband a son of his own. Shmuel. Such ugly sounds those names have. That's him."

Three pages in, a chubby baby, clearly a boy by his blue clothes. Four pictures later, he was a toddler, with a crocheted yarmulke pinned to a head of hair so long and curly he looked more like a girl.

"They don't cut the boys' hair until their third birthday." Helen flipped to the next picture, the same child with his locks shorn.

Then a second infant appeared, almost bald and all in pink. She had Helen's dark brown eyes and a seriousness incongruous in a child.

"They had a girl two years later. Zehava. At least they gave her a pretty name. After that, no more. A great shame, according to the husband. I thought it was a blessing, only three children to be raised as little automatons for *Hashem*."

All of the photographs were studio shots, not a Kodak moment among them—no birthday parties, trips to the zoo, the beach; nothing casual, snapped at home, candid, unposed.

There were a handful of empty plastic pages at the end of the album.

"They're beautiful children," I said.

"Yes." Helen took the book from me and returned it to her purse. She slammed the metal door closed and walked off, pullover in one hand, bag in the other.

That was the last time she'd spoken to me, until that particular October Wednesday when Janis and I made our first post-September 11, post-Barbara's funeral, post-body in the vacuum press pilgrimage to Tenth Street.

Eight

IN SPITE OF THE OWNERS' ATTEMPTS TO TART THEM UP, THE baths are a funky place. Janis and I climbed the high stoop of the brownstone, with its tile entry still intact. The door was open to let in some of the crisp air.

Vera was in her usual place behind the high wooden counter. She turned her back as soon as she saw us, and slid out two of the long metal bank-vault boxes kept under the cash register for customers to stash their valuables.

"Good morning, ladies," she said. "Everyone is okay?"

It was the standard greeting in those days, when anyone was likely to know someone who could be counted among the missing. Yes, we told her, while we took off our watches and put them in the boxes along with our wallets and Janis's beaded wrap bracelet.

"Is everyone you know all right?" I asked in turn.

"Two customers I lost. Maybe more, I don't know. Sometimes people don't come in for weeks."

There wasn't much to say to that. Janis made sympathetic noises while Vera locked the long boxes and handed us keys to the rickety clothing lockers. The changing area is one large room with green metal lockers lining the walls, a ring of battered wooden benches, and a cluster of beds with thin vinyl-covered mattresses in the center.

We helped ourselves from the stacks of freshly laundered towels and cotton robes. Janis took the top robe, light blue.

I went for my favorite color, a deep rose. The shower shoes we ignored. The floor, covered with a meager layer of indoor-outdoor carpeting, is always warm from the radiant heat room below.

It was just after ten, opening time. The dressing room was crowded and unusually quiet. The faces looked unfamiliar to me; mostly I knew the regulars by their bodies. Not only the odd piercings, like the woman with five rings above her navel, and the distinctive tattoos—we called the one with a snake that climbed her left leg, ankle to knee, Serpent Woman—but also the shapes. Janis liked to name them: Pendulous, Flat Butt, Ten, Perky Tits; you get the idea.

We snapped the tiny locks closed. I used the rubber band attached to my key to put my hair up. Janis stopped at the top of the stairs to weigh herself on the big scale. Me, I didn't want to know.

I held the rail as I went down the steep steps. When I opened the door, I was in an echoey vault of cement and pipes. Along with the radiant heat room, the lower floor also houses a sauna, steam room, showers, and a few stalls for the special *platza* massage, which involves being beaten with a bunch of wet oak leaves. I'm sure it feels better than it sounds, but I've never tried it. I prefer the heart-stopping cold plunge, a rectangular pool with steps down to the five-foot depth. Only the brave make it all the way in and swim the seven strokes to the far wall and back. I'm one of them.

I shed my robe and hung it with one of the towels at the far end of the row of hooks. The other towel I wrapped around my waist before I entered the radiant heat room, a world of dripping moisture. The heat comes from a mysterious source behind a concrete wall in one corner. The two adjoining walls are lined with narrow tiers of built-in concrete benches. The higher the bench, the hotter the air. On the upper level, where I've never seen anyone sit, the wood planks meant to protect one's body from the concrete are scorched dry from the heat.

I started on the lowest level, my feet cooled by the overflow of cold water from the large white plastic buckets set under a half-dozen spigots that jut out from the walls. As I sat down, the black woman who wore a strand of colored beads around her waist—yes, Janis referred to her as Belly Beads—picked up a bucket and dumped it over her head. She laughed at the jolt of icy water and did it again.

There were five other women in the room, our uncommunicative elderly friend among them.

"Down four measly pounds," Janis announced when she came in. "A month of Weight Watchers, and that's all the progress I've made."

"Better than gaining," I said. One advantage of a Berkeley upbringing is that weight is a topic I don't spend much time on. As long as it works, my body is fine with me. Sure, I've gained a few pounds over the years, but I prefer a little rotundity to gauntness. Janis, in my opinion, is just about right.

"I know, you're not interested. You've got a husband, what difference does it make how you look?"

That got a scowl from a woman with spiky green hair. Ah, an angry young feminist. Good for her. I poked Janis in the ribs. "Cut it out, girlfriend. You wouldn't have a husband if he was offered to you on a silver platter with an apple in his mouth."

"Well, not if it was a Macintosh, but for a Granny Smith, I might . . ."

That got a smile from Lime Jell-O. There, I named her myself.

Janis and I moved up to the second level, where there was enough unoccupied space to spread our towels on the narrow bench. We stretched out with our heads together in a corner so we could talk.

I'd told Janis about the body in the vacuum press the day after I'd found it, and she was eager for an update. The humid air, the concrete walls and floor, make for acoustics heightened by the hiss of steam and the constant watery plash from spigot to bucket. All I had to report was the lack of progress identifying him, but still I tried to keep my voice down so we wouldn't burden the whole room with our conversation.

Janis had no such scruples when the topic skipped along to her latest project, staging a one-woman theater piece called "Mooseface: Naked in My Birthday Suit." Intrigued by the title, Lime Jell-O asked a question, and next thing I knew, she and Janis were off upstairs to exchange e-mail addresses. When I got up to douse myself with a bucket of icy water, I noticed that Helen—dubbed Raisin Woman by Janis, for her wrinkled and shriveled physique, a mean but accurate moniker—had left the room.

I lingered another ten minutes before heading to the cold plunge. When I rose from the water, my skin steaming, Helen was sitting on the tiled edge of the pool.

I wrapped myself in a dry towel and sat down a few feet from her.

"How old was the boy you were talking about?"

The question, or at least its source, was so unexpected my jaw literally dropped.

"I asked how old was the boy you found," Helen insisted.

So much for trying to talk quietly in the radiant heat room; she'd obviously overheard what I'd told Janis. "They're not really sure. Somewhere between sixteen and twenty," I said. "Why?"

I didn't really expect an answer, but I got one.

"My grandson is missing."

"Why would you think—"

"You said he was a Jewish boy, he wore tzitzis."

"Well, yes, but there are . . ." thousands of Jewish teenagers in the city, I was going to continue, but the distress on her face stopped me. "I have a photo of him, if you'd like to see it."

Does it seem odd that I carried a copy of the police missing person flyer around with me? Not in those days, it wasn't. All of lower Manhattan was covered with posters of the missing, an octopus of hope with tentacles that stretched into every borough. There were faces and descriptions I passed so often I felt they were my relatives, too. In a sense, the boy in the vacuum press *was* mine: I needed to know who he was. These weren't entirely rational times.

I wrapped myself in dusky rose and headed upstairs to the locker room. Helen followed me, in a forest-green robe so much too big for her that it dragged on the ground. She had it wrapped almost double in front, and still the armholes gaped around her skinny arms.

I took the folded flyer out of my bag, expecting we'd sit right there on one of the beds. But no—Helen jerked a thumb at the ceiling.

"Upstairs."

Even better. Upstairs meant the open deck on the backside of the second floor. I brought my cigarettes and Barbara's lighter, the one memento I'd requested from her daughters, up into the open air where it was still legal to indulge.

I know, I know, smoking isn't an indulgence, it's an idiocy.

So, I keep it under three a day. I don't smoke in the apartment; never around Clea; rarely even in front of Benno unless we're out having a drink. Being clandestine means I have to leave the house in order to sneak a smoke, so I actually get more fresh air and exercise.

Yes, I'm rationalizing. You can take the girl out of social work, but you can't separate the social worker from the girl. Call it a trade-off: so far, what I got out of smoking outweighed the potential costs. Although I have to say, six dollars a pack is serious sticker shock every time.

Helen paused at the top of the stairs and surveyed the weight room. A half-dozen exercise machines, like a herd of shiny chrome creatures at a watering hole, clustered in the open center area. Along two walls, there were doors identified by brass numbers, one through eight: the massage rooms.

At this hour on women's day, all but one of the doors gaped open. Helen went up to the closed door, number three. After listening for a moment, she pushed it open—empty like the rest.

Satisfied, Helen went out to the deck. At the far end, there were three more little massage rooms, barely enough space for a masseuse to circle the table as she worked someone over. The women who worked up here could often be found lounging in the white plastic deck chairs, but it was still well before noon and we were alone.

Nine

THE SKY WAS A WONDERFUL BLUE, AS IT HAD BEEN FOR MOST OF that surreal fall season. To the southwest, we could see the upper edges of the cloud that hovered over the smoldering Trade Center site. I turned my face away and watched Helen make sure the little rooms across the deck were unoccupied.

Not only was Helen's body slight and bony as a bird with wet feathers, but her head was also slightly too large for her shoulders, the way a baby bird seems out of proportion. Her hair was iron-gray, short, and straight. She probably cut it herself, lopping off anything that stuck up in the morning with a pair of nail scissors. I'd never seen her hair when it looked as though she'd combed it.

We sat on a wooden bench facing east, with the sun on our faces. The branches of a tall ailanthus, the weed tree of the city's backyards and vacant lots, cast a net of shadows at our feet. Somewhere, birds sang to each other. For just a moment, the past few months fell away, and I was back in an August where tall buildings stood their ground and Barbara was going to beat the cancer.

"I'm sorry, will you tell me your older grandson's name again?"

"Simon." From the way she spoke the single word, I could tell he was precious to her. "Shimon, they call him now. He was named for my father, an unpleasant man if ever there was one."

I offered her the flyer, still folded, but Helen didn't take it. She sat with her arms crossed over her chest, her hands tucked into the opposite sleeves of the green robe.

"Were you close to him?"

"After his bar mitzvah, I was no longer welcome in my daughter's house. For four years I didn't see my grandchildren. This past summer, Simon ran away. The Fourth of July, he came to me."

"Nice choice of date," I said. I had the sense that this was more about Helen needing to talk than it was about any real possibility that her grandson was the boy I'd found in the press.

"I took him in, of course. The next day I called my daughter to let her know the boy was safe. She said okay, she'd have to consult with her husband and the rebbe. My daughter, who is now known as Rivka, doesn't sneeze without consulting the rebbe to ask if it's all right to blow her nose. Not an original thought in her brain. No wonder Simon got out of there."

"Did she allow him to stay with you?"

"Allow." There was scorn in Helen's voice. "For ten years, my daughter didn't set foot in my house. That same afternoon, she was knocking on my door, begging him to come home. If he insisted on staying with his *apikoros* grandmother—that means I'm a heretic, because I turned my back on God, as if she knew anything about it. My God doesn't require—ach, never mind. If 'Shimon' wouldn't go home, Ruth said, he left them no choice, they would have to sit shiva for him."

It seemed to me that acting as if he were dead was a pretty extreme response to a runaway teenager who'd strayed no further than his grandmother, but I stayed neutral and asked what happened next.

"Rivka went back to the rebbe, and we made a bargain. First there was a trip to Israel they wanted him to take. One of the yeshiva teachers had it all arranged already, six boys going for three weeks. Then Simon stayed with me for the rest of the summer. He went home to Brooklyn for *Shabbes,* and moved back when school started. Those Orthodox did bend, I'll give them that. I was afraid the fact I don't keep a kosher house would be a sticking point, and I had no intention of starting up with the dishes again. Since I am a vegetarian, the rebbe in his infinite wisdom decreed that was acceptable."

"So Simon went home for good in September?"

"Yes. After that, I saw him only twice more. He came to me late on Saturday nights. We painted together on Sunday afternoons, ate a little supper, then it was back to Williamsburg. The schedule suited us both." Helen exhaled, a sigh of regret mixed with relief.

"It wasn't easy for me to have a teenager in the house full-time. I've lived alone for many years. Simon is a good boy, only the stepfather is hard on him. Always criticizing, until no wonder the child had no confidence. Well, all that praying would warp anyone."

"How did Simon spend his time with you?"

"What difference does that make?" Helen shooed my question away.

"It might help to find him." I didn't say the rest of what I thought, that if Simon had been hanging out in the East Village with the street kids, the punks, druggies, runaways . . .

"He had a job, something in a warehouse near the Brooklyn

Navy Yard. He went there every day. It was boring, and we didn't discuss it."

"What did you talk about?" My career as a furniture finisher notwithstanding, the social-work hat still fit.

It was the first time I'd seen her genuinely smile, the kind of grin that lifts not only the corners of the mouth but reaches up to delight the eyes. Hers were a deep brown, so dark the irises were almost the same color as the pupils. With the lines of her face wreathed into pleasure, Helen looked—not younger, but—different. As if she'd lived an entirely other life, one that had brought her satisfaction rather than sourness.

She spoke to the trees, to the clutter of little brown birds who came and went from the top branches rather than to me. "He wanted to know about my life, my work. So many questions. For Simon, I found the good memories from my childhood."

She took her hands out of her sleeves and let them lie open in her lap. "And we discussed art. Simon was a blank canvas. They teach them nothing in those yeshivas, nothing about art or culture that isn't Jewish. I gave him books to read. I allowed him to play with my paints."

The wrinkles realigned themselves to bitterness. "Play. He didn't know what to do. I brought out colors I haven't used since art school. Rose madder, blue lake. Here was a child so stunted he couldn't make an uninhibited mark on a sheet of paper when we began."

I let my own curiosity have a turn and asked what kind of work Helen did herself. In her answer, I saw the arrogant confidence of the artist.

"I do what interests me. I fit into no category, I prefer no single medium."

I got out a cigarette and lit it, letting the silence be until Helen was ready to talk again.

Two masseuses, a heavyset bleached blonde with cropped hair followed by a thin woman with a pointed, foxy face, her hair hennaed a pale auburn, wandered out onto the deck. They both wore shorts and low-cut, sleeveless T-shirts, with flip-flops on their feet. The blonde went into each massage room and inspected it. With a distinct Russian accent, Fox Face bummed a cigarette from me. She leaned on the rail to study the absent view while she smoked.

She had the sleeves of her T-shirt rolled up over her shoulders, showing biceps capable of pressing the kinks out of the knottiest muscles. The cleavage she had on display spoke of curing other conditions. Not that there was any officially sanctioned sex-for-money going on at the baths; one of Benno's buddies had once been offered a below-the-waist climax to a massage, but in more than ten years of monthly visits, that was the only time something salacious had ever been suggested.

The blonde finished with the rooms, said something in Russian, and disappeared down the stairs. Fox Face took a long drag of the cigarette and flipped it, still lit, into the backyard of the brownstone next door, then followed her comrade inside.

As if by tacit agreement, neither Helen nor I spoke until the intruders were gone.

"How old are—Shmuel and Zehava?" Their names rose out of the depths of my memory from when she'd shown me their pictures, over a year ago.

"Ten and eight. They are strangers to me." Helen rose and paced the perimeter of the deck, hugging herself, hands in her sleeves, then leaned against the railing and faced me. "When

Zehava was three, she could already knead the challah and parrot the blessings right along with her mother. Seeing her bowed over the candles with a little *shmatte* on her head, like my mother and my grandmother, the whole line of shtetl women with nothing better to do with their lives than cook and clean and bear children . . ."

Helen walked another circle around the deck. "My daughter thinks her religion is beautiful, with its rituals to liberate the mind from the mundane and free the soul to join with God. What I felt in that house was oppressive."

I nodded. What was there to say? A breeze rustled the ailanthus, bringing with it a faint taste of the acrid odor in the air. "Did Simon have friends?"

"I don't know."

"Why do you think he's missing?"

"September sixteenth, that was the last time he came to visit me. This past Sunday, I called the house. My daughter had only just realized—Simon was supposed to be in the Catskills, again with the teacher on a three-week retreat. He was expected home that morning. When he didn't arrive, she called the rebbe. According to him the person in charge of the retreat said Simon never went. They couldn't have called his mother to ask why not? No, apparently Simon told them he wasn't able to go because his mother needed him at home."

"Did she report it to the police?"

"Police. Everyone loves them now, but they haven't changed." Helen scowled and turned her head away. I thought she was going to spit. "Yes, she went to them. They told her it sounded like he planned the whole thing. Teenagers run away from home every day. Simon was over sixteen, and he'd done it before. They said they would call the hospitals and the morgue, but she should wait to hear from him. 'Runaways usually come home on their own,' they told her."

"Simon didn't call you either?"

"No. I told Ruthie something was wrong. If Simon ran away, he would have come to me again." She took three paces across the deck. "Let me see it now."

I handed her the flyer, still folded in half.

Helen opened the sheet of paper, stared at it a long moment, then crumpled it in her fist.

She sagged against me. I tried to support her, but her weight brought both of us down to the deck. I gathered her small body into my lap, where she curled, head to drawn-up knees, the flyer clutched to her chest.

I stroked her back, rocking her as I would a crying child.

We stayed like that until Helen straightened away from my touch. She looked around the deck, at the sky, the branches, as if trying to remember where she was.

I took her hands so she would face me. "Helen. Are you okay? Can I get you some water?" Idiot thing to say. Your grandson is dead, would you like a drink? Vodka, maybe.

Helen stroked the creases out of the flyer and shook her head, no. "Inez Collazo," she said. "This is who I should call?"

"Yes. Would you like me to—"

"There you are!" Janis stalked onto the deck and plopped herself down on a plastic chaise lounge. "I should have known you'd be up here smoking!"

Helen shoved the flyer into the fold of the loose robe and held it hidden against her chest.

"Janis—" I tried to warn her away.

"What's going on?" She wasn't oblivious, just curious.

I shook my head. This wasn't something to be shared, not yet.

Helen had gotten to her feet. I stood up and turned away from Janis.

"I'd be happy to go with you, if you'd like."

"No. Thank you." Helen said it without meeting my eyes, then brushed past Janis on the lounge.

I started to follow her, an elderly woman negotiating the steep stairs down to get dressed and go to the police to identify her dead grandchild.

"Leave her be, Anita," Janis said.

My best friend, as usual, giving voice to my own thoughts. Whether I had a job in the profession or not, I was caught in the same old social-worker dilemma. Should I persist in offering help, or step back and allow a person to make her own choices?

In this case, Helen wasn't my client. Having found her grandson's body still didn't make us more than acquaintances. I let her go.

Ten

I MOVED PAST JANIS TO HEAD DOWN THE STAIRS. THE WOMAN with the cropped blond hair was on her way up, a tall man in a black fedora right behind her. I took a step backward and bumped into Janis.

"What the—"

I turned around and hustled her out to the deck.

"Man on board," I whispered.

"What are you talking about? This is a women-only day, Anita, no men allowed."

"Shh, keep it down."

Trust Janis to raise her voice. I had no problem with the masseuse accepting a male client an hour earlier than the rules allowed; presumably he was a good tipper.

"Well, I'll be!" Janis breathed into my ear.

The woman paused at the top of the stairs and said something in Russian to the man, who from his black fedora, lack of *payess*, and black jacket worn over a white shirt buttoned to the neck was clearly an Orthodox Jew. He avoided looking at us as he strode past the exercise machines. I got a glimpse of closely trimmed russet beard before he stooped down to fit under the doorway to one of the massage rooms.

Janis stalked down the stairs and over to the register. Fortunately, Vera was busy with another customer. Not that that stopped Janis. "Hey, Vera, what's with—"

I slid my arm through hers and marched her off to the

locker room. "Didn't anyone ever tell you that silence is a virtue?"

Janis was pissed. "This is women's day. We're practically naked, and they're parading some horny Hebe up there for a look? I don't care what those Russian masseuses get up to, but not on my time."

"It's not your time," I pointed out, "it's theirs. They have to make a living, too, and it's hard enough without—"

"Don't give me that sisterhood crap," Janis fumed. "I know, I know. I just—the hypocrisy of those men—he's probably got eight kids and a wife pregnant with the ninth at home—"

"You're jumping to some pretty big conclusions there, girl-friend. Come on, you can finish steaming downstairs before you soak your head in the cold plunge."

I wasn't upset by the mere presence of a man, but I will say I was surprised by the appearance of this particular one. Call me naive, but I did think that blatantly religious people should be, as a rule, more pure than the ordinary citizen. They had an image to uphold, and stopping off for a massage in the middle of the day—it was none of my business, but still . . .

We sweated another couple of rounds in the radiant heat room, showered, and headed over to the Second Avenue Deli for borscht and pastrami sandwiches. After all that *shvitzing*, we needed meat. You can only be so pure.

I didn't have much to say. Janis kept up a running commentary on our waitress in an eventually successful attempt to make me smile. The woman was short and dumpling-plump, in her sixties probably, wearing the standard server's uniform of white top and black bottom. This woman, however—the skirt was six inches above her ample knees, and she'd paired it with a sheer nylon blouse, heavily endowed with concealing embroidery but still offering a view of lace-edged bra cups and satin straps.

At the end of the meal we had tea with lemon, and Janis got serious. "You know, Anita, you're wasted on woodwork. With all due respect to Benno's profession, you were born to be a social worker."

"You've got mustard in the corner of your mouth," I told her.

Janis tapped the back of my hand with her teaspoon. "I'm serious. You've got a gift with old people, or else some very heavy karma to work out. No matter what you do, they seem to find you. Like your neighbors, right? Now—"

"There really is mustard on your face." And I really didn't want to talk about my abandoned career in social work.

This time she believed me, and wiped it off. "Better?"

"No, but at least you got the *schmutz* off your face."

"Oh, good. Now will you stop sulking and tell me what that was all about with Raisin Woman?"

"I showed her the picture of the boy I found in the vacuum press and it turned out to be her missing grandson."

"Really?" Janis sat back, bemused. "New effing York. I mean, how weird is that? Where else would you get that kind of coincidence? You find the body of a complete stranger, and it turns out you know his grandmother."

I didn't know then how truly odd the coincidences were about to get, or how many fewer than six the degrees of separation were in Williamsburg's Jewish community.

"About as weird as your theory that I'm a magnet for old people," I said.

Janis had a point, though. All my life, even before I took care of my grandmother, I seemed to get involved in the lives of elderly people. In high school, I cleaned house for my boyfriend's grandmother and several of her friends. I hadn't intended to specialize in geriatrics when I started social work, but my first field placement was with an agency serving Holocaust survivors, and my next two jobs were at agencies dealing with senior citizens. Not to mention my neighbors, and now Helen.

We paid the check. Former waitress that I was, I left a healthy tip.

Janis headed uptown to prepare for a rehearsal of "Mooseface." I hadn't intended to go to the shop that day, but I found I needed to see my husband.

Benno is my anchor, my roots, my source of comfort when I'm troubled. And I was, by Helen as well as the boy in the press. Knowing a member of his family would make it easier for me to satisfy my curiosity about the why of his death, but then—it brought the question of my right to pry into sharper focus.

Benno was glad to see me, too, but not for the same reasons.

He was just hanging up the phone when I climbed the stairs to the office.

"Hey, Anita, you're in the nick of time."

I bent and kissed him. "What's up?"

"The cops are keeping the vacuum press. Evidence, they said."

"You want it back?" I couldn't imagine even looking at the thing, let alone using it.

"No, of course not. Even if I replaced the bag, there's probably stuff in the motor . . ." Benno ran a hand over his thick hair, gilding it with a streak of sawdust. "But I'm out a thousand-dollar machine. The police suggested I get in touch with the Crime Victims' Board and see if we can get some kind of compensation. Maybe you could deal with them—it's more up your alley than mine."

"Sure. But first I have to call Inez." I perched on the two-drawer filing cabinet while I filled him in about the possible identity of our young mystery man.

"Weird," was Benno's response, too. "You don't think someone put his body in our press because they knew you knew his grandmother?"

"How would anyone even know that, when I didn't myself? No, it's just one of those things."

"They say there's no such thing as coincidence," he pointed out.

"*They* say lots of stuff. That doesn't mean they're right!"

Benno shrugged. "So call your friend the detective and see what she has to say about it."

I did, but Inez wasn't in. I left a message, and then spent half an hour explaining to various levels of the Crime Victims' Board what exactly a vacuum press was and why we wouldn't be able to use ours anymore. Time well spent; it looked like we'd be reimbursed for replacement value. Miracles never cease.

I gave Benno the good news, and told him I was heading off to Clea's cross-country meet in Riverside Park on my way home.

"My wife, the soccer mom," Benno teased. "Tell her I said 'break a leg.'"

"I don't think so," I said, not amused.

"Hey." Benno read my reaction and wrapped his arms around me. "What'sa matter, kid, can't take a joke?"

Not in those bruised days, I couldn't.

"You know what the head of the school calls her?" Benno tried again.

I shook my head.

"The fastest girl in the sixth grade."

"That's not funny either!" But I had to smile even as I thumped him on the chest. "I'd better get going."

"Do you have time to drop some money off at Grant's on your way to the subway?" Benno asked. "He was here all morning helping me frame up the walls for your new spray room."

He pointed across the shop, where a corner was now defined by two-by-fours and sheets of plywood. I hadn't even noticed.

"Don't start crying, now"—Benno shook a gentle finger at me—"I know it seems like you'll be working out of my back pocket, but I had to put the finishing operation somewhere. The next stage of this job will be ready for you in a few days."

"It's fine," I said. Getting back to work would be good for me, I knew that.

Benno opened the file cabinet and took out his secret stash of twenties. "Grant asked for cash rather than a check. It's only a couple hundred, but I didn't want him to know I kept that much on hand. I told him I'd drop it off after I hit the ATM at lunch, then I forgot. You don't mind?"

"No problem." What with Benno having set up a new spray area, taking this errand off his hands was the least I could do.

"I'll call and let him know you're on your way so he'll buzz you right in," Benno said. "He'll be happier to see you than me, anyway. Grant's none too pleased with me these days—it was like working with a volcano just dying to erupt this morning."

"What's his problem?"

"You forgot about the boy in the vacuum press already? Grant was pretty pissed that I gave his name to a member of New York's finest, even one as easy on the eyes as your friend Inez."

Eleven

I WALKED PAST THE HULKING SANITATION TRUCKS AND TURNED up Jay Street. The stop would make me a little late to the track meet. Not that Clea would care; I was the one who enjoyed seeing her cross the finish line just behind the fastest boys. For her, it was all hard work.

Grant Farrell's studio was on the corner of Front Street, a former warehouse now divided into a warren of irregular spaces. I'd been there a few times before, and I preferred to walk up to the fourth floor rather than wait for Grant to fetch me in the rickety freight elevator. The stairwell and the massive overhead pipes were painted battleship-gray, with the railings a dust-encrusted but still startling chartreuse. The frosted windows, reinforced with chicken wire, let in a chilly light.

I was conscious of how deserted the building seemed, although I knew there were plenty of worker bees busy expressing themselves in media too diverse to catalog. Probably all contemplating their output to their own personal soundtracks, headphones over their ears. I felt like a rat in a maze.

Artistic anarchy ruled—none of the doors had numbers on them. It took me three wrong turns down meandering hallways before I recognized Grant's. He'd installed a spy hole and surrounded it with sharp curls of scrap metal. They looked playful, like an attempt to imitate bushy eyelashes, but in reality they served to keep anyone on the outside from getting close enough to dare a look in.

I debated just sliding the envelope under the door, but I realized I could use a pit stop before I spent a couple hours in Riverside Park with its lack of facilities, so I knocked.

The fish-eye darkened, and Grant's voice came through the door. "Hey, Anita, hang on a mo."

It was a good minute before I heard the sound of the police lock sliding aside and the clicks of the two Medecos. I was feeling awkward about having waited and what I might be interrupting, but Grant was his usual relaxed self when he finally got the door open and bowed me in.

"It's so nice to see you, Ms. Servi, rather than your worser half." Typical Grant, flattery for me and insult for Benno in the same sentence.

I smiled, more from nervousness than pleasure. Not that I minded flirting, I just didn't care to do it at Benno's expense. As soon as I stepped inside, Grant locked all three locks behind me.

I couldn't see any reason for the delay in opening the door. Grant appeared to be alone, and fully clothed in baggy Levi's and an orange T-shirt with the sleeves rolled up over muscular biceps. He'd shaved his goatee and had his hair cut so closely that a comb would be unnecessary for weeks to come. With rimless glasses, it was definitely a look—half intellectual, half dockworker—although the three thick silver hoops in his left earlobe and the braided silver bracelet on one wrist pushed the image over the line to artist.

"Tell your hub I said thanks, huh?" He took the envelope I held out and added it to a pile of papers on one end of a table made from a half sheet of plywood balanced on a pair of sawhorses.

Grant had one of the larger spaces in the building, with

partition walls that went all the way up to the barrel-vaulted brick ceiling. He'd installed a forced-air heater in the main space and it was going full blast. I unzipped my leather jacket and looked around, curious to see what he was working on.

A third of the room had been blocked off with a six-foot wall. A ladder propped against one side led to what appeared to be a storage space. I knew, from attending a party here last spring, that the cardboard boxes piled along the front edge were really camouflage for a sleeping loft. Behind the wall on the main floor was a mini-kitchen, complete with double hot plate and microwave, next to a bathroom with an illicit shower—an ingenious construction that had the shower up on a four-foot platform so it could be drained by a hose into the sink.

Grant shoved his hands in his pockets and watched me, head cocked to the side, as I stepped over to the long metal shelf under the windows that held his recent work.

It took a minute for me to understand what I was looking at. The foot-high welded figures progressed from people created literally out of nuts and bolts—yup, the women all nuts, collections of orifices; the men all bolts, studded with protuberances. Almost cute, in a Freudian kind of way.

Then the figures changed, became more complex. The women were assemblages of pliers that had been sawed apart and welded into forms that featured pincers for not only mouths and vaginas but breasts as well. There were fewer males, made from chisels with sharp edges sticking out at lethal angles.

When I got to a female figure with genitals fashioned from small saw blades, I had to smile. The vagina dentata is old hat; once you've seen Giacometti's "Woman With Her Throat Cut" everything else loses its power to impress.

"Interesting stuff," I commented. Always a safe response. Grant nodded, amused, but I thought he looked disappointed that I wasn't shocked.

I threw him a bone. "Looks like you're working on gender issues—is there a particular significance to the choice of tools as a medium?"

And was immediately sorry I had. For all his cool posture, Grant was like a geeky kid who rushes into any opportunity to pontificate on an obscure area of interest only to him. I lost the thread of sense when Grant got into a riff on "pulling apart and reordering the abstracted narrative of sexuality" with something, something about the "geometry of genitalia and the quality of primitive representation."

I managed a few intelligent grunts before there was a lull long enough for me to ask to use the bathroom.

"Why, I'd be right honored to have you piss in my toilet, ma'am." Grant snapped back to ironic adult without missing a beat.

I kind of preferred the enthusiastic boy with his jargon.

IT WAS THREE-THIRTY WHEN I LEFT GRANT'S STUDIO. I DIDN'T enjoy the subways at that hour, when they were crowded with jostling teenagers freed from the constraints of school. They filled the cars with backpacks, music, and cursing conversations, oblivious to other passengers. Or worse, openly contemptuous of anyone who looked as though they wanted the kids to rein in their behavior. I understood how hard it was to sit at desks in rooms that could hardly contain the physical energy coursing through adolescent bodies, how much they reveled in bumping shoulders and talking at the top of their voices—but that didn't mean I wanted a front row seat.

I got off the subway at Seventy-second Street and headed for the track in Riverside Park. On the way, I passed Greenwald's Kosher Bakery and stopped in for a loaf of Benno's favorite, corn rye. I also picked up a pound of *rugelach*, dense buttery snails of cookie dough wrapped around chopped walnuts, raspberry jam, and chocolate.

Call it divine intervention or sheer impulse, the thought crossed my mind that *rugelach* in a box clearly labeled as being from a kosher bakery would be an appropriate thing to bring along when making a shiva call to an Orthodox household. You can't go wrong with sweets on a sad occasion.

Twelve

THE NEXT DAY, INEZ CALLED ME BACK AT THE SHOP AND CON-
firmed that the boy had been officially identified.

"Thanks for making the connection with Helen Baum," she
said. "Odd, isn't it, how small-town New York can be?"

"So who was he?" I asked.

"The name on his birth certificate was Simon Warner, although he went by Edelman—his stepfather's last name."

"He was adopted?" I asked. That would give him something
in common with my own daughter.

"No, not legally. According to the mother, Simon's father
dropped out of the picture when she remarried and he stopped
sending money. She didn't even know how to contact him."

"Do you have a cause of death yet?"

There was a moment of silence. I crossed my fingers and
waited for Inez to decide how forthcoming she wanted to be.
Like I said, this wasn't the first time I'd shared her interest in
investigating an unnatural death. The extent of my involve-
ment was totally up to her, however, and I was hoping that she
knew me well enough to remember that I could be discreetly
helpful.

"The toxicology scan showed that he had traces of
MDMA—commonly known as Ecstasy or E, the hug drug—in
his system, along with a significant amount of methamphetamine, crystal meth."

"He died of a drug overdose?"

"Not exactly." Inez hesitated. "Ecstasy is rarely fatal. The deaths that do result from its use are usually due to extreme dehydration. Methamphetamine-related fatalities tend to occur among long-term abusers, although high doses can cause respiratory arrest."

"So what exactly killed him?"

"The official cause of death was suffocation."

"He was smothered?"

No response.

"Inez, please just tell me."

She did. "The medical examiner's report stated that Simon Warner was alive when the vacuum motor was turned on. They could tell from the way the blood was drawn to the surface of his skin, and vented from all of his orifices."

The information was enough to conjure up the image of Simon's bruised and blood-streaked body. In order to dispel it, I asked the first question that occurred to me.

"What did the drugs have to do with it?"

"Ecstasy use is fairly common among Jewish youth, as is marijuana—especially with the Hasidic boys. I've been told that their founding father smoked it centuries ago, that it was the basis for divine visions or something."

I'd read about that somewhere—maybe a bit of propaganda from NORML, the National Organization for Reform of Marijuana Laws—how the Ba'al Shem Tov was inspired by smoking pot.

"I thought Simon was Orthodox, not Hasidic," I said.

"That's right, but there are thriving drug markets in all of Brooklyn's Jewish communities—Borough Park, Crown Heights, even Williamsburg," Inez answered. "Smugglers recruit young Orthodox men as mules, provide the plane tickets, and pay them a couple thousand for a 'vacation' in Amsterdam. A few months ago, an Israeli teen got busted bringing in a suitcase of Ecstasy, which led to a raid on a whole family that was distributing the stuff. Father, mother, two uncles, as well as the boy."

"Jeez. If even yeshiva students are doing them, I guess drugs really are everywhere."

"Kids," Inez agreed. "They'll try anything. Ecstasy is supposed to be like a spiritual experience, that's the appeal it has for religious people. The high makes them feel rapturous, like they're in tune with the higher powers."

Yes, I'd heard about Ecstasy. It sounded like the kind of drug, if it had been around when I was a teenager, I'd have tried myself. Amazing, though, what maturity will do for you. Life came with more than enough side effects for me.

"Crystal meth, though, that's the substance we really don't want to see making an appearance in the city. It's highly addictive, easy to manufacture, causes bizarre and violent behavior. Habitual use results in permanent brain damage."

"Would it make someone crawl into a vacuum press and—" flip the switch himself? It was a stupid question. Inez answered anyway.

"No, but it might lead you to put someone else in that situation. Simon Warner's death was definitely a homicide."

"How old was he?"

"He would have turned seventeen in two weeks."

We both sighed.

"Do you think it would be all right for me to pay a condolence call to the family? It's a Jewish custom to sit shiva for seven days after the funeral, and people come over to the house."

Another silence. This time I didn't wait it out.

"All I need is the address, Inez. If you can't give it to me, I'll just look it up. Edelman is the last name, right? And they live in Williamsburg?"

"Yes. At 236 Heyward Street." Inez paused. "Since you're going over there anyway, Anita, I'd like a report. It's hard to get any of these people to talk to outsiders. Maybe you'll have better luck, being Jewish, even if you're not observant. We'll take all the help we can get."

IT WAS MONDAY BEFORE I HAD ENOUGH FREE TIME TO MAKE THE trip. There I was, one o'clock in the afternoon, on the other side of the East River with a pink bakery box in my hands, all dressed up and unable to make myself go in.

Dressing had been the simple part.

I had a perfectly suitable black velour dress, midcalf length with long sleeves. Accessorizing wasn't a problem—opaque black tights, and to hide my hair, a loose-knit black angora beret borrowed from Clea's hat collection. No makeup, no jewelry. Add a black wool winter coat, and there I was: the ur-New Yorker, ready for a gallery opening or an Orthodox mourning visit.

It had taken me over an hour to get there, what with the three train changes, and another ten minutes to walk over to Heyward. It was on the less-prosperous edge of the area, a two-story row house in a street lined with similar dwellings. Like its neighbors, the Edelmans' residence had a large mezuzah mounted on the right-hand side of the door frame. There was a separate entrance under the high stoop, probably for the garden apartment. That doorpost was also adorned with a long, slender box containing the requisite prayers.

The time I spent in transit had done nothing to alleviate my nervousness. I didn't know much about Orthodox shiva customs, but extrapolating from my experiences with Benno's family I knew there would be morning and evening prayers. I'd timed my arrival to be after one and before the other.

Facing the house, mounting its seven steps was more than I could bring myself to do. My mere presence seemed like an intrusion. What could I say, after "I'm so sorry for your loss"?

The truth. That I came because I found the boy's body, and I helped to identify him.

In the face of my inability to ring the bell, I had to ask myself why I thought those were reasons enough. Because they may have gotten me dressed and to Brooklyn, but they obviously weren't strong enough to get me to the door.

I walked past the narrow brick row house and crossed the street. When I looked back, a group of men had appeared on the top step. All but one of them wore black fedoras, their faces shadowed by the private-eye curves to the deep brims. The odd man wore a distinctive, high-crowned beaver hat, the *streimel* of the Hasidim.

One of the men moved down a step and scanned the street. He looked both ways, as if searching for someone. I had the sensation of his gaze traveling over me without in the least registering my presence; I was of less than no interest to him. It gave me the freedom to watch him without worrying about getting caught. As he looked back in my direction, though, I realized that I recognized him: Dovid Fine, Benno's landlord.

Now what was he doing here? He wasn't a friend; Inez had shown him the photo of the dead boy, and Mr. Fine had said he didn't recognize Simon.

Exactly. And for all I knew, Mr. Fine lived in the community, and a personal acquaintance with the deceased wasn't necessary for a man to make a shiva call on a bereaved family.

Still, Simon had died on his property. I had to wonder if Mr. Fine had known who the boy was all along, and for reasons beyond my ken had kept it to himself. Reasons such as—? Nothing occurred to me at the moment.

Suspicious mind you've got, Anita.

I watched the men take out cigarettes and light up. There didn't seem to be any conversation going on. Nor did anyone glance again in the direction where I hovered.

Along the sidewalk, women came and went. An impossibly young mother—no, that was her own hair held back by a velvet band, she was more likely an older daughter—pushed an English-style pram. The spoked wheels flashed in the sun. Two women with wigs and head scarves reminded me how easy it was to differentiate marital status among the women.

For the moment, the men's presence on the stoop had resolved my dilemma. No way I was approaching a house with five of them on the doorstep. I balanced the box of *rugelach* against my knee, fumbled with the catch on the black velvet purse I reserved for special occasions, got out a cigarette, and flicked Barbara's lighter.

I didn't know how people managed it, so many funerals in those months, so saturated in grief. I'd lost my best friend, and this call on the mother of a boy I'd never met was more than I could bear. You don't have to, I told myself. You don't belong here. This is not a moment to be intruding. What makes you think the mother wants to see you, of all people, the woman who found her son's body?

The truth of the matter was, I hadn't come to see her; I was hoping Helen would be there. Blame it on the social worker in me, or the bored cabinetmaker's wife. I wanted to know that the elderly woman was all right.

And yes, I was still looking for *Why*. I'd discovered who the boy in my vacuum press was; I knew his grandmother; now I wanted to know more about what kind of family Simon Edelman came from.

One by one, the men in black flipped their cigarettes toward the sidewalk. I was amused to notice that they did it with the same finger and thumb gesture any street tough would have used, and with the same disregard for where the still-burning ember would land. Men. Honestly.

I stepped to the curb, dropped my filter, and stepped on it.

When I looked up, I caught sight of a boy on the corner who looked as out of place as I felt. At least I had the protective black coloration right; the kid, with his hatless head of slightly-too-long blond hair, tan trousers, and navy sport coat—well, he stood out like a Jehovah's Witness in a synagogue. Which in a sense he was.

I recognized him even without the anonymous varsity jacket he'd been wearing the first time I'd seen him—it was the young man from York Street. A Witness in Williamsburg, that was odd enough. The same one who'd been tearing down the flyers with the face of the now-identified Jewish boy—what's the opposite of coincidence?

He had to have a reason to be there, and I wanted to know what it was. The fact that it was none of my business didn't deter me in the least. Age has its perks, and one of them is the ability to speak to teenagers and expect to be answered. Not necessarily politely answered, or even printably, but nevertheless . . .

I started walking toward him and he took off. Not running,

but at a pace my pumps had no hope of matching. I watched him turn the corner of Bedford Street and disappear.

With my adrenaline up, I felt brave enough to do what I'd come all that way for. I crossed the street, climbed the stairs, and rang the Edelmans' bell.

Thirteen

A YOUNGISH WOMAN WITH A SHORT BLACK WIG, IN A BLACK SUIT with a long skirt, opened the door. It was clear that she was surprised to find a stranger there, but she took the pink bakery box with a politely murmured thank you. Another woman, older, in a black dress with an ivory lace collar, appeared from the back of the house, took the *rugelach* out of her hand, smiled warmly in my direction, and disappeared.

The sound of hushed voices came from a room to the right of the entry. A metal rack had been set up in the hall, crowded against the foot of a staircase, and the woman indicated that I should hang my coat with the half-dozen others already there. She didn't introduce herself, so I started.

"My name is Anita Servi."

"You know Rivka from before?" she asked.

"No, I'm a friend of her mother's." I held out my hand.

"Oh?" The woman shot me a look, frankly curious, and ignored my offer to shake. Maybe I'd violated some custom I was unaware of; I knew Orthodox men who worked in stores would lay change on the counter rather than risk touching the hand of a non-Jew. She hadn't told me her name, either. I was nervous enough about being there, and the coolness of that single "oh" did nothing to reassure me.

"I was hoping that Mrs. Baum would be here," I tried again.

"She left an hour ago." This time the woman frowned at

me. "Rivka's upstairs. I'll just let her know someone's come on her mother's behalf."

"Oh, no, please don't disturb her if she's resting." My timing, apparently, was terrible.

"I'm sure Rivka will want to know. I'll be right back."

It seemed clear that she intended me to wait at the foot of the stairs, which I did for several minutes. I was acutely uncomfortable, debating whether to bolt, when a door down the hall opened.

"There you are!" A woman with a toddler on her hip and her wig slightly askew gestured at me with one arm, as if I were a marvelous apparition. "Come, please, come in. What was Rochel thinking, to leave you standing alone out here?"

She gave me no chance to answer. It was just as well.

In the center of a patterned rug stood three low benches. Close to the ground with grief, that custom I understood.

The seats were empty.

I looked around at what was evidently the dining room, its table moved out of the way and jammed into a corner next to a glass-fronted china cabinet. Toward the front of the house, a set of pocket doors had been slid closed—separating off the living room, where from the sound of deeper voices the men were gathered. At the opposite end, there was a swinging door with a round window.

Here came the lace-collared woman, with my *rugelach* now on a china plate that she made space for on a table already crowded with baked goods, plates, cups, napkins, spoons, and a polished brass coffee urn. The air was alive with the comfortable chatter of female voices, and I relaxed a little. I should have remembered that women are women, wherever you go.

"It's very nice to see one of Rivka's old friends," Lace Collar said. When I'd seen her in the dim hallway, I'd thought she was a generation older than me. Now I saw her wig was blond rather than white, and we were probably the same age, late forties. "I'm Esther Swersky. Such a terrible thing, and so nice of you to come. Please, help yourself to coffee and a *bissel* to eat. I'm sure Rivka will be down soon. Meanwhile, you'll sit with us?"

"Rivka's resting," the woman with a fat baby on her hip whispered to me. "Her mother was here, and after she left, Rivka was so upset."

"I'm sorry," I said. "I know she and her mother . . . but at a time like this . . ."

The two women looked at me like I'd just mentioned having a ham sandwich for lunch. Was it not polite to allude to family troubles in public? Mrs. Swersky might have finessed the situation, but her attention was claimed by a toddler tugging at her skirt.

The younger one, however, seemed all too eager to confide in me. "Shimon, you know, Shimon was not her husband's son. It's hard sometimes, when a child isn't born into the community. My husband teaches yeshiva, and he said Shimon was a *vilder mensch*, a real rebellious one."

"Teenagers do go through phases," I said, trying to keep it neutral.

But I had a fledgling yenta here, and she went on. "He kept himself apart. No one is surprised he died a *miesse meshina*."

"A what?" My reliance on the consonance of German and Yiddish failed me.

"A *miesse meshina*, a strange death. Unnatural."

I couldn't argue with that. "Do you know if Mrs. Baum is coming back today?"

"Oh, I don't think so! Not after what she said. Mr. Edelman, he made her *gey aveck*, even though she was Rivka's mother."

"Shaina! *Loshen hore!*" The woman who'd abandoned me in the hallway was back. She hissed her admonishment to the young mother, then raised her voice loud enough for the whole room to hear. "You are gossiping to a friend of Rivka's mother."

The various conversations stopped completely. Heads turned toward me, then quickly away. Whatever Helen had said or done, it must have been a serious breach of protocol.

For just a moment, standing among these Orthodox Jewish women, I'd started to feel myself at one with them. The looks on their faces now told me I wasn't, not by a long shot. The communal hostility was so pronounced it pushed me back toward the door. I mumbled an apology to no one in particular and turned to leave. I was shaken, and grateful to find Mrs. Swersky at my elbow, helping me into my coat and muttering reassurances to me.

"There, now, you didn't know, how could you know? So nice of you to come, really, all that way."

A man appeared in the doorway across the hall, drawn I supposed by the sudden silence.

"What is it, Mrs. Swersky?" he asked. "Did my wife—"

"No, no, she's still upstairs. An old friend is here, she's just leaving now. She didn't want to disturb."

Rivka's husband I presumed, a well-built man with an arrogant jut to his beardless jaw. He stood with his shoulders back and his chest out, the lord of the manor asserting his dominance over we mere women in the narrow entry. He wore a tallis, a prayer shawl, white with blue stripes at the ends, over the shoulders of his regulation black suit.

He made no acknowledgment of my presence, and Mrs.

Swersky clearly wasn't going to introduce me. Manners are manners, I thought. I'd come to express my condolences, and that was what I did.

"I'm very sorry for your loss, Mr. Edelman." I managed to remember not to hold out my hand.

"Yes." A glance that flicked from my face to my feet before he nodded once. He wasn't wearing a hat, just a black velvet yarmulke.

As was the man who came up behind him.

I opened my mouth to greet Dovid Fine, but was stopped by the appearance of a third man. Tall, with a neatly shaped russet beard, and an aura of authority that didn't need a puffed chest to make itself felt. Even without the hat, I recognized him from the baths.

"*Nu, Dovid, vos iz der mer?*" he addressed Mr. Fine. He stroked his beard, twice, lovingly, then gave it a small tug before turning to stare at the man of the house.

Adam Edelman, in turn, scowled at Mrs. Swersky. "*Vos meynt es?*"

Never mind understanding the Yiddish, I got the gist of it— I was the dog in this hierarchy, about to be kicked out.

Right on cue, Mrs. Swersky had the door open and was not-so-subtly motioning me to leave. "You have everything? Good. Thank you for coming. Good-bye now."

I nodded to the men as the woman practically pushed me out the door.

I was halfway down the block, my cheeks stung with embarrassment, before I registered the look on Dovid Fine's face when he'd recognized me. He hadn't just been surprised, he'd been shocked white by my presence in that house.

Fourteen

I YANKED CLEA'S BERET OFF MY HEAD AND SHOOK OUT MY HAIR. So much for trying to fit in. I didn't slow down until I hit Lee Avenue, which was too crowded with pedestrian traffic for me to keep up my furious pace.

Once I calmed down enough to look around, I decided to do what I would in any unfamiliar place where I was a visitor—shop. There's no better way to get to know a culture than to see what's on offer in the stores. I started with a different bakery, and picked up a chocolate *babka* as a treat for Benno.

I was about to cross over to a deli for a take-out supper when I noticed a sign for Swersky's Drugs. Cough medicine for Clea, that was something else I needed. If this store belonged to the lace-collared woman who'd been so kind to me, it would be nice to give her my business.

And I was curious to check out the makeup. The women at the Edelmans' had been quite smartly dressed, their faces tastefully done, and their wigs clearly made from real hair styled as if it were their own. I didn't quite get the point; the rules said a married woman's hair was for her husband's eyes only, so she hid it from the world by putting on a wig as close to natural as possible? Vanity, alive and well wherever women are.

I jaywalked across the middle of the block. No one gave me a second glance. I hesitated outside the store, studying the window display. Through the plate glass, I got a glimpse of the counter at the rear of the store. I could see a young girl in a pharmacist's white smock and the back of a hatless customer. Darned if it wasn't the same young Jehovah's Witness who seemed to be a step ahead of me wherever I went these days.

I ducked into the store and loitered in a side aisle, hoping the kid wouldn't recognize me with my hair loose. As I approached the back of the store, I could see that he'd stacked more than a dozen boxes of cough medication on the counter. Very interesting, but for all I knew he was supplying the medicine cabinet of whatever kind of communal living arrangements the Witnesses had in their building on High Street.

Why was he doing it in Williamsburg? And why did this boy in particular keep turning up? First taking down the posters with Simon's picture, then hanging around on the Edelmans' street, now shopping in this neighborhood where he obviously didn't belong. What was the deal?

Their voices were too low for me to catch what they were saying, but from the tone and rhythm of the exchange I got the impression they were flirting. A little cross-cultural romance? That would certainly explain the boy's presence in Williamsburg.

I supposed their attraction to each other wasn't so surprising, really. Teenagers were teenagers, and the restrictive cultures of the Orthodox and the Witnesses had a lot in common when it came to limiting the social activities of their young people.

But how on earth had these two met in the first place?

I studied a rack of face powder and eye shadow. Amid the Revlon and Maybelline was a brand I'd never heard of. I picked up a box of cake eye shadow with a little pad applicator and noticed that it had a *hecksher*, the symbol that indicated that it was kosher—kosher makeup? It had never occurred to me that animal products might be used in makeup, but who knew what they put in the stuff? Kosher makeup suddenly struck me as a good idea.

"This is the last time," the girl said. She no longer sounded like she was flirting. "My uncle is asking why we sell so much of this."

"Didn't you tell him October is cold season?" The boy's voice was light, trying to persuade.

"No more. Please. I already told Shimon—"

"Shh!" He hissed at her. "Okay, no more. We don't even need it yet. I just wanted to see you."

"I can't." There was more regret than resolve in her voice. "After what happened, I can't anymore."

"That had nothing to do with us!"

A little bell rang as the drawer of the cash register slid open. "That will be one hundred forty-two dollars and twelve cents, please."

"Leah," he said. "I promise you, nothing bad will happen."

"A bad thing already happened, Richard."

Silence, except for the rustle of a bag being opened and filled with the boy's purchase, followed by the clink of coins in the register and the drawer sliding closed.

"It was a mistake, okay? Besides, he brought it on himself. Please, Leah—"

The sound of a hand slapping down on the counter. "No!"

I was about to interrupt when Richard lowered his voice. I froze, trying to hear what he was saying.

". . . next week, and we can . . . come on, Leah, it'll be okay, I promise—"

"Leave me alone!" Now she sounded angry. "It's wrong, what we did was wrong. I can't see you anymore. I'm sorry."

I cleared my throat. I didn't want to get involved in a Romeo-and-Juliet affair, but it sounded to me like the lady was looking for a way out.

I walked around the end of the aisle, so they could see me, and came upon the cold remedies. Just what I was looking for. There was a large gap in the display of cough suppressants. I picked up boxes of two different brands and carried them to the counter.

Once again, I got a good view of the boy's back as he hurried away from me. Richard. And he knew something about Simon's death. As did Leah.

She'd retreated behind the shelves of prescription medications in the back of the store. When I put my purchases next to the cash register, she emerged.

Leah looked to be in her late teens at the most. Even without makeup and her light brown hair held back by a tortoise-shell headband, she was pretty. Especially with her cheeks flushed with color from the encounter.

"You're Leah Swersky, aren't you?" Between the name of the store and having overheard the boy call her Leah, it wasn't much of a gamble. I said it with what I hoped was a disarming smile.

"Yes. How did you—?"

"Esther Swersky's daughter, right?" I kept up the smile.

"Yes." She was still puzzled.

"I just met your mother, at Mr. and Mrs. Edelman's house. I made a shiva visit for their son, Shimon. You knew him, didn't you?" I shook my head at the tragedy of it, but didn't wait for her to answer. "Anyway, I was talking with your mother, and she told me all about her wonderful daughter. When I saw the name on the store, I decided to stop in."

I positively beamed at poor Leah. She wilted into speech-lessness under the weight of my delight at having identified her. I pushed on.

"Your mother said that you and Shimon were close. You must be devastated by his death." That was a bigger leap.

Leah took a step back. She stared at me as if I were her worst nightmare.

"My mother said that?"

"Not in those words exactly . . ." I was trying for the role of ditzy busybody, rushing in where someone more tactful would hesitate to go. "That young man who was just in here, he knew Shimon, too, didn't he?"

That got me a flicker of frightened eyes before Leah turned to fiddle with a display of small padlocks hanging on the wall to her right.

"I saw him when I went to the Edelmans', and he seemed like a nice young man."

"He went to their house?" The words were out before she could stop herself.

"On the street outside, not in the house." I channeled Aunt Rose and took on a protective, motherly tone. "Was he bothering you just now?"

"Oh, no." Leah shook her head. "Not at all." The panicky expression in her eyes contradicted her words.

I was ashamed of myself, but not enough to shut up. "Well, that's all right then. It's so nice to see young people from different backgrounds getting to know each other. I can't help wondering, though, how you all got to be friends?"

Rather than answering, Leah looked down at the two boxes I'd left on the counter. "Would you like both of these?"

"Which one is better, do you think?" I asked. I kept talking to allow Leah time to regain her composure. "My daughter's got a sore throat but she's not running a fever, and I'm not sure which to get. They make these combinations so confusing, don't they?"

"Both are good," was all she said.

"Well, this one doesn't have any alcohol in it. Do you know if it works just as well as the other?"

"Oh, yes." Now she relaxed. "That one is excellent."

"I noticed that the young man who was just here bought an awful lot of it," I said, still in Aunt Rose mode. "Someone buying that many boxes of anything is a good recommendation, don't you think?"

Leah nodded.

"Does he live around here?" I asked.

This time she shook her head. The panicky expression was back.

"No, I didn't think so," I kept on with the chattiness. I figured if I ignored her reticence, the manners of her upbringing would eventually compel her to respond. "I could tell from the way he was dressed, that's why I was worried that he was bothering you."

"No." The one small word was all she seemed able to muster.

"But you do know him, right?"

In answer, Leah rung up my purchase and said, "Six ninety-nine, please."

What the heck. I tried one more time. "It didn't look like that nice young man came in here just to stock up on cold medicine . . ." I trailed off suggestively.

It worked, but not the way I'd intended. Rather than confiding in me, Leah found a way to parry my intrusive questions. "The Jehovah's Witnesses often shop in our stores. They like it that we don't put unnecessary ingredients in the kosher medicines."

"Of course." I smiled at her. It wasn't much of an answer, but I left without further upsetting the girl.

Besides, Leah had as much as admitted that she knew Richard when she referred to him being a Jehovah's Witness. Anyone could tell from the way he dressed that he wasn't Jewish, but nothing proclaimed what his religion might be.

On the sidewalk, I hesitated. I was midway between the subway back to Manhattan and the B57 to Dumbo. I wasn't dressed for the shop, but then, the first time I'd seen Romeo Richard it had been on the bus. That settled it.

I kept a lookout for the boy as I hiked down to Flushing Avenue, but I didn't get a glimpse of him till I was a block from the stop. New York luck—the bus pulled up for the one person waiting to board, and was gone by the time I'd broken into a run. And wouldn't you know, the passenger was a young man with sandy hair that spilled over the collar of his navy sports jacket.

Fifteen

SO MUCH FOR THAT. I CONSULTED THE BUS MAP AT THE STOP
and realized that the B57 in the opposite direction would take
me to the Flushing Avenue subway station, where I could
catch an ordinary old J train back to Manhattan. I had pity on
my feet in their dress pumps and took the easy route. I'd had
enough of chasing teenagers for the time being.

Tuesday morning, I was back to work. Benno was cutting
parts for the next phase of the job, and I was his extra set of
hands.

I took an odd satisfaction in my role in this shared labor.
Benno had all the measurements and cuts laid out; I was there
to help launch the awkward sheets of oak plywood onto the
sliding table of the carriage saw. I removed and stacked the cut-
off pieces without conscious thought, anticipating Benno's
moves as if I were in fact his third and fourth hands. As I
squatted, positioned my grip, lifted from the knees, it occurred
to me that maybe these religions had a point about women
subsuming themselves to their men. It was so restful, to be the
helpmeet and simply do what I was told.

The rising whirr of the table saw as it bit through wood was
like white noise to my thoughts. I let the sound fill my brain
until there was no room for anything else. My machine-
induced meditation lasted all of two days before the job re-
quirements shifted to jointer and planer, which made a high
whine as the blades shaved the boards Benno fed into their

steel mouths. The sound would have driven me out of the shop, but I couldn't face the nothing there was to do at home, either.

I pestered Benno to come up with a task for me. "Okay, you want to make yourself useful, you could clean the bathroom. And the fridge could use defrosting."

I was so desperate, I did it. Took a whole half hour. The freezer occupied another half hour, once the ice melted enough so I could go at it with an old chisel. That lasted until Benno caught me.

"Anita! Haven't I told you, never use a tool on a material it wasn't intended for—and certainly not in a refrigerator!"

So I was exiled from the shop, which put me on the street at eleven-thirty on a ridiculously sunny Thursday morning. Not that I was complaining. It was a gorgeous fall—day after day, clear, blue, crisp, sunny. It was the disconnect between the weather and my own internal state that was so unsettling.

It wasn't just me. Everyone was off-kilter. The September 11 death toll that changed daily, the obituaries, the funerals with no bodies, and then the anthrax business to add a drumbeat of anxiety to everything—I just didn't feel like getting back on the subway.

I'd sat through fifteen minutes of an inexplicable, midtunnel stop on the 1 train that morning. The long-suffering, ironic camaraderie of New Yorkers at the mercy of an irrational transit system was gone. These days, every time a train paused like that, the silence that descended on the car had an uneasy edge to it. We were all aware of the shared thought in each of our minds as we looked furtively at our fellow passengers: Are these the last faces I'll ever see?

So no, I wasn't in any hurry to head back under the river and uptown to home.

I went to Los Papis instead, thinking I'd have a cup of coffee and read the *Times* I'd cadged from Benno.

"Where's the boss this morning?" Arsenio asked. It amused him that I worked with my husband; cabinetmaking was not, in his world, what women did.

"Busy as usual, but there wasn't enough for me to do." I smiled back.

The place wasn't much: a handful of battered red Formica tables surrounded by gray chairs, their plastic seats patched with duct tape, and a deli counter behind which Arsenio and his brother, the Dominican *papis*, prepared sandwiches and daily specials.

I ordered bacon and egg on a roll to go with my coffee, then took my paper to a table. It was enough to give a person *agita*. The war preparations—the flag-waving populace—updates on the work at Ground Zero—the world was too much with us.

It was a relief when I looked up from the paper and saw Carlos Sanchez ordering a cup of coffee. I admired him for a moment before he noticed me. Carlos, an artist from New Mexico, lived and worked in a small studio in the one official residential building in the neighborhood. Benno and I had struck up a luncheonette friendship with him, and we often ate together.

He had a lovely head of hair, black curls softer and longer than Benno's, and wide shoulders flowing down to an impossibly boyish waist and narrow hips for a man in his late forties. The slenderness was deceptive; I knew from watching Carlos lift his heavy pieces how much strength there was in those ropy arm muscles.

Hawklike profile shifted to full, thin face that was all dark eyes and generous mouth accessorized by a wisp of hair centered under the lower lip. I got the smile of a man who genuinely liked women, and once again regretted, not in this order, that I was married and that Carlos loved too many women too well to suit Janis.

"Anita, what a pleasure for a Thursday morning. I was just on my way over to your shop, and now you've saved me from intruding on you at work." He set a green paper shopping bag, its handles held closed with a raffia bow, on the table, then slid into a chair across from me and unwrapped the buttered roll he'd gotten to go with his coffee.

"What's that?"

"A gift. I'm just back from two weeks in Paris. The gallery here put me in contact with a gallery owner over there. Since he was paying, I brought along four pieces that hadn't been in the show. He sold three while I was there." Carlos stroked the soul patch under his curved lower lip. "It was a very profitable trip, and Paris . . ."

"The only city that can hold a candle to New York." My one visit to the City of Light had been a decade ago, a sort of pre-marital honeymoon with Benno. "You brought me a present?"

"A small something for everyone in the family. I am indebted to your husband for the frames." Carlos the diplomat. But I was glad it wasn't just me he was buttering up. "Now that I'm back, I'm interested in renting the vacant half space on the third floor of your building. I was just on my way over to see how it takes the morning light."

Carlos had had his place for ten years, since before Dumbo became the new hot location for artists to rent lofts. Not that his long tenure did him much good now that he was looking for a separate studio space. Over the summer, he'd had a one-man show that had not only sold out but also got gushing reviews in the art-world press. I guessed Carlos could now afford to do his work somewhere other than in a corner of his small loft.

"Do you have a key?" Letting Carlos into the space unescorted was not very Fine-like behavior, if I knew my landlord.

"Not exactly." I swear, he winked at me. "Mr. Fine was not in this morning, and the office manager with the lovely long braid informed me in strictest confidence that there was a key kept on the premises in case the owner needed emergency access."

Uh-huh. Trust Carlos to charm even an efficient and unmarried Orthodox woman into unprofessional behavior.

"I was hoping Benno would let me into the building from downstairs." I got the full-on Carlos smile. It might have been irresistible if I hadn't resented how sure of himself he was.

He bit into the roll. A crumb caught in the tuft of hair under his lip. In spite of my better judgment, I had an urge to flick it off for him. I kept my hands in my lap and Carlos wiped the crumb away himself.

"You know we're moving out of the spray room?"

"No, why? I thought Benno had plenty of work lined up?"

It turned out that Carlos, having been in France for two weeks, didn't know about the dead boy in the vacuum press. I told him.

"So this dead person was in your space?" Carlos said. "And you were the one who found the body? What a terrible thing for you, Anita."

"I was just glad that they found out who he was." Then it occurred to me—"Carlos, didn't the police get in touch with you?"

Carlos arched an eyebrow. "There were some messages on my machine, and a note under the door. A female detective. I didn't see any reason to return her call. Now that you've told me what it was about, I don't know what help I can be."

"I'm sure it's just a matter of routine. They talked to everyone who knew about the vacuum press."

"It is an intriguing method of death. Perhaps the emanations from next door will add a dimension of the macabre to my work."

Not that he needed it. Carlos did an intricate kind of collage, layering images cut from magazines, art books, postcards, whatever caught his eye, between sheets of glass that gave the pieces depth and dimension. The images tended toward beautiful, ethereal women watched by men who'd taken on the shapes of animals—half wolf or coyote, goat or zebra—compositions more nuanced than they sound.

"You couldn't pay me to stay on that floor," I said.

"What I'm working on now—it's exactly the mood I'm in. This whole thing—" Carlos waved his long fingers at the paper open in front of me, the color photo of the ruins at Ground Zero. "Fire and smoke and falling birds have invaded my dreams."

We finished our coffees and fell silent. Carlos shook it off.

"Are you heading back to the shop, Anita? Would you like to see my future space?"

I wasn't, but I did, so back to Plymouth Street I went.

Sixteen

sixteen

THE REMAINS OF TWO BROKEN POLICE SEALS WERE STILL STUCK to the door of the spray room. I tried to ignore them. Carlos made for the fuse box next to the elevator and reached up for a key. It was a Medeco, just like ours. At least Mr. Fine believed in good-quality locks.

The door opened on a sunlit space. Dust motes danced in the air above narrow bands of light that lay along the floor. Something skittered in a corner behind the open door.

I shied back toward the hall.

"Mice?" Carlos peered around the door. "Perhaps I'll have to get a cat."

It was only a snack-size yellow Lay's potato chip bag, probably disturbed by the movement of the door. "Cats are good," I agreed.

Not that ours did much in the way of mouse control. Formica, that was his name, spent long afternoons prepared to pounce on the pigeons that flocked on the ledge outside, never mind that he'd have to smash through the double-paned windows to get at them. For the occasional odd mouse, Benno set a trap.

Carlos surveyed his potential domain. A large, rectangular space, with Sheetrock walls newly painted a flat white and the floor a gleaming battleship-gray enamel. Nice of Mr. Fine to have had the place spruced up. I was a little jealous that he'd taken so much care before renting it out; when we'd moved into the other half of the floor, I'd done two coats of linen-white myself.

"They did a nice job getting it ready for a new tenant."

Carlos spun around, arms extended. "I can't wait to spread out. You have no idea how constricted I am in my little studio, living and working in the same place. There's only room for one piece at a time, while other ideas come knocking, and no way to put the images aside when I need to sleep."

The room wasn't entirely empty. A partition across the back wall hid the toilet and a five-foot-long industrial sink with the same stained enamel as the one in our shop upstairs. A wobbly wooden table occupied one corner, along with two metal folding chairs, one blue and one bright green. I walked over for a closer look. There was a layer of what I now recognized as fingerprint powder on both table and chairs.

"It looks like the police were here." If they'd found anything, Inez hadn't deemed it worth sharing with me.

"How do you know?"

I pointed out the gray powder. "They were looking for fingerprints."

He turned his hands up, a quick gesture, and frowned at them. When he saw I'd noticed, he slid them into the pockets of his black jeans.

"You've been in here before, haven't you?"

Carlos shrugged.

"Hey, it's none of my business." But I couldn't resist teasing him. "I just wouldn't have thought that a woman whose idea of art was spray-painting umbrellas gold would be your type."

"Not her." Carlos's lovely mouth curled with disdain. "Piles of broken umbrellas! It's showmanship, not art."

"What then?"

"You didn't know your building had a nightlife?" Carlos walked to the wall of east-facing windows and gestured across the street to his building. "I'm third from the left. I have a direct sight line over to here."

His studio was on the fourth floor of the building directly opposite, with a perfect view across to the room where we stood. New Yorkers don't watch birds, we watch each other. Binoculars, telescopes—anyone who doesn't draw their curtains at night is fair game. It's a harmless hobby, mostly. Those with venetian blinds know to close them in the opposite direction so people in other buildings can't see down through them.

"This place has been empty for months."

"Except after dark."

"Stop being so mysterious, Carlos, just tell me."

He leaned back against the windowsill, his hands still in his pockets. "Back in August, I noticed lights on over here late at night. The umbrella lady was gone, and I was curious. I couldn't tell what they were doing—most of the action seemed to be toward the back of the room, behind the partition. I saw there was usually a man lurking by the door downstairs. People would stop by and be let in for five or ten minutes. It didn't take a genius to realize what was going on. I thought, hey, why not me too?"

"You just walked across the street and they let you in?"

"No, Anita, I am much more devious than that." I got the wink again. "I used the side exit of my building and walked around the block so I would be coming from the same direction as the others. I nodded at the watchman, the door was opened, and I was told 'third floor.' "

Hand it to Carlos, secret agent. "So what were they dealing?"

"Ecstasy."

"Ecstasy?" I felt as stupid as an echo.

"Surely you've heard of Ecstasy, Anita?" Suddenly there was something sharp lurking underneath the charm.

"Yeah." Two could be cutting. "The boy who died had it in his system."

Carlos raised his eyebrows. "Really? It's a difficult drug to overdose on, and what they had was quite good."

"You bought some?"

"Sure." Carlos eyed me with amusement, the knife edge still in his voice. "It deserves its name. The way you feel on E is like nothing else I've ever tried, and I've sampled most of what's available in the way of consciousness-expanding substances."

Not for the first time, I realized there was a whole new world of chemically induced, mind-altering experiences out there now. When I was coming up in Berkeley, we had—in the sales pitch of the dealers who strolled Telegraph Avenue—"grass, hash, acid." Okay, coke for those who could afford it, and Percodan and Quaaludes, but in my set we never went much beyond a bit of marijuana. I'd done mushrooms once, but you really had to chew those suckers and the heightened experience wasn't worth the nasty taste.

"It was the vacuum press that killed him, not the Ecstasy. He also had a lot of some amphetamine—crystal meth?—in his system."

"Ah, Christina—beloved of the driven. I know people who swear by Tina. I've heard you can work twenty hours straight on a single hit, but it's not my speed." Carlos arched an expressive eyebrow, and I gave him the laugh his pun didn't deserve.

"Were they selling meth in here, too?"

"All I bought was a few hits of E." An uncharacteristic flush colored Carlos's olive skin. He pushed off from the sill. "I stay away from addictive substances."

"Do you know who the dealers were? Or how they got in here?"

Carlos laughed. "Don't be naive, Anita. One of the sellers worked for Fine. I suppose he knew the place was empty, and where the key was. Nice yeshiva boy, he probably smuggled the E in himself. Israel is one of the main sources."

"How do you know he was one of Mr. Fine's people?"

"This is one of Fine's buildings—the kid was wearing one of those black velvet caps, and he had those fringes sticking out from under his shirt. You figure it out."

I wished I still had the flyer with Simon's photo on it in my bag so I could show it to Carlos. We'd had one pinned to the cork board in the shop office, but after we found out who the boy was, Benno had taken it down. If he hadn't emptied the trash . . .

A door closed above us, followed by the quick thud of Benno's boots on the stairs.

"Hold on." I touched Carlos's arm to stop him on his way to the door. His skin was warm under my hand. He waited, as quiet as I was, until we heard the street door slam shut. A man used to the subterfuges of women who were up to something behind their men's backs, I thought. Me, I had no such ulterior intentions. It was just that Benno, having shooed me out once already, would not be happy to see I was still hanging around.

"Come upstairs for a minute," I said.

Sure enough, the flyer was in the wastebasket. Carlos thought Simon Edelman had been the person who'd sold him the Ecstasy, but he wasn't positive. "It was dark, Anita. No overhead lights, just candles."

"How many people were there, altogether?"

Carlos hesitated. "I want to rent that space. Whatever was going on, it's over now."

"How many?" I asked again.

"One other Hasid, like your friend."

"You mean with the *payess*?" I curled my finger in the hair in front of my ears. "Did the boy you bought the E from have them, too?" Because if he did, it wasn't Simon.

"No, only the other one. Why?"

I didn't bother explaining the distinctions between Orthodox and Hasid. "Did you ever see him before? Around the neighborhood? Do you know his name?"

"It's not considered polite in such a situation to exchange names."

"You could describe him, though, couldn't you?"

That got me an unambiguous Carlos twinkle. "I can do better than that."

He flipped the flyer over to the blank side, sat in Benno's swivel chair, and picked up a pencil from the desk. Two minutes later, I had the image of a nondescript Hasidic man a little older than Simon. It could have been Heschel, the assistant I'd seen at Mr. Fine's office; it was hard to tell. Carlos had given him an almost sinister expression, a little edginess around the eyes. It was a generic face, and yet particular—the man in Carlos's sketch looked like a person with something to hide.

"Listen, I've got to get a move on." Carlos stood up.

"Do you have time to walk over to the precinct right now? I'll go with you, if you want, and introduce you to the detective."

"No police." Carlos snatched the sketch out of my hands and crumpled it into a ball.

We glared at each other.

"Why not? You have to talk to them anyway—they're interviewing everyone who knew about the vacuum press. You might as well get it over with."

"Not right now, Anita. I'd like to consult a lawyer first."

"Why? You didn't do anything wrong, did you?"

Carlos snorted. "That makes no difference. I am not stupid enough to walk into a police station and confess that I bought an illegal drug from a dead person."

I went through what I knew would be Inez's spiel: they're not interested in a petty drug buy, not with a murder on their hands.

Made no difference to Carlos.

"I would never have said anything to you, Anita, but I thought I could trust you to keep a secret."

I was beyond the manipulations of innuendo and long eyelashes. "What if Simon was killed because of those drugs? The police—"

"—will be all over the place for weeks, and Fine will never rent to me." There was an edge of anxiety in his voice.

"Okay, then I'll tell the detective what you told me. Give me back the sketch, and I promise I won't say anything about where I got it. An anonymous source, I'll tell her."

"Yes, of course they'll let you get away with that story."

"Please, Carlos. It could be vital information."

He smoothed out the sheet of paper with the sketch. "If it will make you happy, Anita, as soon as the space is officially mine, I will speak to your lady detective. But you must promise you'll let me take care of this myself." His dark eyes convinced me he would do what he'd said.

"How soon do you think you'll sign a lease?" I wrote Inez's name and phone number on a slip of paper from the message pad on Benno's desk.

"I'm going there right now. If Mr. Fine is in—" Carlos folded the sketch in half, then thirds, and slid it into his back pocket along with the information I'd just handed him.

We walked up Jay Street together.

At the foot of the metal stairs to the office, Carlos gripped my arm. I tried to pull away and couldn't. "Give me your word, Anita. You'll leave this to me."

"Okay, okay." I was startled by the fierceness in his eyes. "You're hurting me."

Carlos let go of my arm and ran up the stairs. I rubbed the spot where he'd squeezed too hard and watched as he was buzzed into the office.

You think you know someone, and then—as much as I wanted to find out why Simon had been killed, I wasn't sure I wanted to know what was behind Carlos's reaction to sharing information with the police.

Seventeen

I SLID MY METROCARD AND WALKED DOWN THE RAMP INTO THE York Street subway station, into the chill dark like Persephone descending to Hades. This time of day, not many people from around here were heading into Manhattan. It could be a wait on the empty, echoey platform; midday trains weren't all that frequent.

I thought I was alone until the inevitable Jehovah's Witness appeared silently from behind a pillar to urge a copy of the *Watchtower* on me. Caught off guard, I took what she was offering. The Witnesses are a constant presence in the neighborhood, unavoidable but easy to dodge. My usual response is "No thank you, I'm Jewish." It's the equivalent of holding up a silver cross—Jews are one group the Witnesses don't try very hard to win over.

The regular Witness in this station was a middle-aged black woman in a dark skirt and cardigan. This one was a teenager in a blue Fair Isle pullover who looked to be straight from the Midwest, light brown hair pushed behind her ears, in a pleated skirt and penny loafers.

Our eyes met. I realized she'd been one of the kids I'd seen on the corner the week before. Which meant she knew the ubiquitous Richard.

"Thank you," I said.

It was enough to launch her into the start of the Witnesses' standard spiel.

I let her rattle on while I thought about the implications of running into her. Finally she paused to see if I had any questions. I did, but not the ones she expected.

"Do you by any chance know a young man named Richard?" I worked on an innocuous smile. "He's kind of tall, with short sandy hair, and he wears a dark blue jacket with tan sleeves?"

I watched her face shift gears from rote patter to actual thought.

"Richard—. That's— Is he doing home Bible study with you?" Her narrowed eyes said she didn't think he was, but why else would I be asking about him?

Home Bible study? Oh, boy. "No, not yet, but we're talking about it." I laughed, I hoped disarmingly enough to prevent her from trying to convert me herself. "You don't know how I could get in touch with him, do you?"

"Would you like to attend the public talk this Sunday? There's a Kingdom Hall just around the corner. You could be my guest."

"Um . . ." Great. Just what I needed, an introduction to the Jehovah's way of life. Actually—it might just be. Don't slam any doors here, Anita. "Well, I promised Richard—I mean, I don't want to step on any toes or anything, if I went with you. Maybe I should just talk to him first, and be sure it's okay?"

"Oh, it won't be a problem. Any one of Jehovah's Witnesses will help you." The girl's face glowed with pleasure. Lovely. I'd made her day, if not her week and month.

"I think you'd be more comfortable with me, too. Richard got counseled by the friends, because he doesn't always keep integrity." She lowered her voice. "He likes to talk to girls his own age, and I'm better with older people—oh, I'm sorry, I didn't mean—"

"That's okay, I don't mind. In fact"—I decided to throw a little truth into the mix—"I'm friends with a girl Richard's been meeting with. Leah."

"The Jewish girl?" Now she was openly curious.

I nodded. "Do you know her too?"

"Not really. Richard has some Jewish friends, though. That's why he got counseled. When you're a Bethelite, you shouldn't have so much contact with Babylon."

She sounded to me like a talking doll, using words the way a recording might, rather than a real person.

"So if you want an hour of free home Bible study, I'd be happy to come to your house. Maybe tomorrow morning?"

"I don't think so. I feel obligated to talk to Richard first. I guess I could ask Leah how to find him, then maybe after that . . ."

The wind from the tunnel picked up, announcing an F train on its way into the station. The girl looked over my shoulder, scouting for her next victim.

"If you told me Richard's last name, I could call him." I went for the direct approach.

"It's Linden, like the tree?" She didn't seem happy about saying it. "My name is Dawn, Dawn Hymers. You could give me your address and I'll talk to Richard about—" It was impossible to hear the rest of what she said with a train screeching down the tunnel.

She handed me a pen from the crocheted bag on her shoulder.

Providing a Jehovah's Witness with my name and home address was more than I was willing to do. The Manhattan-bound

F came to my rescue, pulling in with a squeal of brakes. I felt mildly guilty about it, but I scribbled a fake phone number on the small notepad Dawn provided.

The train doors opened, and I stepped inside.

WHEN I SAT DOWN AND LOOKED AT THE *WATCHTOWER,* I WAS glad I'd accepted it. All those times I'd turned away, I'd had no idea what I was rejecting. Like Mayor Guiliani getting bent out of shape over a painting of the Virgin Mary with a breast molded out of elephant dung. When we saw it, the material turned out to be unidentifiable as excrement, elephant or otherwise, on what was the most beautiful piece in an odd exhibit. Now, if hizzoner had seen the show, he might have raised a more understandable stink about the fiberglass statues of pubescent boys and girls with penis noses, vaginal ears, and nippled breasts on their knees.

Let us please base our opinions on fact.

Did you know that the Witnesses have their own version of the Bible—the *New World Translation of the Holy Scriptures*—available, whole or in part, in forty-two languages, with 114 million copies in print? Or that they don't believe in the Trinity?

Nope, me neither.

But numbers don't make right any more than political authority does. It only took a couple articles for me to realize that the logic of what I was reading was all internal. To an outsider, the difference between tithing and voluntary giving seemed a matter of semantics, as did whether or not you refer to God as Lord or as Jehovah. Well, I hadn't expected to be converted by the thin newsprint publication.

.   .   .

WHEN I GOT HOME, I FLOATED AROUND THE APARTMENT, WA-
tered the African violets, made myself a cup of coffee, did the
crossword puzzle.

I finally settled at the table with a stack of the Nation
Challenged sections of the *Times*. I'd gotten into compul-
sively clipping captions from the Portraits of Grief—not the
names, but the one-line subheads: Young But Mature, Sub-
urban Dad, Modest Helpmate, Open to Adventure, Happy in
New York.

Clea caught me at it when she got home from school. "What
are you doing with those?"

I had the snips of newsprint sorted into categories and sub-
categories. Hobbies: cooking, golf, other sports, quirky. Family-
related: father, mother, aunt, uncle . . . Career: firefighter,
trader, administrative assistant . . .

"I'm just collecting them."

Clea started arranging the scraps into columns. "You could
do a collage like the Towers. Make them again out of the people who died there."

I sat back and watched her shape two tall rectangles. Such an
iconic image, those doubled geometries.

"Like that." Having sketched out her idea, Clea was done.
She draped herself over my shoulders, waiting to see what I
thought.

I nodded. "That's it, Bops. I can arrange them by what they
did." I reached for the hobbies, spread them out.

"How come you don't have their names?" my literal-
minded child wanted to know.

"Because I didn't know any of them personally. It's about
their lives—what they liked to do when they were alive."

"Whatever." Clea went off to do her homework.

I studied the gray columns. It was the terrible randomness of fate that fascinated. Why did Barbara have cancer, and I didn't? As I read the individual stories of the people who were lost with the Towers, I found comfort in the idea that when it was your time, it simply was. And if it wasn't, well, you were stuck in traffic, or stopped to buy a pair of socks—and you showed up for work too late to be killed that day.

The boy in the vacuum press, his death was intentional, not random. Simon Edelman had been chosen; he was known to his murderer, who had a specific reason to kill him, Simon, and no other.

And I had to know not only whose hands stuffed him into that plastic bag and flipped the switch to suck the air from his lungs, but why.

I stopped reading the captions and concentrated instead on enlarging Clea's towers. While my fingers were busy making order, I thought about the unconnected scraps of information I'd gathered about Simon's life.

He ran away to live with his grandmother, then went back home, then left again. He took Ecstasy and crystal meth. Along with a young Hasidic man, he sold Ecstasy. He was friends with Orthodox Leah Swersky, and with Jehovah's Witness Richard Linden.

Benno opened the door. The sudden draft transformed the newsprint buildings into a scrap pile.

"Hi, honey, I'm home," he said.

I swept my hoard of clippings back into their envelope and turned to greet my husband with a kiss.

"I've got a hot rumor for you, Anita. I heard Carlos Sanchez is going to rent the other half of the third floor," Benno said.

"One of Fine's minions came by to check if we were moved out of the spray room, and he told me."

"I know, I ran into Carlos at Papis. He just got back from Paris." Then I remembered our gifts. "Yo, Mademoiselle Clea, I've got something for you!"

Whatever it was, it would be special. The man knew women as well as the French knew how to wrap a gift. A shiny black cardboard box, understated elegance to set off a bow of pink satin ribbons, tied in some ornate way that made a nest for a pair of heart-shaped barrettes encrusted with rhinestones. Inside were six slender, stretchy hoop bracelets, a rainbow of hot color—red, pink, purple, silver, magenta, lavender.

Made me wish I were twelve again.

He had Clea right. She ran off to experiment with her goodies, then twinkled in with rhinestones in her hair, bangles on her arm, and a swirling purple and green Indian skirt from my hippie days. That's my girl—anonymous in her private-school uniform by day, her own sense of style by night.

"Didn't Carlos bring you a present, Ma?" Done preening for us, Clea occupied Benno's lap.

"Actually, he brought something for Dad and me both." Trust Carlos to get that right, too. He might flirt when alone with me, but Benno was the one in whose good graces he needed to stay. Our package was wrapped in two-sided paper, green with an exposed lip of dark blue, and tied with paper twine. It was white wine tarragon vinegar, and olive oil flavored with garlic and peppercorns in a pair of bottles with curved bellies. One concave, the other convex. They fit together like the married couple we were.

I wanted rhinestones.

I rubbed my arm where Carlos had gripped it earlier in the

day. There'd been a red tinge to the whites of his eyes, as if he were one of the salacious half-human men from his collages. They say art doesn't come from nowhere, it's a mirror of its creator's soul.

Eighteen

FRIDAY MORNING I TOOK THE SUBWAY DOWNTOWN. I INTENDED to do some early holiday shopping for Clea, and on the way to visit the vast, impromptu 9/11 memorial that had formed in Union Square. I wanted to be among people, to have a smoke and a think while I contemplated the outpouring of the city's grief—the drifts of cards, drawings, poems, stuffed animals, wilted flowers, melting candles.

When the train pulled into Fourteenth Street, the doors stayed inexplicably closed for an extra minute. I saw the uncertain expressions of the people on the platforms, not sure whether they should be prepared to flee or to jump on the train if the doors ever opened. Which of course they did. Those waiting to board actually stood back and allowed the rest of us to get off before they crowded on.

It was the oddest feeling, to be suddenly in a city of courteous people. Uptown and aboveground, it was possible for hours at a stretch to forget the destruction. Underground, the ripple effects of the tragedy were more tangible. We were all among the walking wounded, respectful of each other's bruised boundaries. I almost longed for the day someone would curse me out in the subway.

I waited patiently for the throng to move up the stairs. By the time I got to the turnstiles, though, I changed my mind about where I was going. Helen had been on my mind since last week's unsuccessful shiva visit, and I still felt an urge to pay my respects in person.

The subway is the only truly cell-phone-free zone in New York. Unlike movies, concerts, museums, doctor's waiting rooms, places that depend on people having the courtesy to remember to turn their phones off, in the underground tunnels of the city there is simply no reception. The corollary of not having to overhear other people's private telephone conversations is that the stations are supplied with usually operational pay phones.

And getting information from a public phone is the last free service in town. Dialing 411 will set you back forty-five cents at home, but on the street numbers and addresses cost not a dime. Of course, you don't get a real person on the other end of the line without going through the rigmarole of speaking to a recording first—hey, this is progress we're talking about here.

After James Earl Jones thanked me for using a Verizon pay phone, I told the canned operator that I wanted a number and an address for Helen Baum, please. Yes, I'm polite even to machines. When I got a human being, she told me there was no Helen Baum in Manhattan. "How about an 'H.' Baum?" I inquired sweetly. No smarter than the recording, I swear.

"I have an H. Baum at 236 East Tenth Street." No politer, either. Without another word, I was shunted back to the recorded voice for a phone number.

I did the math. The Tenth Street baths, between First and A, were in the two hundred block. That meant Helen was just down the street, and I could take the L train three stops to First Avenue.

It was a good plan. Expressing condolences in person is always appropriate, but even more, I wanted to offer Helen my friendship. Prickly though she might be, I liked her. I was curious to see her artwork, and yes, to learn more about her grandson.

As well as his circle of friends, who spanned the gap between Orthodox Jewish and Jehovah's Witness. Assuming Carlos had told me the truth about Simon selling Ecstasy, it occurred to me that the drug might be the link that had brought such disparate young people together.

It wasn't such a leap. Helen lived half a block from Tompkins Square Park; there was certainly no shortage of mind-altering substances available in that neck of the woods. Simon could well have invested in E and brought it back to the neighborhood to sell. Illegal or not, it was a commodity like any other.

I wondered whether Helen knew that her grandson had taken Ecstasy. She was an artist. Free-thinking stereotype notwithstanding, she might be tolerant of a drug that expanded consciousness. Like Carlos.

HELEN'S BUILDING WAS A FOUR-STORY BROWNSTONE WITH A HIGH stoop and garden apartment below. There were only three buzzers by the main door, labeled ground, first, and upper—the one with Baum next to it. That meant the top two floors were one unit? Probably rent stabilized, and Helen would be paying *bubkes*.

I pressed the buzzer and waited. There was the sound of a window opening above my head. I stepped back and looked up.

"Yes?" It was Helen's birdlike head peering over the sill.

"I'm sorry to bother you—I just came to—"

The head disappeared. A second later it was back, along with a hand that dropped something. "Look out," Helen warned.

Too late, but I'd already dodged the falling object—a red Frisbee with a little metal tail. Dropping the key out the window of a walk-up rather than going down to open the door for a visitor was a custom I'd heard of but never before seen.

At least she was letting me in.

The downstairs door had an oval of beveled glass, untouched by the vandalism that afflicted several of the other brownstones I'd passed. Inside, the stairs were covered by a runner of dark red carpet secured with brass rods at the base of each riser. They were immaculately kept, not a speck of dust in the corners. The walls were papered in a fading pattern of dark red stripes. Old, but no seams coming unglued. The banisters were the original wood, as were the steps themselves, stained dark.

I climbed two flights to the third floor, where Helen waited for me with the door ajar. I stepped past her and watched while she twisted two locks into place.

We were in a sort of foyer, lit only by light that filtered in from the larger room beyond. I caught my reflection in a gilt-framed mirror. The woman who met my eyes seemed to be scowling, an unhappy, pained apparition. I tried to relax the muscles of my face, to make my voice pleasant.

"I don't know if your daughter told you, but I stopped by her house last week when they were sitting shiva. You'd already left, but I wanted to express my condolences to you in person."

"Would you like some tea?"

"Yes, please."

Helen turned her back and walked off. I followed, not knowing what else to do. The place was amazing—in some respects it looked like the furnishings hadn't been changed in sixty years. When I looked more closely at the paintings on the walls, the lamps, the vases, and other tchotchkes that stood on the sideboard and filled the china cabinet, I realized some surreal hand had been at work.

We passed through the dining room, skirting a huge mahogany table with six matching chairs. The centerpiece was a bowl of fake fruit with doll-size plaster arms in multiple shades of brown that reached up from among the grapes and pears as if grasping at air. Lovely.

Each prismatic drop dangling from the crystal chandelier above the table was attached by a miniature hand with long delicate Barbie fingers. They were a riot of color—red, blue, green, silver, purple, pink, yellow. The sideboard held a small forest of candlesticks made from doll legs of various heights and widths, all painted a deep blue, with gold toenails.

I wanted to linger and examine everything, but Helen had vanished through a door whose frame was decorated by plastic roses woven together in an arch. I ducked under the bower and found myself in the kitchen.

The appliances looked like they dated from the fifties. An old-fashioned bulbous refrigerator with a large red hibiscus painted on its side dominated the room. The sink was a one-piece white enamel job, with drain board and cabinet attached. They, too, were painted with a liana of tropical plants. Each bloom had a cluster of tiny human arms waving from its centers, done in eerie, meticulous detail.

"Is this your work?" I asked.

"No," Helen said. "Would you like herbal or Lipton's?"

"Lipton's is fine." I had the feeling I was going to need the caffeine, in whatever form it came.

The white enamel table was reassuringly free of human appendages, but it wasn't without decoration. Oh, no. At each of four places was a painted place mat. They appeared to be the four seasons, nothing wrong with that. Except on closer inspection, a tundra of blue-tinged snow had a lean gray wolf drooling over some freshly killed creature in the lower right corner. Directly opposite, a tiger stalked a herd of gazelles on a scorching yellow savannah.

A riot of greenery framed a hungry grizzly bear emerging from her den with two uncute cubs. I chose to stand beside a glade of trees turning from green to crimson, gold, and brown, which featured a relatively small red fox with a dead rabbit in its mouth. The mind of an artist can be a terrible thing, even when engaged in something as domestic as eating. I was getting an entirely new image of the woman I'd known as a naked waif for all those years.

The kettle wailed. Helen poured water into restaurant surplus mugs, thick white china with no embellishments. Whew.

After we did the milk and sugar thing, Helen said, "Come. It's better in the other room."

She went out a door on the opposite side of the kitchen. I carried my mug of tea through a short hallway. No art or surprises here, just floor-to-ceiling bookshelves filled with paperbacks. So far, it was the only normal area in the entire place.

Helen led me into an odd little room at the back of the building. The old sash windows had been replaced by tall, narrow casements opening onto a narrow balcony. It was very French, although the view was over a cluster of weedy, trash-strewn backyards rather than a cobbled street.

A pair of armchairs were placed on either side of the window, a diagonal patch of sun slanting across their arms. A matching sofa in worn burgundy plush, complete with crocheted lace antimacassars across its back and arms, stood against the wall on the left. The lamps on the end tables had silk shades trimmed in beads. Their bases, however, were lapped in the slender arms of Barbie dolls, layered like leaves and painted in shades of green.

"You didn't make these pieces?" I couldn't resist asking again.

"No. They're a friend's work."

"They're wonderful," I gushed. If macabre, I didn't add.

"Do you think so?" Helen sounded skeptical.

I glanced around the room and noticed the two framed paintings above the sofa. They were abstracts, done in muted but vibrant colors, one with an autumnal palette of golds and glowing reds, the other in blue with delicate slashes of carmine. What appeared to be mica, a flaky iridescence, was scattered about their surfaces.

I got up for a closer look. "Who did these?" I asked.

"I." Queen of the short answer, Helen.

The paintings were simply wonderful, gorgeous and complex. Every artist basks in praise, and I had no problem in honestly piling it on.

Helen finally made me sit back down. We sipped tea in sunlit silence for a few minutes. I had of course thought about what to say to her. I wanted to ask about Simon and Ecstasy, and I was also curious about the scene at the Edelmans', what she'd done to upset her daughter.

I had to begin somewhere, so I picked up with what I'd started to say when I arrived.

"I hope you don't mind my stopping by like this. I know I never met your grandson, but I feel, in a way, connected to him. It may sound strange, but I'd like to get to know Simon a little bit."

Helen had her hands wrapped around her mug. She stared out the window, at the top of an ailanthus that had reached tree proportions, rather than facing at me.

In the silence, I kept going. "I met a woman at the house— Mrs. Swersky?" I paused, to see if Helen would acknowledge knowing her. "Her daughter, Leah, was a friend of Simon's."

"Oh?"

"She seemed like a nice person. I guess I had the idea that your grandson didn't have many friends in that community, and I was surprised that a boy and a girl could—could— socialize, get to know one another, if they weren't—" I had no idea what I was talking about so I stopped.

Then I realized I'd been on the receiving end of the oldest interview technique in the book: keep quiet until the other person gets uncomfortable and starts rattling on.

"She was not Simon's intended, if that's what you're asking," Helen said. "We discussed many things, but if Simon went with girls, he didn't tell me about it."

Okay, blunt is as blunt does. "Did you talk about drugs?"

"I know he had them in his system when he was killed." Now Helen stared at me, as if she could convey her thoughts directly through eye contact. I noticed her pupils wobbled slightly, side to side. I wondered if she was on some kind of drug herself, a medication with odd side effects.

"Simon experimented with drugs while he was staying with me. Marijuana, of course, and something he called 'E,' as in Ecstasy. He said it was a most remarkable experience, and it did seem to open him up. After he used it, he wanted to hear stories about my childhood, about Ruthie when she was a girl."

"Do you know where he got it?"

Helen sat with her head tilted back, her eyes focused on the ceiling. The band of sunlight had been narrowing, and now it disappeared. We sat in the chill left in its wake, the room gone gloomy as the conversation.

"We lived upstairs. My parents in one room, we three girls in with my father's mother. Our brother slept in the parlor. Typical Lower East Side. When I married, we rented this apartment. It was the perfect arrangement, to have my parents always above us." The tone of her voice contradicted the words. "Extended family, extended *tsuris*. My husband left. My father died, then my mother. Now the building is mine."

"You own it?" I found that hard to believe. Maybe it had been affordable decades ago—but now, a four-story brownstone, it had to be worth at least a couple million. The taxes alone—

"You're not the only one who admires my work, you know." Helen, acerbic in response to my obvious skepticism. "But you are right, I did not purchase it myself. I do, however, earn enough to cover the taxes."

"Do you have studio space here, too?" I asked, to cover my embarrassment at having jumped to a conclusion.

"Upstairs. Come."

Nineteen

THERE WAS NO INTERNAL CONNECTION BETWEEN THE TWO floors; we went out to the landing and climbed the stairs. Helen used a set of keys she'd taken from an alabaster vase on a table below the gilt mirror to unlock the door on the top floor. She flicked a light switch, illuminating one vast room. Interior walls between the parlor and the bedrooms had been removed, and the space was dominated by a bay window overlooking Tenth Street. Two easels had been set up to take advantage of the north light.

One held a piece similar to the paintings downstairs, except the lush colors had been replaced by shades of gray and black and instead of mica, the surface of the canvas was dotted with flakes of charred paper and ash.

"Not so pretty, is it?"

"A terrible kind of beauty." I turned to the other easel. The work in progress was somewhere between representational and abstract. The finger of an angry God, in perfectly rendered anatomical detail, pointed down from the upper left corner. In the lower right a small silhouetted figure shook a fist at the finger. In between, it was all diagonals, harsh slashing colors, an overworked cross-hatching of defiance. Even an untutored eye could tell it had not been done by the same woman who created the subtle, evocative worlds of Helen's paintings.

"Simon's?" I asked.

Helen nodded.

"It's—" I didn't know what to say.

"It doesn't matter what you think." Helen batted my opinion away and took a seat on a stool by a long trestle table loaded with the tools of her trade. "The boy had talent. Conceptually he was a child, with preoccupations appropriate to his age and lack of experience. He would have grown into a deeply thoughtful artist. I don't think that drug would have helped him in the long run, but it did enable him to set down visions like this."

"Did you try it yourself?" Impertinent maybe, but the question popped out. Ecstasy seemed like the kind of drug an artist would love. If my circumstances had been different, I could see myself being tempted.

"Simon wanted me to understand what it was like. I didn't care for the experience."

"Really?" My turn to be skeptical. "I thought everyone liked Ecstasy."

"Clever marketing, isn't it? To give it that name."

"I heard it was more like truth in advertising."

"I don't require chemicals to help me interpret and express what I feel."

I looked again at the piece on the other easel. No, Helen had no problem with communicating her vision of the world. The painting had a haunted quality that I knew would stay with me.

"Did Simon's parents know about his drug use?" It was a dumb question.

"Of course not. Simon told his stepfather nothing. For his mother, he made up stories. If he had a problem, Ruth didn't want to know. He never spoke to her about what bothered him. She thinks that husband of hers can do no wrong, and refuses to see the truth."

Helen glared at me. I met her eyes. "What truth is that?"

"He uses their religion to keep her under his thumb. Every penny accounted for, every step outside the house approved in advance. No decision is made without consulting him, and the rebbe. Hypocrites. The women must obey, but the men, they do whatever they want with whoever they want." Helen's eyes were wobbling again, the irises jerking from side to side.

"Are you saying Ruth's husband is cheating on her?"

"That one? Maybe, maybe not. I wouldn't be surprised. Those k'nockers he hangs around with—I tried to tell her. She didn't want to hear it." Helen turned away and picked up a paintbrush. She tapped the bristles against the palm of her left hand.

"Tell her what?" I asked.

"I was introduced to Simon's teacher, a member of her precious rebbe's entourage. I recognized him from the baths, where he went with one of those Russian shiksas, but I didn't know who he was until I saw him at her house."

The man with the neatly trimmed beard. Curiouser and curiouser.

"You told your daughter?"

"I told all of them, the women. Ach, it was stupid to blurt it out in front of everyone. No wonder Ruth hates me. I could never talk to that girl."

"Well, it wasn't the best choice of timing," I said, muting the criticism with a mild tone. I figured I'd get further by expressing an honest opinion rather than being polite for the sake of appearances, but tact is always appropriate. After all, her daughter had just lost a child; to tell her that someone close to her son and her spiritual leader had feet of clay . . .

"What's his name?" I asked.

"If I remembered, I'd write their rebbe a letter and expose him." Helen shot me a glare, then slid off her stool.

There was a smaller table near Simon's easel, its surface likewise littered with rags, brushes, tubes of paints, and a row of books. Helen brought one of them over to me. It was quite old, bound in well-cared-for brown leather. The fading gilt characters on the cover were Hebrew. Clearly a Bible.

Helen held it so the page side was in the palm of her left hand. With her right, she slid the spine up and off to reveal a hidden chamber, maybe six inches long, two wide, one deep. It held a packet wrapped in ivory silk.

"Go ahead." Helen nodded for me to take it out of the niche.

I folded back the fabric to reveal a plastic bag that held a lot of yellow pills with smiley faces stamped on them. Cute.

"Ecstasy?" I asked the obvious.

"I suppose so." Helen sat back down on her stool. "The Bible was specially made for my father. He was a courier, and he used it to carry diamonds from Russia to Austria—and once, to America. He abandoned a wife and two children when he came here. Stolen diamonds paid for his passage, and this building. We lived like any poor family on the street, cursing the landlord. My father never let on. After he died, my mother had to tell me."

"What happened to his first family?"

"It's likely that they were punished or murdered when the theft was discovered. Even my mother didn't know his real name. Diamond is what he told them at Ellis Island."

"A logical choice," I said.

It was just something to say, but it drew Helen's glare.

"My daughter filled Simon's head with tales of what a pious man my father was, righteous, hardworking, thrifty. When she

was a child, she didn't like him very well. He was very strict
with her. Now that she's religious, he's a respected elder. Well,
I told Simon what kind of man his great-grandfather really
was. Harsh, deceitful, selfish, unforgiving."

I thought about Simon selling tabs of the Ecstasy he'd hidden in the family Bible. Painting wasn't the only talent he'd
inherited.

"Do you know where Simon got these pills?"

"No." Helen twisted her hands. "The one I took was green,
shaped like a clover. I thought he bought it in the park."

"When did you find these?" That got me the glare again,
but she answered.

"I ran out of umber a few days ago. There was a tube on
Simon's table, and I noticed he'd left the Bible here."

"You haven't given it to the police." A statement, not a
question. Followed by, *Why are you showing it to me?* which I
didn't ask out loud.

"So they could write my grandson off as a drug addict? No."

More like a drug dealer, you want my opinion. That bag
held more than a one-person supply. I'd bet that at one time
the secret chamber had been full. I didn't say that, either.

"You give it to them." Helen jerked her chin at me. "That
detective woman knows you. Tell her you found it near where
you found my grandson. Tell them he stole it from a dealer,
and he was killed in revenge."

"Is that what happened?"

"What else could it be?" She clutched my wrist.

"I don't know." I felt sorry for her. "But I do know that in-
venting a theory for the police won't get them any closer to
the truth."

"You must not bring the police here." She put the bag in

my hand and wrapped my fingers around it. "If the police find out the drugs were here, they'll want to search everything. I can't have any attention from the police."

And I can't be walking the streets of Manhattan with a quantity of illegal drugs on me. Murphy's Law: I'd get busted for jaywalking, or my purse would be snatched. Or my real fear—I'd try a tab myself.

I'd read recently that they were experimenting with Ecstasy as a way to help people with post-traumatic stress disorder. Apparently, while on E in a safe, therapeutic environment, many people were able to relive and exorcise a traumatic incident. It was neither addictive nor hallucinogenic; Carlos liked it; I was already tempted.

Call it the undertow of a safe life.

I'd felt it before, when I held Barbara's supply of OxyContin—a synthetic, time-release opiate. She'd been titrated up to a dose that would have killed a horse, parceled out in a maxi-sized pill container with compartments for four hits per day. It had done a wonderful job of controlling her pain, allowing her to be out and about right up to the end.

OxyContin, however, could also be smashed to get a pure, heroinlike high. Not that I've ever wanted to try H—but there I was, with all those little blue ovals.

Of course I didn't do it. Having caught myself thinking like the teenager my daughter would soon be, I exercised the same good judgment I hoped she would when faced with opportunity and peer pressure.

I'd popped the lids of each little compartment and emptied them into the toilet bowl. Even underwater, the pills looked dangerous. I felt lighter as soon as they were on their way to the sewage treatment plant.

With the Oxy, I'd known I was holding the start of a lovely habit in my hands. Trying it would have been the first step on a path I had no intention of walking. E, on the other hand, could be a onetime thing. For the experience.

For the sense of release from sadness. For the easing of the shock, the exhaustion, the unbearable sights and sounds and smells that permeated the city.

"I can't do that," I told Helen. "I'll tell Inez, the detective, that I have reason to think Simon was involved with Ecstasy, but I can't bring her evidence and lie about where I got it."

Helen said nothing. I waited her out while she rewrapped the plastic bag and replaced it in the secret compartment. She fit the spine back into its groove and returned the Bible to the pile of books on Simon's table. In the clear north light, I could see how the black of her turtleneck was faded, as worn out as Helen herself.

"The best thing would be if you told Detective Collazo yourself," I said.

"Perhaps." This time when she met my eyes, hers were calm and sad.

We were all heavy with grief, but I didn't know my own burden would soon be increased.

Twenty

AS I APPROACHED THE BATHS, HEADING WEST ON TENTH, I NO-
ticed a man in a fedora at the top of the stairs. He turned his
head to glance up and down the street. Tall, beard shaped to a
blunt point; nothing remarkable in that.

I wasn't close enough to distinguish the individual from the
uniform. He could have been the man who'd been there for a
massage on women's day, or not. Anyway, Fridays were coed;
whoever he was, he may well have come for a simple *shvitz*.

I felt silly dawdling. What did I care if this Orthodox man
saw me? I wasn't a naked woman in a cotton robe, disturbed
in what she'd thought was a private place. If anyone's reputa-
tion was at stake it would be his, not mine.

The man didn't seem to be in any hurry to move. He stared
across the street as he stroked his beard, twice, followed by a
tug, as if to make sure it was still securely attached to his
chin—the exact gesture the man in the entryway at the Edelmans' had made, but I still wasn't sure it was him.

If it was, I hoped he wouldn't remember my ejection from
the shiva visit. I looked right at him as I passed the stoop. For
his part, the man made an effort not to see me. Gotta love a religion that gives women so much power that a mere glance in
their direction can tempt a man from the godly path.

And this from someone who might have just taken care of a
bodily need other than cleanliness. Next to God, indeed.

I cut diagonally across the street. On the far side of a newly

opened juice bar there was a small shop that featured home-
made pasta. It was getting late, and I had a sudden urge for
meat ravioli. That and a jar of sauce would make a quick supper.

When I came out of the store, a man in a watch cap and
leather jacket had joined the black-hatter on the stoop. From
the flash of fire between their bowed heads, I realized one was
lighting a cigarette for the other. Smoking as well as sweating
makes for strange fellowships, I thought.

"YO, ANITA!"

I'd just beaten the light on Eleventh.

"Who taught you to cross a street?" Grant Farrell com-
plained when he caught up to me. "And you walk too damn
fast besides."

"I'm a New Yorker, that's how it's done."

"What's the hurry?" Grant grinned. He had a very nice
dimple in his left cheek I'd never noticed. Maybe it was the
two-day stubble that accentuated his amusement. "I could be
here another five years, and I still wouldn't do it. Where I'm
from in Nebraska, when you're in the big city you want to go
slow and take in the sights. Makes a change from the farm."

The only thing remotely corn-fed about Grant was his size.
The unshaven jawline fit right in with the East Village, as did
his leather jacket and jeans. The outfit on every third male,
most of them accessorized with zippers and safety pins.

"What brings you to this part of town?" I asked.

"Gallery down the street is interested in offering me a one-
man show, so I stopped by to set up a time for them to make a
studio visit to see my stuff, figure out what to include. You?"

"Visiting a friend."

"Got time for a cup of Java?"

We were right in front of DeRoberti's, with its window of cakes and tarts. I hesitated, and was lost.

Grant had me by the elbow and through the door. Caffeine is always good, I told myself. So as not to have what my grandmother would call "a dry cup of coffee," I picked out an éclair, to which my partner in pastry added a pair of profiteroles. What the aroma of chocolate will make a woman do.

Grant kept up a steady patter about the possibility of a solo show; how few pieces he had that were good enough; how much work he'd need to finish before the gallery owners made their visit. We were seated at one of the ornate marble-topped tables before he paused for breath. "So, enough about me. What do you think of my work?"

I was a beat behind him; it took the flash of dimple before I realized he was flirting.

I'd been faced with enough temptation for one day, and the sweets were as far as I was going to yield.

"I saw some very intriguing pieces today." I described the doll-part assemblages I'd seen at Helen's.

"Sounds like early Martha Wolfe. Tarted-up kitsch with S-and-M overtones." One of the profiteroles vanished. "The dykes love her stuff."

"You know her?"

"Her work. Small world, the East Village art scene. Wolfe had a bit of commercial success in the late eighties, but then she died. I didn't know much of her stuff survived—where did you see it?"

Somewhere in the middle of my story about Helen, the baths, and the boy in the vacuum press being her grandson, Grant signaled for two more cappuccinos. They came with a raspberry tart I hadn't noticed him order, and two forks. I realized that

while I'd been waxing lyrical about Helen's paintings, Grant had
been paying more attention to the waitress than to my descrip-
tion of another artist's oeuvre.

I shut up and ate my fair share of the pastry.

"This other woman's work sounds marvelous." Now that
I'd stopped talking, Grant made an effort to engage me again.
"What did you say her name was?"

"Baum, Helen Baum."

"Never heard of her." He licked a smear of ruby jam from the
back of his fork with a single suggestive swipe of the tongue.

Flirting, Anita, he's only flirting. With the boss's wife, my
inner moral compass observed. I checked my watch. Clea'd be
home from cross-country practice in half an hour.

"Thanks for the coffee, Grant, and congratulations on your
show." I shoved my chair back. "I've got to get home to my
daughter."

"Hold up, woman, I'll walk you to the subway." Grant unfolded himself from the delicate chair. "You Noo Yawk ladies
sure do like to rush around."

For all his protestations about my pace, Grant's long legs
had no problem keeping up with me on the two-block walk to
the subway.

"So this woman with the Martha Wolfes lives on Tenth
Street?" Grant asked. "The ladies who own Corolis would
cream their pants over those pieces you were describing. Right
up their alley, that oppressed-female Barbie-doll stuff. If I
could get them an inside track at having a look-see, it might
help me nail down a one-man show."

"Well, I don't really think she'd be—" I was taken aback. I
knew Helen well enough to know that finding the charming
and persistent Grant Farrell on her doorstep would be the last

thing she'd want. There was nothing for it but to be blunt. "I'm sorry, Grant, but she's a very private person."

Grant held me at the entrance to the L, trying to persuade me that Helen's private collection would speed his rise to fame and fortune. I turned on some charm of my own and told him that I knew his work, on its own, was strong enough to get him the recognition and financial reward he deserved.

Then a tall woman in a short skirt and a pair of Manolo Blahnik sandals brushed past us. Grant went quiet while he watched her stroll east on Fourteenth.

Talk about transparent. I nudged him with an elbow, amused. "Nice to run into you, Grant."

"Yeah, hey, you too, Anita. See you around!" Grant whistled the first bars of "New York, New York" as he ambled off after the next person who'd caught his eye.

Thank heaven for short attention spans.

Twenty-one

SUNDAY WAS A LOVELY DAY. THE SUN SHONE; THE GIANTS, THE Jets, and the San Francisco 49ers all went down in defeat; Benno cooked a vegetable soup that was heavy on lima beans, the only vegetable I refuse to eat. Nothing was right with the world, and by eight o'clock I was sulky as a teenager.

Clea wanted ice cream. Vanilla, with rainbow sprinkles. In a burst of indulgent motherhood, I decided to go to the store. Any excuse to get out of the house, stretch my legs, sneak a cigarette.

Force of habit—wanting a smoke, I got in the elevator and hit B without thinking about what I was doing. When I pushed the door open and found myself in the basement, I had to tip my hat to Dr. Freud. If that was where my subconscious had led me, I decided I might as well sit in the backyard as up on Broadway.

The round table and two metal chairs stood at the far end of the yard, just as they'd always done. Even the stupid beige plastic ashtray was there, waiting for Barbara and me. I didn't cry, just sat and smoked and watched the few stars visible in the space between buildings.

I put football out of my mind and thought about drugs, about art, artists who used drugs, artists and the police. I'd been hovering over the phone all weekend, hoping Inez would call. Not that there was any reason for her to keep me up-to-date on the investigation, even if Carlos's information about what went on in the space next to our finishing shop had provided a vital lead.

I was dying to talk to Inez about the drug dealing, and to confess that I had independent confirmation about Simon selling Ecstasy. I tried to work out how I could do it without involving Helen, but it seemed pretty well impossible.

I didn't think for a minute that I could hand Inez the Ecstasy and not say where I'd gotten it. If I did tell—Helen would definitely have police invading her home, she was right about that. But wouldn't it be worth it, to find out why Simon died?

With help from Carlos, the police could determine who the dealers were, whether they'd legitimately rented from Dovid Fine or if one of his minions, knowing the place was empty, had purloined a key. And if so, which one it was.

I could call Inez, just to ask how the investigation was going. If they were making progress, I wouldn't need to inform on Helen. Yeah, and maybe if I were a good girl, the Niners and the Jets would make it to the Super Bowl.

"Do the right thing, Anita. Whatever it is, that's what you do." Barbara's voice, advice given years ago to resolve a very different dilemma. I'd definitely be calling Inez Collazo in the morning.

I put the cigarette out and went to get dessert for my family.

NOT GOING IN TO WORK WITH BENNO LEFT ME AT LOOSE ENDS. Clea was way too old to be walked to school, which left me home and awake in my nightgown at eight-fifteen on a Monday morning. I had nothing to do except call Inez and tell her about the Ecstasy. I was going to do it, but not—quite—yet.

I took a shower and stripped the beds. I felt like Pontius Pilate. Washing clothes was a temporary reprieve.

Laundry meant the basement, which meant facing Barbara's absence again. I'd only done the wash once in the month since she'd died. Benno offered, but he was temperamentally incapable of separating darks from lights or using any setting other than hot.

Once the laundry was in the dryer, I felt able to pick up the phone.

Of course, Inez wasn't in that day.

I didn't go out back for a cigarette, although when I saw who was waiting on my doorstep when I came out of the elevator with a full basket of clean sheets, I wished I had. Then maybe Detective First Grade Michael Dougherty would have given up on me and left before I'd gotten back.

Not that I wasn't glad to see him. I first met Michael at the same time as Inez Collazo, back when they were partners patrolling the Twenty-sixth Precinct, and we'd found ourselves together at the scenes of three deaths. I'd introduced Michael to his significant other, my good friend and former coworker, Anne Reisen.

Anne and I had spoken recently, but I hadn't seen Michael since before the eleventh. In other circumstances, I might have called him last night for advice on what to do. Not that his would have been any different from Barbara's—and with a more detailed lecture attached.

I had a feeling his presence outside the door of my apartment was neither an answer to prayer nor a social call.

"Yo, Social Worker, how you doing?" Natty as ever, if casual: black jeans, white shirt, black and white tweed sport coat, no tie. Same smile on generous lips, except that it didn't come near his exhausted eyes.

I put my arms around him. It wasn't an intimacy we'd ever

shared, but Michael held me close. We stood like that for a long minute before I snuffled back tears and invited him in.

I put up water for coffee. It was looking to be yet another gorgeous October day, and I opened a window to the blue sky. Michael inhaled.

"It's good to breathe clean air," he said.

"Have you been spending much time at the pile?" I asked.

"Some, but I got assigned to Homicide South. I put in time over at the site whenever I can, but hey, you know New York, people are still getting themselves killed one by one."

I didn't ask. He'd tell me anyway.

"I thought when you retired from your chosen profession, I'd be done paying house calls except on social occasions. But guess what turns up at the scene of an obvious homicide?" Michael put a plastic bag with one of Benno's silver-gray business cards in it on the table, facedown, so I could read what was on the back.

I'd written my name and home phone number on it three days ago.

"Helen Baum," I said. I had that pit-of-the-stomach feeling, unable to believe what I knew was true. "What happened?"

"She's dead." Michael folded his hands around the mug, holding on to the heat of it. "She was kicked in the ribs, and six of her fingers were broken. Hard to say exactly what caused her death."

I crossed my arms, held on tight to my own rib cage, and tried not to imagine what Helen had gone through.

"Hey." Michael reached across the table and slid a hand under my elbow. "Like I said, Anita, people are still shits. Whoever did it trashed her place, like they were looking for something particular, but we have no idea what. You think you could help by telling me whatever you know about this Helen Baum?"

When I looked up, Michael met and held my gaze. What do you do when the world as you know it ends? Pick up the pieces and try to put them together. The delicate skin under his eyes was a deep purplish brown with fatigue.

Helen not only dead, but tortured. I filled him in on Simon and the vacuum press before I explained about my condolence visit the past Friday, and the tabs of Ecstasy in the smuggler's Bible.

"Art studio? Bible?" Michael shook his head. "What are you talking about?"

"Upstairs," I told him. "Didn't you go upstairs?"

He unhooked a radio from his belt, instructed the person on the other end to guard the stairwell. He paced to the window and back, three strides each way.

"All right, Social Worker, c'mon. Lots of procedures getting stretched these days, you might as well ride along and have a look at the scene. You're all I got so far who can provide me some background on this woman."

On the ride down the West Side Highway, I gave Michael the story of Helen's father's Bible, ending with the secret compartment filled with smiley-faced tabs of Ecstasy. I sat through the predictable—and deserved—lecture about withholding evidence.

In Helen's defense, I explained about her not wanting to have the police tromping around her house.

"Be careful what you wish for, right?" Michael said. "Now she's got cops going through her stuff in spades."

He cut across town on Greenwich, past St. Vincent's Hospital where the police barricades were still up along the sidewalk.

They were papered with "Missing" flyers, the ground around them a jumble of candles in glass cylinders, long-wilted bouquets of flowers, sodden teddy bears. Michael wasn't the type to take comfort in the tokens of grief, and he didn't give the display more than a glance.

We hadn't exchanged the typical greeting of people seeing each other for the first time in those days, either. There was no point in asking "Everyone you know okay?" because for Michael, as for every cop and firefighter, the answer was no.

He parked in front of a hydrant a few doors down from Helen's building.

Michael stopped in Helen's apartment first, to see if the crime-scene team had found any keys.

"Yeah, we picked up a set somewhere around where this stuff got knocked over," a woman in white coveralls said. "Now where'd I put that bag?"

I didn't get farther than a few feet inside the door. Whoever trashed the place had taken pleasure in destruction for its own sake. Every piece of furniture had been overturned and smashed; the floor was a mess of legless chairs, snowed with kapok from the sofa cushions and shards of china and glass. Sprinkled everywhere, like scraps from a macabre miniature abattoir, were doll parts, rainbow hands and blue legs.

Twenty-two

A MAN WITH PAPER BOOTIES ON HIS FEET STALKED AROUND THE room, shooting photographs of the devastation.

"You know what this doll stuff is about?" Michael asked the techs.

"They were art," I said. "Done by a woman named Martha Wolfe." So much for Grant's plan to impress his gallery owners with Helen's collection. It would take all MoMA's restorers to put those pieces back together again.

I described the chandelier, the forest of candlesticks with their gold toenails, the bowl of fake fruit.

"Yeah, I figured it was something like that. Art." The photographer snorted. "Don't tell me—when I get this film developed, I can call it deconstructionism?"

His shots would probably be worth more than the originals, from what I knew of the East Village art scene, but I didn't say so. "Were the paintings in the other room destroyed too?"

The photographer turned in my direction. I thought he was going to take my picture and I ducked behind Michael's broad shoulders.

"Cheese!" He raised the camera in a mocking gesture, then lowered it. "You mean the pair in the back room? Nah, they're okay. Looks like the perps didn't get past the kitchen. That's where all the blood was."

I was suddenly light-headed with the thought of what had happened to Helen. I held on to Michael's arm for support.

"You gonna faint on me, Social Worker?"

I shook my head.

"Good." He withdrew his arm and put on a pair of plastic gloves before taking the keys out of a plastic evidence bag.

"We've got something here that'll help you out, Detective," the woman in white added. She held up another bag with a sheet of yellow lined paper in it. "Bank account info, lawyer's name, insurance company."

"Great," Michael said. "Just hang on to it, will you? I'll be back in a minute."

He took the stairs two at a time. "Let's hope the perps didn't know about this place—door's still locked, that's a good sign."

Helen's studio appeared untouched by the destruction in the apartment below. Michael stopped me from heading immediately for Simon's table.

"Just look around, Anita. Everything the way you remember it?"

"Except for the cloth over that painting." I pointed to Simon's easel.

Michael raised the piece of black fabric that had been draped over Simon's work. "This what was here before?"

"Yes." I circled the room, scanning it carefully. I hadn't paid all that much attention the day before, but it didn't look like Helen had done any more than cover the one painting. I stopped in front of the smaller table and pointed. "Here's the Bible I told you about."

Michael picked it up. I explained how to slide the spine open. The bag of yellow smiley-face pills was still there.

"Hot spit," he said. "Seemed pretty obvious the bad guys didn't get what they wanted before your Mrs. Baum died on them, but what I don't get is why she held out on them. I can't see as how the Ecstasy was so precious that she wouldn't've given it up as soon as they broke the first one of her fingers."

"I don't think that's what she was protecting," I said. I thought about which would have been worse to Helen, the physical abuse or the desecration of her work.

Michael thought about it. "You could be right about Baum having her own agenda, but those bastards had to've been after the drugs."

"How much are they worth, really? It seems to me they went to an awful lot of trouble, for what—a few thousand dollars?"

"You know, I don't think they intended on killing her. For an old woman, she put up a lot of resistance." Michael aimed a finger at me. "Stay put a minute, Social Worker. Don't even twitch."

I saluted, but I stood where I was and watched him stalk around the studio, riffle through a stack of canvases, peer under worktables and into an array of coffee cans that held brushes and pencils, open a half-dozen cardboard cartons on the bottom shelves of a metal storage rack, then disappear into the bathroom.

I heard the sound of the toilet tank lid being lifted and replaced, a medicine cabinet door squeaking open. Michael crossed the hall into the only other room on the floor that was still walled off from the main studio space. I dared to follow him, but stopped outside the doorway.

It was a kitchen with the same ancient appliances as downstairs, except these were free of decoration. There was a modern coffeemaker on the counter and a miscellany of mugs resting upside down in the dish drainer. Michael had the fridge open, revealing a carton of half-and-half and a few containers of Chinese takeout. He lowered the freezer section, which was encrusted with ice and white frost crystals, then let it snap closed in disgust.

"Jesus, Mary, and Joseph." Michael noticed that I was watching him. "I thought I told you—ah, hell. It'll take crime scene to do justice to this place."

But he went through the cabinets, poked a spoon into containers of sugar, cocoa, herbal tea, and coffee; shook all the cleaning supplies under the counter; felt the bottoms of the drawers; came up with the same nothing as in the studio.

On the way out, Michael paused in front of the painting on Helen's easel. "She had it, didn't she? Bunch of swirls, but it's exactly right. Makes me feel . . ." He wiped his forehead with the back of his hand. "I wish I'd known this woman. Not much surprises me anymore, but the kind of individual who'd break the fingers that made this . . ."

Twenty-three

WHEN WE GOT BACK DOWNSTAIRS, MICHAEL DIDN'T MAKE MUCH of the information sheet Helen had compiled about her business affairs. He left it on the kitchen table, after cursing the fact that it wasn't an inventory of the valuables in the apartment.

"At least you've got the insurance info," the crime scene tech reminded him, "and the lawyer's name."

"Yeah, yeah," Michael groused. "So I'll have to visit some Third Avenue shyster's dinky office and find out our Ms. Baum was suing her tenants for leaving trash in the halls."

I picked up the paper he'd abandoned and started reading. "Yo, Michael. Not a shyster and not a dinky office. Unless there's more than one Grace Davis practicing law in Manhattan, Helen's lawyer is an associate in my father's firm."

That got his attention. "Oh, that's rich. Now what do you suppose this nice artist-lady needed a criminal defense attorney for?"

"The firm does family law, too—that's Grace's area. My father's been fighting against the trend of trying juveniles as adults, which means handling the entire constellation of family issues."

"Okay, enough with the social-work speak. What's that got to do with Helen Baum?"

As soon as the words were out, it dawned on both of us that Simon was a juvenile who'd been involved with illegal drugs—reason enough for Helen to have consulted my father.

"But his fingerprints weren't in the system, were they?" It was a rhetorical question. If they had been, he'd've been identified right away.

"Okay, but if it was Grace Davis she saw," I went on thinking out loud, "it would have had something else to do with Simon."

"No point in speculating." Michael handed me his cell phone. "Call her and ask."

Grace Davis, according to the secretary, was in court and not expected back. I figured if it had to do with Simon, the great Aaron Wertheim would know about it, so I asked to be put through to him.

Michael smirked at me while I waited for my father to come on the line. No love lost between those whose job it is to get criminals off the street and the attorneys who look over their shoulders to make sure they do it within the limits of the law.

"Anita. This is an unexpected pleasure, to hear from you in the middle of the day."

We'd only known each other a few years, my father and I, and he meant exactly what he said. From some other man, the words might have suggested that I was interrupting his busy schedule.

"I'm actually calling on business. It's about a client of Grace's—Helen Baum? Or her grandson, Simon Edelman?"

"The names don't ring a bell, but let me check our database."

I could imagine him swiveling from desk to computer in his big gray leather chair.

"For Edelman, I have nothing. Baum, Helen—she did indeed consult Grace. For anything else, you'll have to speak directly with her."

That's my dad, the soul of lawyerly rectitude. He'd give me

what he could, no questions asked, as long as it didn't violate privilege.

"Helen Baum was killed last night, and the detectives found a paper that said Grace was her attorney," I told him, hoping for more.

"If you don't mind my asking, Anita, what is she to you?" Something had gotten his antenna up; Aaron Wertheim didn't go in for idle questions.

"Just someone I knew casually, but I happened to visit her a few days before she died."

"You're not under suspicion, are you?" Sharp and to the point.

"No, nothing like that."

"I recommend that you come along with the detectives to see Grace, Anita."

Now he had me. Surely this was none of my business. "Why?"

"I'll switch you back to Evelyn to schedule an appointment. I trust all is well with Benno and Clea?"

A true lawyer's nonanswer. "Fine, we're all fine."

According to Evelyn the efficient, Grace was free all of tomorrow morning and would expect us anytime after ten-thirty. "That will allow her time to review the relevant files," Evelyn said firmly.

Michael wasn't happy about my father's enigmatic suggestion that I tag along when he spoke to Helen's attorney, but he had too much on his mind to put up a fuss.

"C'mon, Social Worker, I'll buy you lunch."

It was a nice offer until it translated to Cuban sandwiches from a deli that heated them in a microwave—guarantee of soggy heros, although it did melt the Swiss and warm the roast pork and ham pretty well. We both got coffees and headed over to Tompkins Square Park to eat.

The memorial offerings here weren't as overwhelming as at Union Square, although a corner was devoted to the ubiquitous clutter of grief. Most of the candles had blown out, but a few flickered in tall glass cylinders, their flames pale as ghosts in the daylight. The aroma of ash and burning chemicals was faint but pervasive.

I opened my mouth to make some comment intended to start up a where-were-you-when conversation, but Michael stopped me.

"I don't mean to be rude, Social Worker, but I don't want to talk about it. Shit happens, and we deal."

"Good sandwich," I said, with my mouth full. Then we just ate, the sun warm on our faces.

"So how do you suppose Helen wound up with your father's law firm? Kind of a coincidence, isn't it?" Michael broke the silence.

"I suppose." I thought about the eerier coincidence of Simon Edelman being related to Helen, and the quirk of Helen and I knowing each other from the baths. What were the chances of that, compared to the number of law firms in Manhattan?

I lit a cigarette. The trees around us let loose a flutter of leaves. I remembered the conversation with Helen last spring, when Janis had blurted out my father's identity. I hated it when she bragged on my connection to the great defense attorney; I'd spent more than forty years without relying on Aaron Wertheim or the cachet of his name, and I saw no reason to change that even as we grew into being a family.

"Maybe it's not a coincidence after all." I told him about Janis's name-dropping on my behalf.

"So she chose the firm *because* of you? Yeah, it makes a weird kind of sense."

"I guess we'll find out when we talk to Grace," I said.

Michael shook himself, an all-over muscular spasm, like a dog who's been startled out of a half-sleeping daze.

"Life goes on, doesn't it?" he said. "One death at a time, life goes on."

I dropped the cigarette butt and put it out with my shoe.

"You know you oughta quit that habit, Social Worker." There was a tone in his voice, anger and despair, that made me vow right then to stop dying one inhalation at a time. Some deaths are preventable, and I wanted mine to be one of them.

"What next?" I asked.

"I have to tell the daughter." Michael stood and offered a hand to help me up.

I kept hold of it after I rose. "Would you like me to ride along with you?" I asked.

"Yeah, that'd be okay."

We headed back to Tenth Street, skirting the little memorial mound.

Twenty-four

THIS TIME IN THE CAR MICHAEL GOT TO HEAR THE TALE OF THE shiva visit, including how Helen had upset her daughter when she was introduced to Simon's teacher and told the women that she'd seen him come to the Tenth Street baths for an illicit massage.

"So what? One of their *machers* got himself rubbed for lunch—no biggie. Religious big shots can be just as hypocritical as anyone else. How you act in your own community is one thing, but out in the world? All bets are off." Michael shrugged. "And behind closed doors—Bible, Koran, Talmud—doesn't matter what book it is, you got the same bickering, jealousy, domestic abuse. Families are families, and life's a bitch."

"Not too cynical, are we?"

Michael hit the brakes and the horn simultaneously, producing a squawk of protest at the car ahead of us—which had prudently stopped for a yellow light.

I grabbed the dashboard to keep from banging my head on the windshield.

"Hang in there, Social Worker. I'm just blowing off steam. I figured you wouldn't mind, being as you're a professional and all."

That was more like it, the briefest flash of a Dougherty dimple as he twitted me.

"Yeah, make fun of me. Grief counselors live to take abuse."

I waved a white tissue in the air between us. Whatever I could do for him, I would.

"That's my girl, always trolling for tears." Said lightly, but he snatched my peace offering and blew his nose. Men.

In a way, though, they had it right. Tears hadn't helped after Barbara died, and they did nothing to ease the vicarious grief I felt just reading the papers.

"So you'll call Inez, right?" I changed the subject, and got a smile.

"Yeah. The old silver lining, a chance to catch up. She's done good in Brooklyn. You know she got married again?"

And that got us to Lee Avenue, and the turns to the Edelmans' house.

In response to Michael's knock, Ruth opened the door on the chain and spoke through the crack.

"Yes?"

Michael held up his shield. "I'm Detective Michael Dougherty, NYPD. I'm looking for the daughter of a Helen Baum?"

"She was my mother." Ruth made no move to take the chain off.

"Was?" Michael asked.

"She is dead to me."

"May we come in, ma'am?" Michael asked. "There's something I need to tell you."

"If it concerns my mother, I am not interested."

"I'm afraid it does, ma'am. I really need to speak with you, and I'd rather not do it like this, where all your neighbors can see."

Indeed, we were drawing some attention. A pair of black-hatted men had stopped two doors down to light cigarettes and watch what was going on. A young woman pushing a stroller slowed her steps as she approached the scene on the Edelmans' stoop. There were faces in a couple of windows across the street.

Ruth Edelman closed the door, undid the chain, and stepped back so we could enter. Even in the privacy of her home, she wore a scarf low on her forehead and tied at the nape of her neck so that every strand was hidden. It was black cotton with a light blue stripe, as nondescript as the dark blue cotton knit turtleneck dress she had on. What with the bluish circles under her eyes, Ruth was not an inspiring sight.

She ushered us into the first room on the right, where the men had been on my visit to the house. It was sparsely furnished, just a pair of wine-dark sofas facing each other across a glass-topped coffee table with nothing on it except a film of dust.

Apart from two spots of surprisingly vivid color, it was not an inviting room. Both were quilted wall hangings. One was a Garden of Eden minus its Adam and Eve, where Hebrew letters embroidered in bright green wrapped around the trunk of a tree laden with scarlet fruit. The other was a pair of black satin tablets, their Hebrew letters done in silver thread, surrounded by flashing yellow thunderbolts and rays of divine light—the Ten Commandments, I presumed.

"You may wait here while I call my husband." Mrs. Edelman closed the door, shutting us in.

Michael and I glanced at each other. I made a snap decision. "We should talk to her without him."

He didn't argue with me.

I headed toward the back of the house, down a short corridor that ended in a swinging door with a diamond window set in it.

Ruth was bent over the sink, clutching the edge of the counter, taking deep breaths. I pushed through the door.

She didn't look up. I patted her gently on the back.

At the touch, Ruth straightened. "Do I know you?" she asked.

"I don't think so. I made a shiva call after your son died, but you were upstairs."

Michael's face appeared, momentarily framed by the diamond, then disappeared.

"You knew Simon?"

"No, but I wish I had. He seemed like an interesting young man." I noticed she'd pronounced his name the American way. "I came that time to pay my respects to your mother."

"Why are you here now?"

I debated leaving the news for Michael to break, and decided I was doing fine on my own. I didn't mince words. "Detective Dougherty and I came to tell you that your mother was murdered last night."

When they say a person goes white and passes out, well, that's exactly what Ruth did. The blood drained from her face as her legs simply collapsed. I managed to break the fall so her head missed the corner of the table.

"Michael!" I hollered. I stretched her out. I knew enough to elevate her feet, propping them on a footstool I found against the wall.

"Yo, Social Worker, what'd you do to her?" Michael dropped to his knees and felt for a neck pulse.

"It's only a faint," I said.

"Yeah, probably." Michael rocked back on his heels. "So, you told her?"

"I'm sorry. I didn't realize she'd react like this."

Michael nodded at the cabinet under the sink. "Make yourself useful. See if she's got some cleaning product with ammonia in it in there."

Sure enough, Mr. Clean himself, earring and all. How kosher was that, I wondered irrelevantly.

Detective Paramedic unscrewed the bottle and waved the cap in the vicinity of Ruth's nose. It brought her right around.

She coughed as she came to. I knew what it was like, having been on the receiving end of an ammonia ampule once myself. Not pleasant.

"Water," Michael told me. He started to slip an arm behind Ruth to help her sit up, but she recoiled from his touch, scuttling backward toward me.

Physical contact between a man and woman neither married nor related by blood was against the rules. Perceptive as ever, Michael figured it out and backed off. That meant me on the floor, helping Ruth drink a few sips of water. Even in her state, I noticed, she paused to move her lips in silent prayer before they touched the glass.

When I had her seated at the table, Michael pulled out a chair for himself, but kept a respectful distance.

"Mrs. Edelman," he said. "I'm sorry about your mother, and about your son. I know it's a lot to take in right now, but if you could answer a few questions, it might help us to find the person who—"

"Please, I have to call my husband now." She stood up. There was a tremor of panic in her voice.

Michael tipped his head in my direction, just once, then said, "I'll wait in the front room until he gets home, then, and Ms. Servi here will stay with you."

I took the nod to mean that he wanted me to keep her talking. I had no problem with that.

Ruth waited for him to leave, then whispered, "The telephone is in the hall."

"It's okay, you can call him now."

Michael was standing in the doorway to the front room. Ruth stopped abruptly when she saw him.

"Just one thing, Mrs. Edelman. I don't want to disturb you any further, but would you mind if I had a look at your son's room while I wait? If you give me permission, it'll save the hassle of having a whole crew troop through your house when I come back with a search warrant. I'll be very careful, ma'am, I promise."

The Columbo technique—just one more thing, ma'am—was a nice touch, and it worked. Ruth nodded assent, and Michael was up the stairs before she finished telling him it was the second room on the left.

Twenty-five

RUTH EDELMAN'S ARMS HUNG AT HER SIDES, LIMP AS BROKEN wings. I didn't push her to make the phone call; Michael might need every minute he had to search before the man of the house came home and stopped him.

I've seen many reactions to bad news—stunned, shocked, angry, incredulous, grief-stricken, relieved, even glad—but the expression, or rather lack of expression, on Ruth's face was unsettling. Numb was the word that came to me. Like the news of her mother's death was one piece of information too many in a life that had already presented her with more than she could take in.

What had made this woman so cut off from her feelings? The death of her oldest son, obviously that played a role; and the unpleasantness the last time she'd seen Helen—but no matter how vast the rift, a parental bond doesn't snap without some feeling. And Ruth had seen her mother more often in the past few months than she had in years, making it a current relationship as well as a past.

While she stood motionless, her gaze now directed toward a swag of black fabric that hung over what I assumed was a mirror covered in the wake of her son's death, I wondered if Ruth were on medication. Xanax, Ativan, something to counteract a crippling, grief-induced depression.

It was chilly in the hallway. Enough already, I decided.

I reached for Ruth's hands. They were cold. "Would you like me to dial for you?" I asked.

"I can manage." She squeezed my fingers before releasing herself from my grip. For just a second, her gaze met mine, and I saw Helen's spirit in her daughter's eyes.

I listened to the brief conversation, Ruth asking whoever picked up the phone if she could speak to Mr. Edelman, please, then, "There are two people here from the police. Will you come home now?"

Her voice changed as soon as her husband came on the line. From competent woman to humble petitioner in the space of a sentence.

A silence on Ruth's end. From the drone of Adam Edelman's voice, I got the impression he was complaining, at length, about the interruption. When he finally gave her a chance to respond, Ruth said, a bit more assertively, "They came to tell me that my mother was killed. I think Mr. Fine will understand if you—"

Ruth held the phone slightly away from her ear. From the sound of it, Adam had launched into another tirade—not exactly the response of a man consoling his wife.

Fine is a common enough name, and if I hadn't seen my landlord in this very hall, I might have thought nothing of it. But I had, and his presence here made absolute sense if Adam Edelman worked for him. On the other hand—I knew for a solid fact that Edelman was not among the names Dovid Fine had given to Inez when she'd asked him for a list of his employees.

Ruth waited until her husband had run out of steam. "Half an hour is okay. Thank you, Adam." She put down the phone. There were spots of color on her cheeks; embarrassment, maybe, at having been reprimanded while I was standing right there. Not that she'd done anything wrong, so what was his problem?

All I'd have had to say to my husband was "My mother's dead" and Benno would've been home as fast as the MTA could get him there. Okay, so there was no love lost between Adam Edelman and his mother-in-law, but still—isn't honoring thy father and thy mother right up there in the commandments? Yeah, I could hear Benno grouse, after you're done groveling at the feet of the big guy himself.

"Would you like a cup of tea?" Ruth asked.

"Yes, that would be good." I put an arm over her shoulders and led her back to the kitchen. "Shall I make it, and you have a sit?"

I filled the kettle, found a teapot in the dish drainer, a canister of Swee-Touch-Nee on the counter. I smiled at the little red tin tea chest—just like Benno's Aunt Rose had in her kitchen. I measured out three teaspoons and waited for the water to boil.

Not that Ruth was letting me wait on her. She got out cups, spoons, and milk, and set them on the table next to the sugar bowl. The kettle wailed, and Ruth just stared at it. I diagnosed shock and made her sit down. She put her elbows on the table, rested her head in her hands, and didn't look up.

I let the tea steep, then poured us each a cup. When Ruth made no move to add anything to hers, I gave her two sugars and a healthy glug of milk. I had to put the cup into her hands and help her raise it to her lips. The first sip acted like a tonic, and again the spark of Helen appeared in her eyes.

"I love my mother, you know."

"And she loved you, too, very much."

It was the wrong thing to say.

"My mother thinks I'm stupid and insecure because I quit working when I married Adam. We wanted to be a real family. I tried it her way—married a jerk who left me a single mother with no income and no skills. At least I had enough sense not to move in with her, the way she moved in with her parents."

It was good to hear Ruth speak up for herself. Having Helen for a friend was one thing; as a mother, I could see how she'd come across as distant, judgmental, overbearing.

"What did you do?" I asked.

"I was an administrative assistant at the Wise School, in the West Village. I took the job because it came with free tuition for Shimon, and it changed my life. The people were so kind, especially the *rebbetsen*. I was alone, and she helped me to find my *bashert*." As she remembered, her face relaxed.

If their phone conversation was any indication of how a soul mate treated you, I thought, I'll stick with my mere earthly partner.

"Maybe Adam and I aren't the happiest couple in the world right now." Ruth spoke to the skeptical expression I hadn't managed to suppress. "We were once, and someday we will be again. Marriage is hard, the rebbe says, but the rewards are great."

I hoped for her sake that they made it.

"What does your husband do?" I offered her the opportunity to brag on him, always a good way to win a woman's approval.

"He's a property manager." A flicker of satisfaction. "He just bought a loft building that he's going to convert to residential. The first of many, *kanehore*."

Aunt Rose's favorite word, warding off the evil eye so it

wouldn't punish someone with the temerity to actually enjoy her bit of good fortune.

"Who does he work for?"

"No one." There was outright pride in her voice. "He learned the business from someone, and now he has his own office. What does your husband do?"

"He's a cabinetmaker. His shop is near the Navy Yard, in Dumbo?" I made it a question, wanting to know if she knew the area.

"Oh, yes, that's where our building is."

"Is his office near there, too?"

"Yes, for the time being it's right in the building. He drives to work every day, and he parks there, too." Said with the smugness of automobile ownership—a symbol of status even in the outer boroughs.

We both glanced at the clock on the wall. Adam Edelman should be walking in the door right about now.

"Our landlord is Dovid Fine—I wonder if your husband knows him?"

"Yes." Her expression changed from neutral to wary. "Mr. Fine was his boss, before. He's a good man."

I wanted to ask if she knew her son's body had been found in one of Fine's buildings, but it didn't seem appropriate. Then it occurred to me—if her husband had worked for Fine— "Mrs. Edelman, did your son work for Mr. Fine, too?"

"No. My husband wanted him to, but Shimon had other ideas . . ." Her gaze drifted back to the clock.

I waited to see if she was going to continue. When she didn't, I reached across the table and touched her hand. "I am sorry about your mother. I didn't know her well, but I admired her work very much."

Ruth flushed. I think she'd actually forgotten why I was there in her kitchen.

"Yes, her precious paintings. She fusses over them like they're her babies. Tell me then, why is it so hard for her to understand how I feel about my children?"

I noticed that Ruth was now using the present tense to talk about her mother—as if in real death Helen was more alive than she'd been in the imposed death of no contact.

When someone dies unexpectedly, it removes forever the chance to come to terms with unresolved issues. Take Ruth, talking about her mother as though it wasn't too late for them, still needing the approval she hadn't gotten enough of as a child. It's a cliché, but no less applicable for that. As the child of a larger-than-life mother myself, I knew exactly how Ruth felt. I'd had to put considerable distance between my mother and me before we could get to know each other again as adults.

I had a bright idea. "Is there anyone you'd like me to call, to be with you right now? You'll have a lot to take care of, when the children come home—maybe Mrs. Swersky?"

"That old yenta—not in my house. Her or her darling daughter who can do no wrong." Helen's daughter, acerbic after all.

"Leah?" I asked. "She seemed like a very nice—"

"—respectable young woman?" Ruth finished for me. "Beautiful, pious, good cook, knows how to manage a household? That Leah, the one who is too good for my son? The one who runs with goyim, who introduced Shimon to those, to those—"

"Rivka!" And there was Adam Edelman, filling the doorway with an anger as broad as his shoulders.

Twenty-six

"WHAT ARE YOU DOING HERE? YOU, YOU'RE NOT THE POLICE."
The man of the house addressed me, then his wife, "Did she
tell you she was one of them? What did you say?"

"No, nothing," Ruth protested. "She came with the detective—I didn't say anything . . ."

Lovely. I have a strong distaste for men who imply in front of
other people that their wives are incompetent idiots. What was
Adam Edelman so uptight about anyway, that he couldn't spare
so much as a word of greeting for his wife, who'd just lost her
mother?

Michael made a perfectly timed entrance. Under cover of the
pleasantries, I faded into the corner between the fridge and the
back door, where there was a handy stepstool to perch on. Adam
glared once in my direction before sitting himself at the head of
the table; mercifully, he didn't object to my presence. Either he
figured I was a cop after all, or I'd simply dipped below his
threshold of what was worth raising a fuss about.

"Mr. Edelman, I assume your wife told you why we're
here?" Michael took a seat opposite Ruth, at the brown Formica
table.

"Because my mother-in-law is dead, yes."

Typical. Defining Helen in relation to himself, rather than
to her daughter.

"I didn't have a chance to explain the circumstances of her
mother's death to Mrs. Edelman. Let me tell you both." Michael

paused. He had Adam's attention; Ruth, however, was focused on her husband, watching for cues as to how she was supposed to react.

"It appears that Mrs. Baum was murdered, attacked in her apartment by person or persons unknown. We're not sure yet exactly how many perpetrators were involved." I appreciated his use of the royal we, which could be stretched to include me along with the rest of the police force. "Whoever it was searched her place very thoroughly, and did quite a bit of damage in the process."

"Robbed? You think she was robbed?"

"It certainly looks that way. Of course, we don't know yet exactly what was taken. The thieves weren't interested in the television or stereo system, the usual items snatched by a burglar. Easy to carry, easy to unload. Much of Mrs. Baum's artwork, which I understand had a certain value, was destroyed rather than stolen. Furniture was overturned, drawers emptied, and so forth. We believe they were looking for something in particular." He turned to Ruth. "As soon as you're up to it, Mrs. Edelman, we'd like you to have a look-see for what might be missing. Your mother carried insurance on the apartment, but we haven't located an inventory yet. It would help enormously in the investigation, if we knew what to look for."

Before Ruth could respond, Adam interrupted. "Did the gonifs take the jewelry?"

"What type of jewelry did she own? Where was it kept?" Michael had his notepad out, ready for the answer.

Adam glanced at Ruth, a quick warning to leave the talking to him. "Diamonds. Earrings, rings. Very old, very valuable. In a floor safe in the kitchen."

Michael stood up and slid a small silver cell phone out of his pants pocket. He tapped at it with the end of his pen, then stepped away from the table. "Nunez? You still at the scene? Good. Go in the kitchen." He looked at Adam Edelman. "Where, exactly?"

"Stand facing the sink. Turn left, two paces. Left again, three paces. Under the table."

Michael relayed the instructions. "Okay, she's there. Now what?"

Edelman grinned. "One board is shorter than the rest. Press on the near edge, and it will tilt up. Remove that piece and slide the fingers underneath on both sides. An irregular section, five boards in width, can be lifted out."

Again, the relay of information, then: "Bingo. Small safe, intact. You know the combination?"

For the first time, Adam Edelman allowed his wife to answer a question. "Eleven-eighteen-thirty. My mother's birthday."

"Great." Michael repeated the numbers into the phone.

"Who uses their own birthday for a combination?" Adam grumbled.

"My mother never opened it." Ruth, eyes lowered, addressed the table. "Her father installed it, and she never bothered to change the code."

"Are you familiar with the contents of the safe, Mrs. Edelman?"

Adam fielded that one, too. "Diamond earrings. Teardrop pendants, two carats each. Two dinner rings, stones approximately three carats. Also a leather-bound Bible and a set of tefillin in a blue velvet bag."

Ruth opened her mouth, as if to add something. Adam looked directly at her as he listed the contents of the safe, and the expression in his eyes stopped her from speaking. I'd have staked my life that he left something out of the inventory.

Such as unset stones left over from Helen's father's original stash? Gems that could have been sold to finance the purchase of a building with which to start one's own property management company?

"All there except the Bible and the velvet bag with the—what was it?" Michael asked.

There was surprise on the faces of both Mr. and Mrs. Edelman, but she looked apprehensive while he seemed relieved.

"Tefillin. Small leather containers with long straps. They are used in our prayers, morning and evening, bound around head and arm. These belonged to my mother-in-law's father. Items of no value other than religious—perhaps she disposed of them. She was very set against us. It would be like her to do such a thing out of spite."

Ruth looked as if she were about to disagree. Adam turned on her. "They should have been given to Shimon when he was bar mitzvah."

"Yes." A single word, spoken meekly enough, but I detected the hint of an old and unresolved argument below the surface.

It seemed reasonable to me, a grandfather's legacy passed on—but on the subject of religion, I knew Helen could be as irrational as Adam accused her of being.

Michael didn't pursue the issue of the Bible. I figured he made the same assumption I had—that it was the book with the smuggler's compartment, kept in the safe until Helen did, indeed, give it to her grandson. She'd probably given Simon the tefillin, too, and he hadn't told his parents.

As to whatever Ruth was going to add to her husband's inventory—from her narrowed eyes as she considered the plain gold wedding band she was turning around and around on the ring finger of her clenched hand, she was putting pieces together and coming to some conclusions of her own.

"I'll need someone to come to the medical examiner's office to make a formal identification," Michael was saying, "and if you wouldn't mind, then we could stop by the apartment and go over the other contents?"

"Rivka." Adam Edelman spoke sharply to his wife.

Her face slipped back into its blank expression, as if all independent thought was being erased from the chalkboard of her mind. "Zehava will be home in half an hour," she said.

It didn't take a Talmudic scholar to discern whether Adam Edelman would offer to collect his daughter or accompany his wife—because he did neither. "I will go with you," he informed Michael. "My wife will stay with the children."

Michael didn't argue. I decided I'd better pipe up. "Mrs. Edelman, is there someone we could call to take care of them for a few hours?"

"She doesn't need help. Every day is the same for her." Adam Edelman answered for his wife—without consulting her, of course.

Nice guy. "Yes, but she's just lost her mother, on top of her son's recent death, and this is not a time to be alone. If you like, I could stay with her until you get back?" There, I was doing it too—discussing arrangements for Ruth with him rather than with her.

Caught between outright rudeness and an insistent social worker, he caved. "Very well. I will ask Mrs. Swersky to come to you, Rivka."

Clearly Adam didn't share his wife's opinion of the Swersky family.

There was a mutinous glare in Ruth's eye, but she gave a wifely nod. He went out to the telephone in the hall.

"Mrs. Edelman, as next of kin it's your right to be the one to identify your mother's body. If you'd like to come with us also, I'm sure arrangements can be made to look after the children for a few hours."

Good for you, Michael, I thought. Let Ruth know that we'll support her if she wants to go against her husband's wishes. Which she didn't. "Thank you, that's very kind. My husband will see to things."

"Okay then, if you're sure?"

She nodded, head down.

Not sure at all, but—there were her husband's shoulders in the doorway again.

"Mrs. Swersky will send Leah to the cheder for Zehava. They will be here soon, so there is no need for you to stay." This in my direction, but with no eye contact.

"Oh, that's okay, I don't mind." Innocent, helpful me.

"Thank you." Ruth sounded, to my surprise, grateful. She looked up at her husband.

For the first time, I saw compassion in his eyes as he met his wife's. He took a step toward her, as if to lay a hand on her head, then stopped. If they'd been alone, would he have comforted her?

I felt sorry for Ruth. In the days after my friend Barbara died, Benno had stayed close to me; even sitting at the table, he'd pull his chair up so our knees or shoulders were touching. It was enormously reassuring, that slight physical contact reminding me that I was loved.

Until that moment, there'd been no sign of affection between the Edelmans; the only other visual communication had been when he was silently telling her to keep her trap shut.

"I'll see you back at the station," Michael said to me. We couldn't have worked it better if we'd actually been partners. He'd not only put an official seal on my legitimacy to be there, he'd also established that I'd be staying with Ruth until the cavalry arrived.

Which I was more than glad to do, especially since it would give me another chance to talk to that paragon of rectitude, Leah Swersky. I was interested in the relationship between her and Shimon Edelman, and those pesky goyim Ruth had referred to. And, as I was sure Michael intended, I'd ask Ruth about the Bible—along with whatever else she'd expected to be in the safe.

Twenty-seven

RUTH TRAILED FROM THE SUNNY KITCHEN INTO THE DANK
entry hall after her husband, as if reluctant to see him go.
Adam paused briefly in the open door to gaze at his wife. This
time a different type of communication passed between them,
a marital dialog without words, intended to be opaque to an
outsider but clear as a conversation to each of them.

From what I could tell as a practitioner of the art of silent
spousal disagreement myself, he was warning her yet again to
watch what she said. Her response was a challenge of some
kind, like she was asking him a question. He tried to ignore it
with a frown. She insisted. Then his expression shifted to
threat, and she looked down.

"Rivka." Adam Edelman forced his wife to meet his eyes, to
acknowledge and yield to his will before he turned and left.

As soon as the door closed behind her husband, Ruth began
to shake. First a slight negative gesture of her head, *no*, side to
side, *no, no,* before it rippled down her shoulders and set her
knees trembling.

I put one arm around her waist and a hand under her elbow.
"Shall we go upstairs and get you a sweater?" I suggested.

"Yes. I'm very cold."

She allowed me to guide her up the steps. The second floor
was as barren and shabby as downstairs. No rug on the wood
floor, and no furniture in the short hallway. Four doors opened
off the landing, three bedrooms and a bath.

The master bedroom featured twin beds, no headboards, both spread with bright blue and purple quilts in identical patterns of tumbling blocks. Between them was a nightstand with a single lamp. On either side of what I took to be a closet door were two wooden dressers that were not a match in any sense other than location. Under the room's only window a newish Singer sewing machine was surrounded by piles of fabric.

Ruth went for the bed on the right and lay down. I took the quilt—actually a duvet cover, from the feel of a goose-down comforter inside—from the other bed, and placed it over her. The bed linens were a pale lavender, the first really beautiful things I'd seen in the house. The separate sleeping arrangement seemed strange to me, but I wondered if the bedroom wasn't the heart of the marriage.

It's impossible to know from the outside what goes on in the private area between a man and a woman. What appeared to be a relationship where one party held all the power might in fact be no more than a pretense put on in public. This room felt like Ruth's domain, from the prime location of the sewing machine to the gorgeous coverings she'd made for the marital beds. Who was I to say that Adam in his own way wasn't trying to ease his wife's grief just as my husband had comforted me?

Ruth curled into a ball. I sat next to her and stroked her shoulders until the shivering stopped.

"I wasn't just saying that, before," I told her. "Your mother loved you. Did you know she carried that album of photos you gave her around with her? She showed them to me—Zehava in a pink dress, and Shmuel before and after his first haircut. She told me she really enjoyed having Simon stay with her. He wanted to know about her childhood, and yours, too."

I was stretching it a bit, but not much. You've got to give to get. I figured I'd tell her as much of the truth as necessary, and see how she responded.

"She told him stories about her father. The Bible, that wasn't in the safe? She gave it to Simon. He left it in her workroom upstairs, and—"

"Did the thieves ruin the studio, too?" Ruth sat up. All of a sudden she was concerned about her mother's work?

"No. Either they didn't know about it, or they were interrupted before they could break in up there."

"The Bible was upstairs? It's safe?"

"Yes."

"Oh! I have to tell him." Full of purpose, she pushed the covers away and got out of bed.

"They won't be at the apartment for quite a while yet."

Ruth turned on me. "So? He has a cell phone."

"Detective Dougherty took the Bible for evidence."

She slumped down on the edge of the bed, and started shivering again. I wrapped the comforter around her shoulders, but it didn't help.

What was going on here? Clearly the Bible worried her. I decided to put an end to the misery of not being able to talk about it.

"Your mother showed me the secret compartment."

That stopped the tremors. "And the bag of diamonds?"

So that was it. I should have guessed—it wasn't the Bible itself; Ruth expected there to be something left in the smuggler's pouch.

"No. There were drugs hidden in there, not stones."

"Not—what?" She stared at me.

"Your mother noticed the Bible on Simon's worktable after

the funeral. When she opened the spine, she found several dozen tabs of Ecstasy. Didn't they tell you, that's one of the drugs they found traces of in Simon's blood?"

"Ecstasy? I thought—they said something about amphetamines?"

"Yes, that too. Ecstasy is a euphoric, just like it sounds. Simon had taken a combination of the two."

"I don't understand. My mother gave Shimon drugs?"

"No, actually—" But I decided not to tell her that it had been the other way around, Simon getting his grandmother high. The woman had enough to absorb without that particular non sequitur. "I think Simon used the Bible to hide his own supply of Ecstasy. Your mother didn't know anything about it until after he died." I left out the part about his possibly selling the stuff, too.

"But what happened to the diamonds?"

It seemed an odd thing to be concerned about, considering that we'd been discussing her son's use of drugs. Maybe she was just overwhelmed, and having trouble switching her focus from diamonds to Ecstasy.

"Your mother said her father used them to buy the brownstone, all those years ago."

"Yes. And he thought he was paying my mother's tuition for medical school, but she tricked him and studied art instead. My mother sent me to college on them, too. I asked for the remainder of them as a dowry when I married Adam. She refused me."

"Do you know how many were left?"

"At least twenty stones. They were very valuable, because of their age and quality. They were all two carats or more, and very skillfully cut."

"Was your grandfather a cutter?"

"No, he owned a dry cleaners. My grandmother worked behind the counter, and my mother when she was old enough. A pair of Polish women did the hard work. The two pressers were men, and the tailor, Morris Moskowitz. I haven't thought about him in a million years. Uncle Morrie always had a pocket full of hard candies, butterscotch ones, in orange wrappers. I wonder what became of him? I was six when my grandfather died, and my mother sold the business. 'Fine's French Laundry' it is now."

Dovid Fine again? "The same Fine as your husband worked for?"

"No, no relation. It's a common name, and that was over thirty years ago. Uncle Morrie . . . he would come to the front and flirt with the ladies. My grandfather stayed in the office. I don't know what he did all day—drank schnapps, the way my mother tells it."

Remembering her childhood erased the cares of the past few months and allowed a lovely lightness to settle on Ruth's features. It didn't last long.

"We should go down. Leah will be here soon with Zehava." As she said her daughter's name, the light came back to her eyes.

I followed Ruth to the hallway. As we passed the other two bedrooms, I paused for a glimpse. Their furnishings were as sparse as in the master bedroom, and the quilts on their beds as gorgeous. I assumed the room with the rose, yellow, and orange spread was the girl's, a pattern of stars set in circles.

In contrast, the room with bunk beds was clearly the boys'—their spreads were different patterns in the same colors, deep tones of mostly blues and browns with flashes of dark red, bordered in black. A bit on the somber side for children, I thought, but incredible pieces. Their abstract geometries reminded me of Amish quilts.

Ruth came back to stand next to me while I paused in the doorway.

"You made these, too?"

"Yes."

"They're very different from your other work. Much more—depth to them."

"They're made from Shimon and Shmuel's old suits. My husband doesn't like them, and perhaps he's right. They do seem dark . . ."

I let my thought drift with hers. I don't know if our reveries led to the same place, but when I asked, "Do you suppose your mother gave Shimon his grandfather's tefillin as well as the Bible?" Ruth moved to a desk across from the beds and opened the top drawer.

It held an ivory silk bag with a buttoned flap, a prayer book, a maroon velvet drawstring bag with Hebrew letters embroidered on it in gold, and behind that, another drawstring bag, worn blue velvet, with a large Star of David stitched in yellow thread.

"There it is. I wonder why he didn't tell me?" She lifted the bag with two hands, and sat on the bed with it unopened in her lap.

"May I?" I sat beside her. I didn't know how sacred these things were, or even if women were allowed to touch them, but asking never hurt. As Aunt Rose would say, the worst she can do is say no and call you *pisher.*

Ruth nodded permission. I undid the bag and slid the things out. There were long leather straps wound around small square boxes that I was surprised to find were made of paper. Then I realized they were just covers. When I lifted one off, there was a smaller container inside, made of leather or wood—it was hard to tell, the thing was so old and shiny with use—with a larger square base that the straps were attached to. The base seemed to have a piece of leather sewn over it.

"The prayers are inside there," Ruth pointed. "The same ones as in the mezuzah. But that's strange . . ." She took one of them out of my hands and peeled the leather back.

"It should be sewn closed. Oh!"

The tiny compartment was empty. The level of Ruth's horror at this discovery was such that I had to suppress the urge to cross myself—my religion's way of warding off the evil eye of travesty, but not exactly appropriate in this situation.

Then she shook it, and two small yellow pills with smiley faces stamped on them rolled into her hand.

We stared at each other. Perfect, I thought. What better place to carry contraband?

Ruth snatched the other tefillin and pried its bottom up. She had to use a fingernail to extract the contents—not a scrap of parchment covered by minute Hebrew letters, but a square of green paper that, even before she undid its careful folds, was clearly legal tender in the U.S. of A. Twenty dollars, to be precise. About what a tab of Ecstasy would retail for.

Go, Simon. Nice niche market, there at the yeshiva. *Daven*-and-Deal, great name for a start-up operation.

"This is the drug you were talking about?" Ruth asked me.

"Yes," I said, but I didn't elaborate. "I'll need to take these as evidence."

"Of course." She proceeded to refold the bill and replace it in the tiny chamber. "Will my husband have to know?"

Now there's a woman capable of cutting to the chase. Sharper than I'd given her credit for. Confronted with the evidence, she'd figured out what her son was up to as quickly as I had.

"I really have no idea—it depends on where the case takes us." Ah, the royal us again! "I can promise you, though, that I won't mention it to him unless it's absolutely necessary."

"Thank you." Ruth held the bag briefly to her chest, and seemed to draw some kind of sustenance from the contact. When she turned it over to me, she was calmer, as if now she knew the worst and was able to face it.

The doorbell chimed from downstairs, and we heard the high tones of a little girl calling, "*Ema, Ema, let us in.*"

Twenty-eight

THE LITTLE GIRL HAD HER ARMS AROUND HER MOTHER'S WAIST,
her face buried in Ruth's dress. Leah glanced at me over their
heads, then away. If she recognized me from the drugstore, she
gave no indication. She looked for all the world like she was
wearing a Catholic school uniform—gray wool pleated skirt,
navy-blue cotton tights, and a navy cardigan buttoned all the
way up over a white blouse with a Peter Pan collar.

"Zevala, Zevala," Ruth crooned to her daughter. The child
had on a real uniform, again with the navy-blue, a wool
jumper over a white turtleneck, white tights, and black leather
Mary Janes on her feet.

When Ruth disentangled herself from the embrace and
stood up, she was transformed. The loss of a child takes people
in different ways. Some sink so far into grief that they are unable to rise and care for the children who are still alive; Ruth
Edelman was not one of those. In her case, the love she could
no longer express to her eldest child was now being lavished
on her youngest. I was glad to see it.

"Thank you, Leah," she told the girl. Then, "Mrs. Servi, this
is Leah Swersky; Leah, Mrs. Servi. She was kind enough to sit
with me this afternoon."

"My pleasure," I mumbled. If Ruth was dismissing me, I
chose to ignore the hint. I wanted to speak with Leah alone, if
I could.

"Come, *bubeleh*, let's go upstairs and change you out of

your school clothes." Ruth took Zehava's hand. "Please, Leah, help yourself in the kitchen."

"Mrs. Edelman certainly cheered up when her daughter came home, didn't she?" I started conversationally as I followed Leah through the swinging door.

"Yes. My mother says it's the best thing, that she still cares for her surviving children."

A polite girl, parroting her elders.

I thought about what I wanted to ask her and decided it was best not to waste time while we were alone.

I held up the velvet bag. "Do you know what this is?"

"A pouch for tefillin?"

"Do you know whose they are?"

"No, why should I?" Leah was puzzled. "They are for men. Maybe I know what kind of bag my father and my brothers use to carry their own, but this one I have never seen. It looks very old."

"It is. These belonged to Shimon's great-grandfather."

No response. Leah crossed the room to the refrigerator. As at home as if she lived there, she began taking containers out and setting them on the table. I noticed the brands, a mix of the familiar, like Mott's applesauce, and the strange—Menhadin low-fat yogurt, Kedem grape juice and crackers.

"These tefillin were tampered with. Inside one of them, there was a twenty-dollar bill instead of the prayers. I think Shimon was selling the drugs to other boys at his yeshiva—in the other one, I found two tablets of Ecstasy. Do you know what that is?"

Her cheeks flushed pink as she lied. "What happens among the boys is nothing to do with me."

Yeah, I knew that. "I understood from Mrs. Edelman that

there was talk about a match between you and Shimon. Surely you would know—"

"Only once, we went on a date. To the airport. My mother and father felt Shimon was—too worldly. They spoke to the matchmaker, to find someone more appropriate for me."

"How did you feel about that?" It was strictly my own personal curiosity asking.

"I have faith that I will marry my *bashert*. Shimon was not for me." Leah removed the wax paper from a log of strudel and set it on a flowered plate.

"Do you think Richard Linden might be your intended?"

When her pink cheeks turned scarlet, I was almost sorry I'd asked.

Embarrassed or not, Leah sidestepped neatly. "My sister says it's natural to have rebellious feelings at my age. It happened to her, but now that she's married and a little one is coming, she's glad our parents guided her as they did. She had some say in choosing her husband, and so will I."

"And if you wanted to choose Richard? What are the chances your parents would approve of him?"

"I don't know who is this person you're talking about."

"I saw you talking in your family's store, while the Edelmans were sitting shiva for Shimon. Remember me? Richard was buying all that cold medication—"

Leah's face went white. What had I said?

"Many people come into the shop. I don't remember you, and I don't know this Richard."

Nice try. "It really seemed like the two of you were on close terms, close enough that he upset you."

She shook her head, still denying.

"Look, Leah, I'm not trying to get you in trouble. I'm not

a police officer, I'm a social worker, but—do you know that Mrs. Edelman's mother was murdered yesterday?"

She nodded.

"Well, I came here with the detective who's investigating her death. The drugs in Shimon's tefillin weren't all he had—there were a lot more in his grandmother's apartment. I think Richard is involved in this and you know it. Maybe you didn't have anything to do with Shimon's death, but Richard did. At least tell me how to get in touch with him, and I'll try to keep you out of it."

The girl was terrified now. She shook her head, no. I felt like a louse, threatening this young woman, but this was no time for Ms. Nice Guy.

"If you don't want to talk to me, fine. I'll tell Detective Dougherty and Detective Collazo what I know about you and Richard being friends. I know he's a Jehovah's Witness, he lives over in Dumbo. The police will be able to track him down. Once they're involved, your parents will know everything."

It was a good try, but Leah stuck to her story.

"He was just a person who came into the shop. Sometimes maybe he flirted with me. He is not of our faith, and I didn't pay him any mind. I don't know anything about Shimon, or that drug. I'm only a girl, they wouldn't say anything to me."

They, she'd said, not him. Who they? I started to ask when a cell phone chirped. Leah took a blue Nokia out of her pocket, glanced at it before she pressed TALK, and said, "Yes, *Ema*, I'm here at the Edelmans'."

I was treated to one side of a dutiful daughter conversation. Evidently Mrs. Swersky would be here momentarily. Leah put the phone back in her pocket and began to set out plates and silverware for the afternoon snack.

"Who did you mean, they, when you were talking about Shimon?"

"They? I only meant boys, in general. We don't have much to do with them."

Smart cookie, Leah Swersky. I suspected her talents were not being used to best advantage in the drugstore.

Then there were voices from the stairs. I gave up on interrogation and stuck to satisfying my own inquisitiveness.

"That's a nice phone." It was, and very up-to-the-minute. "Do many people in the community use them?"

"Oh, yes." Relieved to be on neutral territory, Leah expounded. "Everybody has one. Well, everybody over thirteen. In my family, there are six of us on the same network. It's very convenient. Even the married ones, my father still provides for them so we can talk wherever we are."

Where could they be? From what I could tell, daily life in the Orthodox community was lived within about a ten-block radius. Not much different from life in my own neighborhood. All those cell phones seemed like overkill—but maybe it was my own preconceived notion that the Orthodox lived without modern conveniences. Which, judging from the Cuisinart food processor and the KitchenAid mixer on Ruth Edelman's counter, was my mistake.

The doorbell rang, and we could hear Ruth and Zehava welcome Mrs. Swersky. At the sound of her mother's voice, Leah shot me a single apprehensive glance before she continued placidly slicing the strudel.

I got my purse from where I'd left it in the corner by the back door, and stashed the tefillin bag before Mrs. Swersky came into the kitchen. While I was at it, I scribbled my home phone number on the back of another of Benno's business cards. Not that it had done Helen Baum much good, but maybe Leah would change her mind.

If she was surprised by my presence, Esther Swersky, like her daughter, hid it well. She did acknowledge having met me before, however, and once again pressed food on me. I decided I'd had enough of Orthodox living for one afternoon and declined a second cup of tea.

Besides, it was getting late and my own girl-child would be done with track practice soon enough. Not being blessed with a cell-phone umbilical, I liked to be home when she got there.

Leah was clearly relieved that I was going. Without prompting from her mother, she offered to see me to the door.

I slipped the card with my number on it into her hand. "If there's anything you want to speak to me about, call me. Anytime."

"I hope the police find out who did these terrible things," she said, polite to the end. "I'm sorry I can't help you."

"Can't or won't?" Given the opportunity, I had to press.

"It was nice to meet you, Mrs. Servi," was all the answer I got.

Twenty-nine

I WASN'T HAPPY ABOUT TAKING THE TEFILLIN HOME WITH ME. I didn't have time for a side trip to drop it off, however, even if I'd known which station Michael had cryptically referred to seeing me at later. The evidence would keep until morning; I'd hand it over at our meeting with Grace Davis.

I stopped off at Zucker's Deli on Lee Avenue and bought six stuffed cabbages for supper. Thanks to the motherly woman behind the steam table, they came with extra sweet-and-sour sauce on the side. The day was already getting dark. I passed Swersky's Drug, which today had a man around Esther's age behind the counter. The patriarch, I supposed.

No sign of Richard Linden in the neighborhood, or any other Jehovah's Witness sticking out like a sore thumb. On the subway ride home, the vinegary smell from the cabbage sauce seemed to short-circuit my thought processes. The only thing I was sure about was that Leah had lied to me.

Whether she was protecting her feelings for Richard or her knowledge of Simon's drug dealing, I had no idea. I couldn't even decide if it mattered which it was. I chased my tail trying to figure out a way to get the truth, and wound up climbing the stairs at 110th and Broadway no closer to an answer.

As it turned out, I didn't have to worry about keeping the tefillin and their illicit contents overnight. I reached Michael by cell phone when I got home, and got read the riot act.

"Jesus, Mary, and Joseph, can't you leave anything alone?

You're not a cop. You have no business poking in people's private property and confiscating evidence. You know what the D.A. is going to say about this? 'So I'm supposed to go into court and defend a chain of evidence that involves a defrocked social worker who happened to be in the victim's home and claims she had the victim's mother's permission—which the mother has now denied ever giving—to look in her son's drawers, where she discovered an illegal substance hidden in a religious object, which she then took home with her before calling the detective in charge of the case to—' For Pete's sake, Anita, what were you thinking?"

"What was I supposed to do, leave the tefillin there so Ruth Edelman could dispose of what was in them? She did give me permission to look, and she saw what was in there, too. I know I'm not a cop, but isn't that what makes it okay?"

That got me a heavy sigh. "Yeah, whatever. Done is done. Listen, I'm going to send a uniform over to pick the whatsis up. Do me a favor, put 'em in a plastic bag, and don't fool with them anymore? Not that it matters, with your prints all over the place already. This whole investigation is turning into an effing mess."

It wasn't just the case, though, it was everything.

TUESDAY MORNING SPORTED YET ANOTHER OF THOSE CRYSTAL-blue autumn skies, so kind to the workers clearing the rubble at Ground Zero, so cruel to those waiting for news and unable to revel in the long spate of low-humidity days, the unusual clarity of light that was so like California.

The law offices of Wertheim and Associates was on Third Avenue in the Forties. As head of the firm my father did have a corner office, but it wasn't what you'd think. Yes, on the fifteenth floor; facing south and east, so while the view was elevated it didn't include any of the city's better-known buildings. It's always nice to be up high, though, and look out at more sky than walls.

Michael was already seated in the small waiting area. Nice location or not, Manhattan real estate comes at a premium. The firm boasted six attorneys, a receptionist, a secretarial staff of three, a conference-room-cum-law-library, all housed in a warren of small rooms that included a kitchenette.

"Would you like coffee, Ms. Servi?" Evelyn asked. No matter how often I asked her to call me Anita, she never did.

"Yes, please."

I don't know much about legal receptionists, but to me Evelyn is an archetype. Of some indeterminate age between fifty and sixty-five, her hair dyed a pale color that was probably called champagne, she invariably wore dresses with belted waists—not frumpy, but not up-to-the-minute either—and tasteful jewelry. Today it was forest-green wool, with a scarf in shades of paler green pinned at the shoulder by a ceramic fish. She'd worked for my father forever.

Evelyn escorted us down the hall to the open door of Grace's office, then went on her way to make the coffee. It would be French roast, freshly brewed, served with cream and one sugar, just the way I liked it. I wished I had a wife like Evelyn. I'd once asked my father if he'd ever been romantically interested in her, and he'd replied that efficiency in the workplace didn't necessarily make a person easy to live with at home. A nonanswer if I've ever heard one.

What with the desk and computer table, credenza under the window, and two comfortable chairs for clients, there was no floor space to speak of. Grace Davis, a slender brown-skinned

woman, stood behind her desk and reached out to shake hands
with us. Her straightened hair was angle-cut to emphasize the
shape of her chin. She wore a lawyerly suit in an unlawyerly
color: deep teal, with a scoop-necked yellow silk shell under the
collarless jacket. I watched Michael to see how he'd size her up.

She was the kind of woman I thought he would appreciate,
firm grip and all. For once, though, he seemed not to notice
how attractive she was—either he was more attached to Anne
than I'd thought, or more preoccupied with the case.

Or with life. At this hour of the morning, the lack of sleep
made for stains like dark bruises under his eyes. Grace's window provided a narrow slice of East River view and a healthy
dose of morning sun. In the brightness, I noticed how the gray
at Michael's temples seemed to have spread.

He took out his pad, flipped it open, and started with the
standard question. His tone suggested that he was anticipating
the usual lawyer's nonresponsive answer. "Ms. Davis, what
can you tell me about the reason Ms. Baum consulted you?"

"She came to me to draw up a will." She glanced down at a
narrow white envelope on her desk before continuing in a
lovely, neutral courtroom voice. "As you know, Anita is named
as the executor."

"I'm what?" I thought I hadn't heard correctly.

"Surely you were aware of this, Anita? I understood Ms.
Baum obtained your consent prior to consulting me. She did
say that you recommended her to the firm."

"Not exactly—she knew my father was a lawyer, but she
never said anything to me about consulting him, or you." And
why would she? My father's name was mentioned often
enough in the press, but he was hardly the person you'd think
of first when it came to estate planning.

Evelyn brought in a tray with three mugs. I figured she must have ascertained Michael's preferences before I'd come in, because his was paler than mine.

"Ms. Servi, Mr. Wertheim asked me to convey his greetings to you. He's very sorry that he's meeting with a client and won't be able to see you this morning. He asked if you would phone him at home this evening."

"Thank you, Evelyn. Please tell my father no apologies are necessary, and I'll talk to him tonight." Damn if they didn't have me talking like them already.

Evelyn nodded and backed out of the room. Like I said, the perfect secretary.

Michael inhaled from his cup like he was taking in oxygen, and sighed at the taste. "Almost as strong as yours, Social Worker." It seemed to revive his prickly side. "So what's in the thing?"

Grace passed the envelope to me, along with an aluminum letter opener shaped like a dagger.

I slit the flap. "And the winner is—"

Michael tsked with impatience while I scanned the document.

"Would you like me to sum it up for you?" Grace asked.

"Yeah," Michael said. "Save Miss Junior Lawyer here from taking all day to figure it out."

I handed the sheaf of papers back to Grace.

"Helen Baum carried two million dollars' worth of insurance on the contents of her home. I have a copy of the inventory in her file." Grace tapped a manila folder on her desk with a manicured nail painted deep maroon. "She left the brownstone and the first five hundred thousand dollars from the sale of her collection of artworks, which includes paintings done by Ms. Baum herself as well as by others, to her grandson, Simon

Edelman. Anything over that amount goes to the Henry Street Settlement for the permanent endowment of an art program for children and teenagers."

"Is there a provision in the event that her grandson predeceases her?" Michael asked. "Which he did."

I admit, I was surprised by his command of legal terminology. The question was right on the money, though—who benefited from the two deaths?

"No," Grace answered. "Ms. Baum did not anticipate that contingency. I assume Simon Edelman had no children?"

Michael and I shook our heads no.

"Then, according to the rules governing intestate succession, his portion of the estate will revert to Ms. Baum's heirs at law."

"And who are they when they're at home?" Michael sought clarification.

"The deceased's next of kin. In this case, her daughter."

"So did Ruth Edelman's mother leave her anything directly?"

"She's to select a painting, along with her choice of items in the apartment that may have sentimental value to her. According to what Ms. Baum said at the time she had me draw up this will, she had already given the daughter and her husband an amount equal to what their portion of the estate would have been.

"To continue, Ms. Baum's jewelry is left to her other grandchildren, Shmuel and Zehava, with the instruction that it is to be sold to pay for their college educations—with the stipulation that the institutions of their choice be secular, not religious. In the event either grandchild chooses not to pursue higher learning, the jewelry is to be held in trust for their children, with the same stipulation. Ms. Baum declined to itemize the jewelry she referred to; my notes from the time indicated that her response, when pressed, was, 'My daughter will know.' "

It was easy to figure that she was talking about the contents of the floor safe. No reference to their provenance, though—such as my mother's earrings, my grandmother's ring. But then, Helen's grandmother had never made it to America, and her mother had hardly led the kind of life where she'd've worn such dramatic jewelry. Odd, I thought. Did Helen's father steal finished pieces as well as loose diamonds?

Grace was still talking. "Ms. Baum provided for her tenants to have lifetime occupancy of their apartments, superseding any right Simon Edelman as owner of the building has to evict them in order to claim the space for the use of his family." Grace frowned. "I did advise her that this might not hold up in court, but Ms. Baum was adamant that she did not want her building to be taken over by—well, I won't use her words; she meant members of the Orthodox community."

Michael stopped taking notes long enough to grin. "Wish I'd met that woman."

"Yes, she was something." Grace's professional reserve slipped for just a moment. "There are several minor bequests as well, such as five thousand dollars each to the proprietors of the Tenth Street baths and Omar's deli on the corner of Tenth and Avenue A. Similar amounts are left to a handful of charities. As I said, Anita is named as executor, and is to be compensated at a rate of one hundred dollars an hour."

Honestly, my jaw dropped. A hundred an hour? Social workers make half that. Where had she gotten the idea—apart from settling my grandmother's affairs more than ten years ago, I had zero experience with administering estates.

Then I remembered. Sometime last spring, maybe; Janis's father had died recently, and we'd been talking about the details of his estate while we sweated. I'd told Janis a story about probating my grandmother's will, which would have been a remarkably simple process if not for a stickler of a court clerk. Had Helen been in the room at the time?

Who knew? Anyway, it was hardly enough to recommend me for the job. For one thing, the point of the story had been my ineptitude in the face of a paragon of bureaucratic nitpicking. For another, I hardly knew Helen.

"I find it hard to believe she didn't discuss this with you in advance, Anita." Grace Davis responded to the expression on my face. "Had I known, I would have insisted that she do so."

"I wish she had, because I'd have said no." How could Helen dump this on me without asking my permission? "Is it usual to just take a person's word in matters like this?"

"Yes, it is. Ms. Baum indicated that she had your consent."

"Couldn't you have asked me about it yourself?"

"No, I could not. I understand your reluctance, Anita—this is no small task she's asked you to undertake. The auction of the art alone—which is why I insisted on the provision regarding compensation."

"Okay, okay." Michael flipped his notepad shut. "I think I've got what I need here. Maybe the two of you could go over the details later? I need some time with you myself, Social Worker. If you can spare it, now that you're a highly paid whatever."

At least he stopped himself from calling me an executor.

Grace nodded agreement. "I think we're done for now, although you should start on the insurance claim for the items that were stolen or damaged as soon as possible." She turned to Michael. "How soon will Anita have access to the premises?"

"Could be immediately if you've got an itemized list of the valuables. I'll go through the place with her myself. Anything stolen, we'll try to track it down and hope it leads to the perpetrators."

"I've made a copy of the inventory Ms. Baum drew up for insurance purposes. It also contains photographs of the artworks. And, Anita—keep track of your time. The clock on your compensation should run whenever you work on Helen Baum's affairs." Grace handed me a large envelope. "Please ask Evelyn to schedule an appointment. Tell her we'll need several hours."

The whole thing made me very uncomfortable. I was beginning to think Janis was right about me being fated to take care of old people. After this whole thing was over, I was going to have to see about some kind of cleansing or whatever you do when you decide you've paid as much as you can afford of your karmic debt for one lifetime. I'd had enough of death and the elderly when I'd left social work. It would be nice if this business with Helen was the period at the end of my sentence.

Thirty

"CAN YOU BELIEVE THIS WEATHER? DAY AFTER PERFECT DAY. YOU look at the sunshine, and you want to be outside. Then you inhale, and you remember. It's like God blinked that morning, and now He's making up for it with this clear spell, so the guys down at the pile can—ah, shit." Michael raked a hand through his hair. "C'mon, Anita, I'll buy you some breakfast."

We looked around for a coffee shop. In spite of the upscaling of the city, there are still plenty of old-style diners. We jaywalked across Third to the Olympia, a narrow place with a dozen stools along a gray Formica counter and a single row of booths. At that hour on a weekday morning, the place was almost empty. A well-dressed woman alone in a booth, three men in suits at the counter, all reading the *Times*. Job seekers, I thought. Collateral damage from the devastation of lower Manhattan, killing time before or after interviews, or just getting out of their apartments to pretend they still had gainful employment.

Michael slid into a four-person booth toward the back, out of earshot of the closest suit. A small man with skin a shade paler than his gray hair came over with a pot of coffee. He set two mugs on the table and poured without asking.

"You need menus?"

We didn't. In a greasy spoon like this, you either know what you want or you're in the wrong place. We both ordered bacon and egg on a roll. Our plates were on the table in less than two minutes.

I watched Michael glop ketchup on his and hoped the natural mellowing agents would do their work. I opted for Tabasco on mine. It wasn't salsa, but hey, this was New York; I made do.

Michael finished a half in three bites before I decided to break the silence. "Did you talk to Inez?"

Wrong opening. He shoved the plate away. "No. She got assigned to Fresh Kills six days ago."

"The dump?" I asked. "Why?"

Stupid question. It slipped out in one of those before/after disconnects. Fresh Kills, on Staten Island, had been the largest solid waste disposal site in the world before it was closed two years ago by Mayor Giuliani. In the wake of September 11, it had been reopened to handle the wreckage of the Towers.

"Scavenger duty. They got detectives pulling twelve-hour shifts, looking for body parts, personal belongings, whatever might identify . . ."

Rather than putting my foot in my mouth a third time, I waited for him to get a grip.

"Anyway, two weeks into the Edelman homicide, Inez hadn't turned up diddly. Her boss kicked the case over to Brooklyn Homicide where they got better things to do than solve some precinct detective's problems. Guy over there said he had no problem losing it. I put in an official request to have it assigned to me and picked the file up last night."

Michael went back to his roll and took a bite. Ketchup oozed out and splatted onto the plate. "Detective thought there was something odd about this homicide, though. Usually one of their own gets killed, there's a flock of black-hatters camped out in front of the precinct until we pin it on someone. This kid, none of the Hasids seemed to care."

"Probably because Simon wasn't one of them. He was Orthodox, not Hasidic."

"So?"

"So, it makes a difference. Don't ask me what exactly in terms of doctrine—they're all very observant, but the Orthodox are more modern about it. The Hasidim cling to the way they dressed back in the old country. There are dozens of sects, depending on what town they came from. Their rebbes are like avatars or something—they like to live nearby, breathe the same air.

"The Orthodox aren't so mystical about it, although their rabbis are the ultimate legal authority. Also, the Hasidim wear *payess"*—I made the twirling-finger gesture to indicate the long curls of hair favored by Hasidic men—"and beards and long black coats and those round black hats, *streimels.* The regular Orthodox men don't necessarily have facial hair. They wear yarmulkes, and when they're out in public a fedora or any kind of regular cap will do."

Most of this I knew from Benno. He'd been raised Jewish—four sets of dishes, kosher outside the home as well as in—but not exactly religious; no daily prayers, or even weekly attendance at the synagogue. Among his cousins, however, were some who had not only remained *frum,* observant, but become more so as the community changed around them with the arrival and increase in the traditional Orthodox and the Hasidic populations.

"Yeah, well, Orthodox, Hasid, black-hatter, my experience with those people is they look out for their own."

I shrugged. "Even Jewish people have bad apples, people whose activities the rest of them don't want to know about. If

Simon was selling Ecstasy at the yeshiva, claiming him as a victim might bring unwanted attention to the less-than-perfect underbelly of Williamsburg."

"That's what I'm trying to tell you."

Michael signaled for a refill on the coffee. The gray waiter topped off our mugs and whisked the plates away. Michael laced his with a stream of sugar and three creamers.

"The search of Helen Baum's place? Kid had another two thousand tabs of E hidden in an old toolbox. Street value, fifty thou minimum. Probably more. Theory is, whoever did Ms. Baum was after the Ecstasy. Whether she was aware Simon had it or not, we'll never know. Either way, it's clear her attackers didn't know about the studio upstairs. For whatever reason she didn't enlighten them.

"Upshot is, that quantity of drugs, I had to call in Narcotics. I'm only telling you this, Anita, so you'll keep out of things from now on." I got a finger wagged in my face. "No more snooping around and slipping me pieces of evidence on the side. This is one for the big boys now."

I couldn't tell if Michael minded this or not; he looked too exhausted to care.

"So what are you doing here if it's not your case anymore?"

"I'm still working the homicide angle. Everybody's stretched a little thin right now. One good thing though—cooperation is more than a code word for guarding your turf by giving the other guy as little as you can get away with."

"Are the two deaths definitely related?"

"Sometimes a coincidence is just a coincidence. My opinion though—it's unlikely a grandmother and grandson would get themselves killed within weeks of each other and it's not connected. Assume the perps knew the kid had all that Ecstasy hidden somewhere in the old lady's place, her death makes sense—they were looking for drugs, she got killed in the process. The weird thing is why the kid wound up in that kinky machine of yours."

"Same reason. Someone wanted the Ecstasy and he wouldn't tell where it was."

"Okay, but why there?"

"Because he was dealing Ecstasy out of the space next door. Didn't you read Inez's file?"

Michael threw a crumpled, ketchupy napkin on the table in disgust. "What are you talking about, Anita? I thought your theory was that the kid was using those leather-box thingies with the straps to sell it at school."

"Tefillin," I corrected him automatically. "Yes, but he was also using a vacant studio in our building. The person who knew about it was supposed to tell Inez."

"What person?"

I hesitated. There was no reason for me not to give up Carlos's name at this point.

Michael banged a fist on the table, rattling saucers and my nerves. "Damn it, Anita, what's going on here?"

"Carlos Sanchez," I said mildly. "He's an artist who lives in the converted building across the street. He told me he noticed people coming and going in the middle of the night and went over to check it out. A couple of Jewish teenagers were selling Ecstasy. Simon, and another kid Carlos made a sketch of. He was supposed to give the drawing to Inez."

Michael flipped open the file folder and went through a stack of forms. "No Sanchez in here. Only one identified as an artist is Grant Farrell. You don't mean him?"

"No. Inez interviewed Grant because he was on our list of

people who knew what the press was and how it worked. He's got a studio in the old factory on the corner of Front and Jay— another one of Dovid Fine's buildings."

"Yeah, that's all here. Says she thought he was living in the loft illegally, but it wasn't worth bothering over. This Carlos fellow, only thing about him in the file is that he was out of the country when she knocked at his door."

"He got back from Paris at least a week ago. He was negotiating to rent that space, and he didn't want to talk to you guys until he signed the lease. If she's been at Fresh Kills, maybe he tried to get in touch with her and the message didn't get through?"

"Anything's possible. Guess I'll have to pay him a visit myself." But Michael wasn't over it yet. "Okay, you know so much, tell me why your building? You got a copy of a lease with Simon Edelman's name on it?"

I let the sarcasm go. "Simon's stepfather used to be a property manager for Dovid Fine, the man who owns the building. I saw Mr. Fine at the Edelmans' house when I went to make a shiva visit. Simon could've known one of the other young men who worked for him, someone who would have known the space was empty. Maybe you could figure out who from Carlos's sketch."

Michael shook his head in amazement and disgust. "You got the dots all connected don't you, Social Worker? They ought to set you on al Qaida's tail. We'd have the bastards in no time."

"Go ahead, be snarky. Why should all the goodwill in the police department extend to civilians? We get in the way, we provide information that gums up the works, we—"

"Okay, okay. I know you're trying to help, but you sure can be a know-it-all. That business with what you took from the kid's room—please."

As apologies go it wasn't much of one, but I let it slide.

Michael was a bit too close to the truth for me to be seriously offended. I'm curious by nature, a solver of puzzles. Maybe I cross the line into busybody territory, but I can't help it. I felt the pieces of Helen and Simon's story beginning to come together and I wasn't about to step back.

"So what did Inez find out?" I tried.

"Not a whole hell of a lot. For one thing, not having an exact time of death made things hard. The M.E. got it to within a two-day time frame based on stomach contents. He didn't eat his last couple of meals at home though, so it was hard to get any closer than sometime on Saturday, September twenty-second."

At some point I hadn't noticed, the unobtrusive waiter had slipped us the check. Michael turned it over, squinted at it, took a ten out of his wallet, and left it on the table. Given the place, it was a generous tip. I approved.

Thirty-one

WITHOUT NEEDING TO DISCUSS IT WE TURNED NORTH ON Third, toward Grand Central. It was the closest subway stop, a nexus of lines that would take us each wherever we wanted to go. I was at loose ends, not sure what to do next.

"Yo, Social Worker, wake up! Where you headed?"

"That's a good question," I told him. "If I could answer that one—"

"Sure, you wax philosophical, but I'm taking the Lex downtown. Some of us have jobs with bosses."

The large manila envelope Grace had given me was tucked under my arm. "Do you have time to go back to Helen's apartment with me? Or I could do it myself, if you're too busy?"

"Not a chance." Michael consulted his watch. "Give me a couple hours. You got the number for my cell?"

I didn't. He jittered with impatience while I got out my daybook and wrote it down.

"So where are you going now?" Michael sounded like he didn't trust me to wait for him.

Not without reason. I had a set of Helen's keys and he was familiar with my ability not to resist temptation.

"I think I'll cruise the food halls while I'm here," I answered. "I never get over to Grand Central, and I just need some saffron from the spice place."

"Shopping. Women." He held up a hand. "Don't bother, I apologize. Whatever gets you through the day is fine by me.

I'll catch up with you later. Just stay out of trouble, Anita, you hear me? No poking around on your own. You call me if you get any bright ideas."

"Yes, dear." I smiled back at his fussing, and he went off with another muttered *women.*

I wasn't really in the mood for shopping. Saffron was essential for arroz con pollo, though, so I strolled across the lobby. In the middle of the vaulted room I paused to look up at the starry ceiling sky, the glittering dots of the constellations connected in the shapes of bears, hunter, ram. I stood still amid the swirls of hurried people, small and insignificant below the artificial heavens.

The new food hall did nothing to improve my mood. On some other day, I might have enjoyed the gorgeous displays, the polished green apples, lush red grapes, the racks of chocolate pastries and kiwi tarts, the perfectly marbled steaks and lamb chops with frilly white booties.

Before the muted light and the scattering of shoppers in fur coats got to me, I made for Adriana's Caravan. On my chicken budget, a pinch of saffron went a long way toward luxury. I shelled out twelve dollars for four grams, and resisted the siren call of the salsas.

I still had a few more hours to kill before Michael would be ready to meet me. As I crossed the main waiting room again, it came to me: there was one area where I could satisfy my curiosity without interfering with the narcotics investigation.

Gone were the days when I had friends I could consult on the latest advances in recreational pharmaceuticals, but the Internet would tell me all I wanted to know and then some. I was just a few blocks from the Mid-Manhattan Branch of the New York Public Library—the world's greatest research facility.

No, not the gloriously restored main building guarded by the pair of lions known to New Yorkers as Patience and Attitude. Fortitude, actually, if you want to be technical about it, but attitude is closer to the mark. The Mid-Manhattan Branch's six stories of books are housed in a building across the street.

You want to see real New Yorkers, go to a library. From a homeless man in rags following a red finger down the columns of the *Wall Street Journal* to an almond-skinned woman with her hair covered by a black scarf carrying a stack of books to one of the wooden tables, all the city's denizens come together to read.

I crossed my fingers that I'd be able to luck into using a computer, though—you have to sign up for the machines with Internet access. The time is scheduled in half-hour increments, and competition is fierce. At this time of day, I expected the next few hours would be full.

The force was with me. Someone had canceled a slot for which I'd only have an hour's wait. I spent the time at a table next to the studious Muslim woman. I made notes on what to look for while I read through the inventory of Helen's artworks. I was amazed by what some of them were insured for. If the Wolfes could be restored—well, Grant Farrell had been right about their importance.

Once I got on-line, I started with the drug that had contributed the most to Simon's death. You don't truly appreciate what freedom of speech means until you walk into a library, log on to the Internet, call up Google, and type in "methamphetamine."

Within minutes, I'd located support sites for people trying to quit, an FAQ page that gave a comprehensive overview of how crystal meth is consumed (smoked, snorted, injected), what it costs (not much—enough to fuel a three-day binge might run you twenty-five bucks), and what effects it produces in the user (an immediate rush or "flash," euphoria, increased alertness, decreased appetite, paranoia, irritability, insomnia, confusion, anxiety, aggression, hyperthermia, convulsions).

That wasn't the half of it. You gotta love a country that makes it possible to order on-line and pay by credit card for a book called "Secrets of Methamphetamine Manufacture" written by a person who identified himself as Uncle Fester. For $15.95 plus $5.00 shipping and handling, the recipes and complete instructions for making all the meth I could sell, smoke, or give away would be mine.

Lovely. From what I read it wasn't all that complicated a process, although the photos of seized meth labs in Iowa looked like the kind of contraption Clea's Mousetrap game resulted in. Flasks, test tubes, metal rods, clamps, buckets, mason jars, a hot plate, some rolls of duct tape, coils of rubber tubing; the collection of items stacked next to the apparatus included acetone, lye, road flares, a gallon jug of ammonia, and—I peered at the screen. It looked like a stack of green Dimetapp boxes.

I went back a few screens and found a list of ingredients. The flares were not for alerting customers to the readiness of a batch; they were a vital part of the manufacturing process. As was the cold medication, which provided pseudoephedrine. And then there was ammonia and lye and Epsom salts and a long list of things you'd never in a million years put into your system. Lithium from camera batteries? If you weren't nuts to begin with, you would be by the time you'd used the stuff a few times.

I printed out what I didn't have time to read from an extremely helpful site run by the Koch Crime Institute, whatever that was.

Given the short time I had left, I moved on to Ecstasy. My initial query got me to another of those general FAQ sites. It's amazing what people put their time into; for every cause or quirky interest, there's someone with a Web site.

I learned that Ecstasy, also called MDMA (short for 3-4 methylenedioxmethamphetamine—try saying it once, never mind three times fast), is a close cousin of crystal methamphetamine—as you might guess from the name. While it is not as addictive nor as destructive as crystal meth, some of the effects are the same. Euphoria, for one; E is also known as the "hug drug" and is especially popular at dance parties and raves.

A very different set of mind-altering substances to abuse than was available when I was growing up. I took notes, not least so I'd have something concrete to show Clea when I sat her down for yet another antidrug conversation. Some parents of my acquaintance feel too morally compromised by their own youthful drug indulgences to urge their kids not to experiment. Me, I have no qualms about it. The fact that I smoked and enjoyed marijuana does not mean I'd recommend it to Clea any more than I'd offer her a glass of wine with dinner.

Yeah, enough with the soapbox. What else I learned about Ecstasy was that eighty percent of it is produced in the Netherlands, with Israel a secondary supplier. I typed in "Ecstasy seizures" next, looking for information on smuggling.

The manufacture of MDMA is no backyard operation. Not only is the profit margin high—pills that wholesale in Amsterdam for less than two dollars each go for thirty or forty in the clubs—but the product is classy. Depending on the supplier, there are various logos embossed on the tabs—Superman's S, Fred Flintstone, a green shamrock—or a yellow smiley face, I thought. Talk about marketing to kids! Free enterprise, alive and well.

Most interceptions were made, unsurprisingly, at international airports—Kennedy, O'Hare, Miami, Los Angeles. From what I read, young Hasidic and Orthodox men were especially popular as mules. Customs agents rarely hassled people in religious dress on their way home from Israel. The boys were told that they were bringing in diamonds and paid a few thousand dollars for the trip.

Simon, to a T. Thanks to his smuggling grandfather he had the perfect tool for the trade, and he'd been to Israel a few months ago. Except hadn't Michael said he'd found a much larger cache of drugs than would have fit in the spine of the Bible?

I tapped the corner of the screen absentmindedly while I thought about it.

"Excuse me." An elderly woman with a red folder clutched to her chest stood behind me. "I believe your time is up, young woman. Please stop that, you're getting fingerprints on the screen."

I was actually hitting it with my nail, and according to the clock I still had two minutes. I bit back the urge to point either of these facts out to her and gathered up the pages I'd printed out.

The woman was literally huffing with impatience by the time I yielded the wonderful Aeron chair to her bony backside. Okay, so I didn't stifle my thoughts; give me credit for keeping them to myself.

I was lucky again to find a working pay phone on the side-walk. Michael said he was already at Helen's brownstone, and where the heck was I?

On my way, I told him. Back in the plebeian subway passage of Grand Central I didn't give the Oyster Bar a second glance as I made for the turnstiles. Let the rich eat cake. I dropped a gold Sacajawea dollar in the outstretched cup of a skinny woman in a shiny gray raincoat.

Thirty-two

I SHOULD HAVE KNOWN WE WOULDN'T FIND ANYTHING OF ANY use whatsoever in Helen's apartment. It was Tuesday after lunch. Nothing worthwhile ever turns up during the least cosmic time of the week.

By the time I got home, though, I was feeling less discouraged. The blue-leg candlesticks were a bit chipped, but all intact. Thanks to the photos in Grace Davis's insurance file, I was confident that the bowls of fruit and arms could be reassembled. The great majority of Helen Baum's own paintings were stored in the studio upstairs.

And Benno was thrilled to hear about my new occupation. Not just for the money, either.

"I think it's great," he said as we finished our wine after supper. "Much as I enjoy having you at the shop, your talents are wasted on finishing."

"I thought you said I had a gift!"

"Flattery." My husband grinned at me. I punched him in the arm.

"You have a lot of gifts, Anita. Spraying lacquer is fine and dandy, but like I said, making the unnecessary for the unappreciative doesn't add much to the greater good. Taking care of elderly people does. What social workers do takes heart and brains and courage. You should be proud of yourself."

For that night, I was.

.   .   .

WEDNESDAY MORNING, HOWEVER, I WOKE UP WITH ACHING muscles from sorting through the chaos in Helen's apartment, and the sinking feeling that I was getting sucked back into a world I'd renounced.

What I needed was a *shvitz*. I thought about calling Janis, but decided not to. Although I think of the baths as an experience best shared with a friend, I needed some time alone. Not that being naked in a room of sweating strangers was a particularly solitary thing to do—which was the point. I could be among people who, other than silently acknowledging my presence among them, wouldn't intrude on my thoughts.

I needed time to ponder the events of the past few weeks, and to think about my future. Benno was right about me and cabinetry. My foray into his world had been a good break from my profession, but ultimately it wasn't the career for me. In the time away from social work, however, I'd gotten clear that I didn't want to go back to working with the elderly, either. I enjoyed setting my own schedule, and not spending my days in bra and panty hose.

The extra income from settling Helen's estate was like manna from heaven, a windfall to carry my share of the household while I figured out what to do next. I pulled on a pair of fleece leggings, a cotton tunic, and a denim shirt. Too impatient to wait for the elevator, I ran down the twelve flights of stairs.

Then cooled my heels for almost twenty minutes waiting for a train—par for the course now. In that time, the sparse crowd on the platform increased to rush-hour proportions. When the 1 finally came, it was already packed. There was the normal pushing of people too impatient to wait for the next train, meeting with resistance from those unwilling to move to the center of the car.

"Yo, people, suck it in!" This from a burly man shouldering his way into the reluctant crowd.

"There's another train right behind this one," a woman scolded.

"Yeah, and Christmas is just around the corner," he answered. "Keep it to yourself, lady, ain't nobody standing on your toes."

Ah, now life really was getting back to normal! It was the first rude exchange I'd heard on the subway since September 11. Not even two months, and New York was already slipping back into old habits. It felt great.

I rode the rest of the way to Fourteenth Street with a smile on my face.

Going to the baths would also give me the chance to share Helen's death with someone else who knew her, someone whose relationship with her was less complicated than her daughter's: Vera.

Peace, Michael, I thought as I walked the underground corridor between the 1 and the L at Fourteenth Street. Yes, I'm curious what Vera will make of Helen's bequest to her, but that's hardly "poking around." I had to tell her about it anyway; why not now?

Benno has been known to call me the queen of rationalization. I prefer to ignore the sarcasm and take it as a compliment.

"GOOD MORNING, ANITA." VERA PLACED ONE OF THE LONG metal lockboxes on the counter in front of me for my valuables, then tilted her head to look past me. "Are you alone today?"

"Yes." I took off my watch and earrings, then reached into

my purse for wallet and date book with its emergency stash of twenty dollars.

Vera locked the box and handed me a locker key attached to a fat rubber band.

"Vera . . ." I wasn't sure what to say. We didn't know much more than each other's names. From what I could tell, she wasn't much closer to any of the other regulars. It was a business; if you wanted frills like therapy or advice, you'd be better off at an Upper East Side spa.

She waited me out.

"Have you heard about Helen Baum?" There was no good way to start.

"She is not here today, I don't think. Is something wrong?"

"Yes. I'm sorry to be the one to tell you, but she's dead."

Vera shook her head. "I'm not surprised. Every week, I think maybe this is the last time."

"Was she sick?" I was startled.

"I think so. We don't talk about it, but since the summer I was seeing in her eyes the look of cancer."

I must've seemed skeptical. Vera went on to explain.

"I don't know how to describe it. I see people, and I know. Like pregnant women, it shows in the eyes."

"How about cheating husbands?" The question was out before I knew I was going to say it.

Vera laughed. "Everyone except the wife can see that!"

Too true, I thought, but I let it go. "I don't know if Helen Baum had cancer or not, but that wasn't what killed her. She was murdered last Sunday."

Vera pushed back from the counter on her stool and said something to herself in Russian. Then, "Those hoodlums! An old woman like that, why don't they leave her alone?"

Was it a second-language grammar thing, or— "Was someone making trouble for Helen?"

"This neighborhood, there are all kinds of crazy people. She gets mugged, what do you expect?"

Well, maybe. It was a nice cover job. I gave her the brutal truth. "Helen wasn't mugged. She let someone into her apartment, and she was tortured and beaten to death. They broke her fingers."

An intake of breath, but her face remained impassive. I dropped the other shoe, just for the heck of it.

"She left you some money in her will."

"Me? Why would she do that?"

I gave her points for not asking how much. "Because she liked you, I guess. It's five thousand dollars."

"How do you know that? You were not friends with her."

"No, but she made me the executor of her estate. Did you know her very well?"

A shrug. Her composure was back. "Like you, to speak to. One time she gave me—wait a minute." Vera bent down and took a box from one of the lower shelves. She riffled through a stack of papers, flyers, business cards, and menus, until she found what she wanted and handed it to me. "An invitation to a show of her paintings. I didn't go."

The opening had been February 6, 2001, at Corolis Contemporary Arts on First Avenue. The name sounded familiar; I might've walked past it every time I came to the baths and never gave it a second glance. There were dozens of storefront galleries in the neighborhood. They opened like mushrooms after a rain and faded just as quickly when their friends' pocket money dried up. This was the East Village, after all, with more art-makers than art-purchasers amid the grunge.

"She was an incredible painter," I said. "I wish I'd seen more of her work."

Vera nodded at a small, framed oil above the tables in the eating area. "She gave me that many years ago."

I walked over for a closer look. It was less abstract than what I'd seen in the studio, a discernible autumn landscape with shadowy shapes flitting past the verticals of bare trees. Grim and evocative, like all Helen's work.

A pair of Goth-girls had come in and were removing their varied items of face jewelry.

I slid the invitation to Helen's opening into my bag. Assuming the gallery was still solvent, it would make a good next stop after the baths—someplace I should probably visit anyway, in my capacity as executor.

"Would you like a massage?" Vera asked the young women. They reminded me of husky puppies, with their boxy shoulders and shorn thatches of hair.

They both declined. Inspiration struck. I waited for them to get their keys and vanish behind the heavy curtain to the locker room.

"You know, I think I'll have a massage today, since I'm on my own."

Without comment, Vera opened the large ledger book.

"Someone told me that—shoot, I forgot her name—a woman, Russian, with short blond hair—was very good."

"Could be Sasha? Tanya? Maybe Irina? Who told you this?"

"I'm blanking on his name. He's Jewish, tall, with a neat beard. He works for my landlord. He was here two weeks ago. Maybe you could—?"

It was enough to get Vera to consult the schedule book. "Irina, but I don't know if you will like her."

I watched where Vera's finger rested against the left-hand column, pointing to a name. Jacob, that was all; no last names here. "This guy said she was very good. Since he's a regular, I figured he knew what he was talking about."

"Irina doesn't give the kind of massage you like."

"No?" I pretended innocence.

"She does Swedish, with oil. Not Oriental like Pai Lin."

"But Pai Lin isn't here anymore, is she?" I hadn't had a good acupressure-type massage since Pai Lin left the baths a year ago, around the same time the man I'd gone to for shiatsu in my neighborhood went back to Japan.

"No, not for a long time."

"So it's time for me to try someone new," I said brightly. "And Jacob said Irina has a very firm touch."

"Yes, the men like her," Vera acknowledged. "She's strong, but I'm not sure for you she is right."

"Well, you never know. I'm willing to give Irina a chance."

Vera hesitated. What was it to her, who rubbed my back? She got paid regardless. She seemed to come to the same conclusion herself. "How long would you like? Half hour or whole hour?"

"Oh, a whole hour." I always went for the max; half an hour just wasn't enough.

"I put you down for twelve-thirty then. That gives you time to finish before the men start to come at two. Room eight, outside on the deck."

"Thanks, Vera," I said. "You're an ace."

That got me a thin smile. I headed for the door, then turned back casually, as if something had just occurred to me. The Columbo technique had worked for Michael; why not give it a whirl? "Do a lot of Orthodox people come here?"

I didn't think Vera was Jewish herself. A lot of recent Russian émigrés were, but she'd been in the States at least twenty years. I hoped I hadn't offended her.

"Some."

"Only the men, though, right?" I was hoping for more. "I thought Orthodox people had their own special bathhouses, and I've never seen any of the women in here."

"Just men. We are not kosher." She closed the book and slid it under the counter, clearly waiting for me to leave.

"Right, I guess not. Don't they have to use rainwater in the ritual baths?"

Vera shrugged. "Don't forget your towels," she said.

Thirty-three

I STARTED IN THE RADIANT HEAT ROOM, STRETCHED OUT ON A narrow bench. Janis had been right about one thing: I did miss an aspect of social work. Not the people per se, but the window I was allowed into other lives. My profession gave me license to indulge my curiosity about people, how they lived, their backgrounds, habits, family constellations. I entered lives in times of crisis, and that gave me reason to ask questions that in ordinary circumstances would have been overly intrusive.

What I was learning about the deviations from Orthodoxy among the religious Jews I'd come into contact with fascinated me. Every culture has its rule-breakers. Some did it more or less overtly; others led secret lives. I found these closeted rebels to be more complex and interesting personality types than those, like Helen, who outright left the tribe.

I had no idea what it meant that a yeshiva teacher frequented the Tenth Street baths in order to be stroked by a woman who most likely gave him more than a standard rub for his money. I'd kept the information tucked away like a squirrel storing nuts, and now I had a chance to take it out and start nibbling. I'd have loved to sit down and talk with him, but I couldn't imagine a context where that might happen. A massage from Irina and some conversation on the side was as close as I was likely to get to an inside view of the kind of man who could cheat on his religion as well as his wife.

I dumped a bucket of cold water over my shoulders and

looked around the room. There were the pierced women who'd come in after me, two black women applying mud to each other's backs, and no Helen. I built up a sweat again, then ducked out the wooden door and did a lap in the cold plunge.

I dried off, put on my dark pink robe, and headed up to the deck for a smoke before the massage. When I got there, the woman I figured was Irina was stretched out in one of the lounge chairs next to another masseuse, a thinner woman with black hair pulled back into a ponytail. I noticed that the trace of dark at the roots of Irina's hair was gone, and it had been cut in the kind of shag that was popular about ten years ago. It didn't really suit her; she was too large-boned for the poodle look.

I took the pack of Camel Lights out of my pocket and offered it to the two women. Ponytail refused, but Irina accepted. We looked at each other over the flame of the lighter as I held it for her. Her eyes were gray, with large dark pupils that gave her a languid appearance.

I broke the eye contact and stepped over to the rail. I stared off to the southwest, toward lower Manhattan, with my back to the women. I wasn't ready yet to let Irina know I was her next client. Timing is everything; that she'd taken a cigarette from me would get us started on a friendly basis.

The masseuses were talking idly in Russian with an occasional word of English tossed in. I caught references to the subway, and Brighton Beach.

The trees had lost their leaves since last I'd stood here. The sky was just as blue, the smell of incinerated plastic just as faintly pervasive as it had been that afternoon. Only two weeks ago. Now Helen was dead, and I was responsible for settling her affairs.

I dropped my cigarette butt to the deck and stepped on it. Irina sent hers sailing over the railing, with a glance at me to see if I had anything to say about it. I raised my eyebrows at her, like, no, it wasn't a good thing to do, but hey, none of my business.

"You're Irina?" I asked. She nodded. "I've got a twelve-thirty appointment with you."

She studied me for a moment before she got to her feet. In no particular hurry, she crossed the deck and opened the rickety door of the middle cubicle. I stepped inside.

The roof was green corrugated fiberglass that gave the light an underwater quality. There was exactly enough room for the massage table with two feet of space on either side. At the far end, a small table covered with a flowered cloth held several plastic bottles of oil, a windup clock, two candles in glass cylinders, and a stack of clean towels on a lower shelf. Irina lit the candles, which didn't do much to dispel the gloom.

"Take your robe off, please, and lie down on your stomach." Her voice was deeper in English than it had been in Russian, less inflected.

I was reluctant to get naked in front of this woman, even though she covered my backside right away with a large towel. "You like lavender, eucalyptus, or spice scent oil?"

"Lavender is good," I said. Not that I was crazy about any of them. Swedish massage is not the same as shiatsu. I'm used to leaving my clothes on, to thumbs pressing and releasing specific points. What I was about to get would leave me slathered in oil and feeling like a loaf of kneaded bread.

As well as propositioned.

I will admit, the knots in my shoulders and neck yielded their grip on my muscles to the insistence of Irina's strong hands. She moved down my back in a pattern of circular, squeezing movements that lingered slightly longer on my buttocks and thighs than I was comfortable with before she moved on to my calves and feet and I relaxed again.

As the circles made their way back up, her hands seemed to be urging my thighs open. I stiffened, and she didn't insist. "Roll over, please."

Again the big towel covered me right away. She began with my face, which was wonderful, and moved down each arm in turn. I hadn't forgotten the earlier awkwardness; when she squeezed out another handful of oil and lowered the towel to my waist, I reached to pull it back up.

I opened my eyes and we looked at each other. "You don't want?" Irina asked.

"No, that's okay," I said. This whole session was not going at all how I'd planned. I should have stopped it when she asked me to turn over; I'd intended that to be when I told her I'd had enough, and just wanted to talk.

"For woman, only fifty dollars extra," Irina offered.

"No, really, thank you. Not today." As if I'd have agreed to it some other time. Always polite, that's me. I wondered how much it was for a man, and what exactly they got. Hand, mouth, the whole enchilada? Suddenly I didn't want to know.

I sat up, clutching the towel to my chest.

Irina shrugged. "Okay. You still have twenty minutes."

I reached for my robe. I had to let go of the towel to put it back on. Irina stood with her arms folded and watched me.

"Hey, no offense," she said.

"No, don't worry about it," I told her. I took the cigarettes out again and offered her one.

She took it, and held out a candle to give me a light.

I perched back up on the foot of the massage table. Irina slid up on the other end of the table, and set a large green glass ashtray between us. We smoked in silence for a minute.

I had a dozen questions I wanted to ask. Not just about Jacob, but in general, such as: Does Vera know what you're up to? Do all the girls provide these kinds of services? How much *do* you charge men?

As if she'd read my mind, Irina opened the conversational door. "You don't complain to Vera?"

"She doesn't know?"

Irina shrugged. "It's like in the army. She doesn't ask, you don't tell her."

"What about the other masseuses?"

"Maybe, if a customer asks. It's more money, but most say no. I think, so what if you rub another body part? Feet are any better?"

That was one way to look at it. I laughed, and she joined me.

"Most people who ask special for me, they hear from a friend. Why you ask for me if you don't want?"

"Honestly? Because I know a man, his name is Jacob, who's"—now, what was the right euphemism to use here?—"who sees you regularly, and I wanted to—"

Irina stubbed out her cigarette. "If you know Jacob, you don't ask questions about him."

Suddenly she was on guard.

"Is he a bad man?"

There was no amusement in Irina's smile.

"Why then?" I asked. "Because he comes to see you in spite of his religion?"

"No."

"Why don't you like him?"

"Like, don't like. It's all the same. You're not Jewish?"

Call me Judas, but I denied my father's contribution to my gene pool. It seemed to be the answer that she was looking for.

"The men, they are all the same. One way at home, another way outside. What I do is nothing special, but they can't ask their wives. It's not *koh-sure*."

She gave the word a mocking emphasis.

"My husband has relatives like that," I said. "Eat kosher at home, but when they go to a restaurant, it's steak and baked potato with sour cream."

I offered another cigarette. I was over my quota for the day, but whatever worked. After we'd lit up I asked, "Do you know what kind of work he does?"

That got a disgusted snort. "Mr. Jacob is a teacher. To teenage boys. They should see him with his pants around his ankles."

It was more bitterness than I'd expected from a woman who supplemented her income the way Irina did. I could imagine how she felt, though. Disgusted, even by behavior that she profited from. It wasn't an easy life.

Irina waved a hand at all the smoke we were making in the little room. "I better open the door."

In the brighter light, I could see how shabby the space was. The walls, no more than sheets of plywood held together with battens, had been painted a medium blue probably intended to be cheerful. The color came across as tacky, as did the green shag carpeting on the floor.

Irina stayed by the door, as if waiting for me to go. I got up from the massage table but made no move to leave. I tossed out a final question on a wild hunch.

"Did Jacob ever give you drugs?"

Bull's-eye. Irina stepped into the room again, pulling the door shut behind her and forcing me backward. I could smell her breath; cigarettes and unbrushed teeth.

"What are you, the cops?"

"No. No, I'm not." I noticed she had her right hand in the pocket of her sweatpants. I had the sudden image of a flick knife and how much damage it could do to me, at bay in the narrow room. I held up a hand. "Really. I'm a social worker, not a cop. I don't care what goes on here."

Irina eased back about a foot. It wasn't far enough for me.

"Why are you asking me these questions?"

Candor, Anita. I gave her a highly edited version of the story, short on facts and long on theory. I left Helen out completely and told her about finding Simon's body, that I knew he'd been selling Ecstasy. I said I knew Jacob had been one of Simon's teachers, and I was trying to find out if that was who'd given him the drugs.

It sounded lame even to me. Irina was shaking her head. "You Americans. You know one Russian person who lives in New York, you think we all know each other. Okay, so Jacob gives me some pills of Ecstasy. You think only two Jews have this stuff?"

There was a knock on the door, two solid raps.

"One minute!" she called out, then took a threatening step toward me. "Now we are finished."

I didn't like that hand in her pocket, not one little bit. I maneuvered around the head of the massage table to the other side, and out the door.

Sure enough, a man in a black fedora was pacing the deck. It wasn't Jacob, or anyone else I recognized.

There wasn't time for another round of sweating before

men were officially allowed in, so I took a shower and got dressed. While I waited to pay up, I eavesdropped on an ordinary New York man, in jeans and a black turtleneck sweater, who was making an appointment for a massage.

"Tanya is good?" Vera asked, and the guy agreed.

He smiled at me as he reached for a towel and robe, just the casual greeting of one passing stranger to another, but I responded with a scowl.

"What's your problem?" he muttered as he pushed through the curtain to the locker room.

Men, that was my problem. I was not feeling kindly toward the unfair sex right at the moment.

Thirty-four

Thirty-four

I CONSOLED MYSELF WITH A BOWL OF RUBY RED BORSCHT AT Veselka before I headed down First Avenue to the Corolis Gallery to see what they knew about Helen and the value of her work.

As it turned out, not much; the gallery was closed. From the look of things, it had been for several weeks at least. In the recessed doorway, a collection of dead leaves, coffee cup lids, and a missing poster for a white-bearded man had accumulated. There was a metal grate over the entire storefront. I peered in one of the large display windows and got a glimpse of various sculptural items still on display.

One of the pieces looked familiar. It stood about three feet high and was made of pairs of pliers that had been separated and then welded back together in a new configuration. The result was a female figure with nipples and genitals poised to pinch the organs of whoever was fool enough to approach her.

It had to be Grant Farrell's work. His current stuff was smaller and more finely wrought, bound by all those obsessive twists of wire, but this predatory woman was a clear example of his style and sensibility.

Corolis—that's why it had sounded familiar, from when I'd run into Grant last Friday, and he'd nattered on about a gallery. A one-person show here? From the looks of it, not very likely.

I peered through the windows at the paintings on the walls.

They were a collection of desert landscapes with suit-and-tie Wall Street types riding armadillos to work in high-rise saguaros. I kid you not, that's what they were. It didn't seem like Helen's kind of place. And with work like that on the walls, it was no surprise the gallery had folded.

There didn't seem to be any sign with information on hours or ownership, so I gave it up. Out of sheer aimlessness, I cruised across the street on the diagonal and headed for P.S. 122, a former public school converted into performance and gallery space. Of what they had on display, the only things I liked were some huge charcoal studies of industrial buildings, multi-windowed brick edifices drawn freehand with a quirky, wavering line. There was nothing that resembled either Grant's or Helen's work. I walked out without a word from the sulky, safety-pinned young man draped around a folding chair just inside the entrance.

So much for art. I headed back uptown. Just north of Twelfth Street I passed another storefront gallery with the un-likely name of Pause, and figured why not. As I browsed the collages of handmade paper and metallic foils that I actually liked, a woman emerged from the back room and asked me how I was doing.

She introduced herself as Willow, a name slightly at odds with her regulation black jeans and the streak of magenta over her left eye. She had a friendly manner and a merciful lack of metal studs embedded in her facial features. We chatted for a bit about the current exhibit before I asked if she'd ever heard of Helen Baum or Martha Wolfe.

Of course, by then Helen's death had made the papers. Unlike Vera, Willow was up on the news. "Oh, that was so tragic. Her work is wonderful. The way she used pigment and line . . ." She discoursed at some length about the plastic qualities of oil paint and embedded tactile materials.

I tuned out the art-speak until she took a breath. "I just saw my first Helen Baums last week. You don't represent her, do you?"

"I wish! Robert, that's my boss, he approached her when the shit hit the fan at Corolis, but she turned him down. It's too bad, because the prices for her paintings were just beginning to get really serious. I suppose now she's dead they'll go through the roof."

"Corolis?" I prompted.

"Down the street. There was a break-in over the summer and a couple of Helen's pieces were stolen. After that, she pulled all her stuff out. I don't know what happened between her and Diana and Ronnie, those are the owners, but they got enamored by this painter from Arizona who calls herself Tempe—that's the name of a town, but I don't think she's even from there—she just uses the one word, Tempe. You should see her stuff—" Her nose wrinkled in disgust.

Despite the avant-garde hairdo, I had a feeling this young person was not from around here. She was way too chatty for a true New Yorker. We do tend to run on at the mouth, but usually what you get from a native is ranting. I've found it's the elderly who routinely tell you more than you asked for, and newly transplanted Midwesterners.

I made an all-purpose, sympathetic tsking sound.

"The worst part about the robbery was that Diana had let the insurance lapse. The things that were stolen were worth at least fifty thousand dollars each. Can you imagine?"

I could, actually. I wondered if the robbery was random, or perpetrated by a member of Helen's own family. Simon? It didn't seem likely, but—a boy who took drugs? Or Adam Edelman? A hundred thousand would have made a nice down payment on a building. But how would either of them have known where to unload such paintings? It wasn't like selling old diamonds—which would be impossible to trace. Especially if they were loose stones . . . I put the ideas that were forming aside for later.

"Have you ever heard of Martha Wolfe?" I asked the voluble Willow.

"Martha Wolfe! She's practically a legend in the art world. I've seen the catalog from her very first show at Corolis—really groundbreaking use of mass-produced cultural icons."

I refrained from asking if she meant the doll parts. "When was that?"

"In the late eighties, I think. Right before she died."

"Corolis has been around that long?"

"Oh, yes. It was the first art space to open up in the neighborhood." She frowned.

"So why did they close?"

"Well, I guess because of the robbery. Helen Baum had agreed to let them exhibit some of Martha's pieces from her private collection, but then she changed her mind." Willow lowered her voice in a very un-East-Village-type whisper. "Helen and Martha lived together, and after Martha died, Helen sort of withdrew. Corolis was the only place she'd let handle her own work, and even then it took Diana years to convince her to show Martha's work. It really is incredible, right up there with Joseph Cornell's boxes."

"Do you know how I could get in touch with Diana or—Ronnie, was it? I'm not much of a collector, but when I see something I really like . . ." I let the sentence dangle.

"Oh, sure, they're probably in Robert's Rolodex." She returned from the small office two minutes later, with a slip of paper that she handed to me. "There you are. Diana Coroman and Ronnie Arliss. That's where they got the name, Corolis. Dropped one of the esses, I guess, to make it look better."

"Thanks, Willow," I said. "Do you mind if I ask where you're from?"

"Minnesota," she said, proud of herself. "I know I still talk too much, but you can't tell by my accent, can you?"

Now that she mentioned it, I did recognize the slightly flattened a's. I gave her the compliment she obviously wanted anyway. "No, you don't have even a trace of the Midwest. I think it's great that you haven't lost the friendliness, though. New York could use a little more of that."

I smiled gamely while she went on about how nice people had been to her since she moved here three years ago, and how her parents wanted her to come home—after what happened—but this was home, especially now. I knew exactly how she felt. The attack on the Trade Center hadn't made me feel any more patriotic as an American—for my money, you can keep the flag-waving—but it did cement my sense of being a New Yorker. I loved the irritable residents of my city and the way we all came together in the face of disaster.

"Thanks, Willow," I said again. "I've got to run—my daughter will be home from school any minute." It wasn't quite true, but it was an excuse the polite young woman couldn't argue with.

I STOPPED AT A PAY PHONE ON FOURTEENTH STREET AND TRIED the number for Diana and Ronnie. I wasn't surprised to get a recording—out of service. I should've asked for an address, but then, I was guessing that if she'd had it, the helpful Willow would have told me.

Well, I'd done enough poking around to come up with a hot prospect for Michael to follow up on in terms of the Ecstasy trade. Jacob, variously known as a *macher* in the Edelmans' rabbi's entourage, a yeshiva teacher, provider of drugs to Irina—it seemed to me he was worth a closer look by someone with more investigative authority than I had.

First thing when I got home, I called Michael. I was hoping for a pat on the back, but he was in an extremely pissy mood. My input on Jacob did nothing to improve his outlook on life.

"Look, Social Worker, I told you to stay out of this. Narcotics already has an eye on your Jacob and there's stuff happening that I can't let you in on. If you go anywhere near the guy, you could mess us up royally. The narcos were not, you'll pardon the expression, ecstatic about your gift of the tefillin. The only reason they didn't haul you in for interfering in a police investigation was that the whoosies helped them get warrants for the school. So give your overactive brain a rest—if you don't mind, we can take it from here."

Far be it from me to horn in on a drug investigation, but I still considered the murder fair game. "Is Jacob involved with either of the deaths?"

"I swear I'd hang up on you if I thought it would put an end to the questions. Short answer is, we don't know yet. Trust me, you'll be on my must-call list as soon as we've got Jacob Stern in custody. Maybe you'd like to sit in on the interview?" Extremely heavy on the sarcasm.

"Okay, I get it. Just please *will* you let me know?"

"Anita. Leave it alone, will you? I've got work to do."

Thirty-five

THURSDAY MORNING I FUTZED AROUND AT THE GREEN MARKET on 116th, then found myself walking circles around the living room. I was ticked at Michael for his dismissive attitude even though I knew he was right. I felt like the bull in the china shop. I had no idea what I was doing; I just bumped into things and then thought every item I broke was connected in some way. Yeah, by my own ineptitude.

With a glare at the bowl of pears I'd just bought, I grabbed my leather jacket and took off for Brooklyn. I intended to put in a few hours at the shop. I'd sweep if there was nothing else to do; at least I'd be busy.

I took the pages I'd printed out at the library along for reading material on the train.

I learned how to identify a clandestine meth lab (strong odors of cat urine or acetone, renters who pay cash, isolated or industrial locations, lots of nighttime traffic) and what steps to take in getting rid of the toxic residue created by the process of cooking meth. There were no official guidelines; recommended solutions ranged from total demolition to doing nothing. The site advised that at the very least, the former lab should be aired out for several days, all surfaces thoroughly scrubbed, and rugs, drapes, and upholstered furniture removed. A complete paint job was also a good idea; the paint would "lock" the contaminants to the wall so they couldn't escape into the air.

By the time I walked up the ramp at York Street, I was in

dire need of caffeine. One of the advantages of the minor gentrification going on in Dumbo is the opening of more places to eat. While we are staunchly loyal to Los Papis for lunch and Benno still picks up his morning brew from the Hispanic luncheonette on Jay and York, I've converted to the place across the street.

"D" Space is basically a combination of cafeteria and deli where you can get Asian dishes like chicken with green curry and coconut milk as well as regular sandwiches, gourmet muffins, or egg on a roll. To apply the word decor to the interior would be stretching it. The place is a large, open room with a painted concrete floor, a mélange of mismatched tables and chairs, and a wall of windows that could use washing.

Nevertheless, they serve Green Mountain Roasters coffee. I don't need vegetable lasagna for lunch, but give me a cup of freshly brewed French roast and I'm happy. As I walked past the front, I caught sight of Grant Farrell at one of the tables. The person sitting across from him had a nice short haircut and a dark blue jacket with cream sleeves.

Neither of them looked up at the window as I approached. I knocked on the glass and startled both of them. Grant smiled when he realized it was me, but his companion ducked his head like he didn't want to be recognized. Too late; I already knew who it was.

I helped myself to a cup of coffee from the self-service carafe on a side table. The downside of good coffee is that you pay for it. Cost Benno fifty cents for his American brew; I had to shell out twice that for mine.

While I stood at the cash register, Richard Linden left. Rather than following him, I took myself over to Grant's table. He flashed me a dimple. Why is it that men with unshaven jaws are so sexy? When you get down to it, they're no fun to kiss.

"Hope I didn't scare your friend off," I said.

"You did me a favor. I'm glad for the interruption, especially from you." He tried a lascivious raising of his brows, the male equivalent of batted eyelashes.

Yeah, as if I'd even be tempted to follow him upstairs for a quickie.

"It looked like you were having a pretty serious conversation."

"Nah, I was just fooling with him. The kid's a Jehovah," Grant said with a wink. "I like to torture him with the intricacies of biblical text."

"You're a Bible scholar?"

"Honey, I was raised in the Bible belt. Enough years of Baptist Sunday school, and I can pretty much quote chapter and verse on any subject you like. That stuff adheres to the crevices of the brain and no amount of recreational drug use can scrub it out."

That got a genuine laugh out of me. "Well, good luck with trying to unconvert the kid." I stood up to leave.

Grant rose and bowed. "Always a pleasure, Anita. Especially when I can put a little glow in your cheeks."

Which, as intended, made me blush. As I walked down Plymouth, I thought about what a change working in Dumbo was. With its mix of artists and craftspeople like Benno, it was a much more male-infused environment than your average social services agency. I wasn't always so sure the testosterone-laden ambience was an improvement, but a little flirtation did raise the spirits.

When I got to the shop, Benno was building a set of cherry

bookcases. For a moment I thought I'd be able to do some real work with one of the machines. Uh-huh. I was perfectly capable of operating the drill press to make holes for the adjustable shelves, but Benno wanted me to sand—every woodworker's least favorite task. Being the boss, he won.

I guess I wasn't paying quite enough attention to the orbital sander, because I accidentally sanded through the veneer on the third shelf by staying in one place for too long. When Benno saw what I'd done, that was it.

"Who do you think you are, Shel Silverstein's dish dryer?" He was referring to Clea's favorite poem, which goes something like, "If they ask you to dry the dishes, and you break a few, then they won't ask you to do it anymore."

"Hey, I said I was sorry." I was, too, and on the verge of tears. "Maybe I'll just go back home."

"Yeah, that might be a good idea. Fortunately for you, I cut an extra shelf, but that's all the cherry I've got." Nothing like a mistake on the job to turn my amiable husband into Simon Legree.

I STARTED DOWN THE STAIRS. WITHOUT THINKING ABOUT IT, I made for the spray room on the third floor. With the keys in my hand, I was ready to retreat to the sanctity of my own space. The remains of the police seal stuck to the door brought me up short. Old habits die hard.

Although the place wasn't off-limits anymore, I hadn't been in it since the morning I'd found Simon's body. Now that I was there I thought I'd take a moment to commune with Simon's spirit, see if he had anything to tell me.

Chalk it up to being from California, but I believe the dead communicate, even if only by the thoughts we allow them to inspire in us. Especially the restless dead, the unavenged, among whom I counted not only Simon Edelman but also Helen Baum. I pushed the door open and reached automatically for the lights.

Of course they didn't go on. Benno had had the power turned off as soon as he moved all our things out. The windows provided plenty of illumination for the neatly swept, utterly empty room. I stood for a moment in the center of the space. I felt no sense of unease, no hovering spirit other than that of the dust motes set in motion by my presence.

"Simon? Helen? Care to help me out here? Anything you think I should know about why either of you died, or who killed you?" I spoke out loud and got no answer. What did I expect?

I left the room, closed and locked the door behind me.

Then I reached on top of the fuse box on the wall next to the elevator and felt for the key to the next-door space. It was right where I'd seen Carlos leave it the other day. A Medeco, exactly like the one to the spray room. I still had my key ring in my hand. I don't know what impelled me; I held the two keys together and compared them.

Identical.

Thirty-six

I TRIED MY KEY ON THE OTHER DOOR, AND IT OPENED. UNBE-lievable. I used the fuse-box key on my door, and don't you know, that one worked too.

I felt a wave of fury at Dovid Fine and his lame business practices. The same key for both places—anyone could have gotten in at any time and done anything. And they had!

I relocked the spray room and went back to Carlos's future studio space. Early-afternoon sun slanted in the open windows and shone on the white walls. I walked over to the sink and sniffed at the drain. So, it smelled like paint thinner. From the glossy look of the paint, it was probably oil-based rather than latex. That would account for the open windows, too—letting the smells out.

I'd noticed it when Carlos brought me here, and now the fact that Mr. Fine had painted before renting it out really bothered me. Why had he gone to the trouble? It cost money, and if the tenant wanted paint, he could do it himself. We certainly had.

I did a circle of the room, thinking: night traffic; cash rent; easy to set up, easy to dismantle; toxic waste; smells that wouldn't be noticed with a finishing operation next door.

Simon with meth in his system when he died. Richard Linden buying all that extra-strength cough medicine at Swersky's Drug. Carlos scoring Ecstasy from Simon. Carlos reluctant to talk to the police.

Carlos, from whom I'd gotten the distinct sense that he knew more than he was saying.

Like what might have been going on along with the sale of Ecstasy.

But maybe Carlos didn't know about it. For one thing, he was too fastidious to knowingly rent a place that had been contaminated by toxic chemicals. For another, he'd made his night visit in August—I had no idea whether a meth lab was in operation then.

Which meant Simon might not have known about it either. No, that didn't make sense. Simon had crystal meth in his system; clearly he used the stuff himself. Could he have overdosed? Sure. And then crawled into the vacuum press to sleep it off?

There were too many permutations. I knew nothing about the timing except that Simon died on September 22. Did his death force an end to the manufacturing operation, or was its demise due to the police presence on the corner after the eleventh? Pretty hard to sneak drug buyers in after midnight with a squad car parked in front of the building.

And when did the paint job happen? Was it intended to cover up the lab, or something else? I wondered if Dovid Fine was in on the whole deal, if he'd rented the space for cash, to— whom? Not Simon; Mr. Fine had looked at his picture and denied knowing the boy.

Maybe he was lying.

Maybe Heschel and Sroeli and the girls in the office were, too.

I paced the length of the room, hitting dead ends in my thought processes with the same regularity I reached a wall and had to turn around.

All of these questions would be better handled by the police.

For all I knocked my brain out, Michael was the one with the authority and resources to find out the facts, establish a timeline. All I'd done was collect a cast of characters who may or may not have been connected.

Time to think outside the box. I locked the door behind me and pocketed the key instead of putting it back on the fuse box. I know, I had nothing left in the spray room to protect; it just seemed like a prudent thing not to leave it lying around so anyone could have access.

Access, that was still the thing—whoever put Simon into the vacuum press had to first get into my finishing room. Dovid Fine and all his minions probably knew about the hidden key, the duplicate Medeco locks. The Hasidic man Carlos had done the sketch of, for example—he could be the one who provided the space to set up the lab. Then who would have known how to cook the stuff?

Difficult to imagine Sroeli at his computer, ordering Uncle Fester's recipe book. But was it impossible? Now I had a full-blown conspiracy theory centered out of my landlord's office. And what about Jacob? He and Dovid Fine knew each other . . . Sure, Anita. Make it complicated.

When I hit the sidewalk, I scowled up at Michael's bright blue sky. Now what? Go home and call my friend the real detective? Yeah, and while I waited for him to get back to me, I could lay on the couch, read a novel, and eat bonbons—live my mother's idea of the good life.

I crossed the street to Carlos's place.

The former factory building was a bona fide residential conversion, complete with buzzer, intercom system, and trusting tenants. A woman actually held the door for me on her way in.

It would have been better manners if I'd allowed Carlos an

extra minute of warning by buzzing from downstairs, but I didn't think it would matter. I was in a hurry to share my conclusions with someone willing to listen. Carlos, it seemed to me, had more of a reason than even Michael to be interested in the previous use of the space he'd put good money down on.

Why I didn't realize he already knew—well, call me naive.

The woman took the stairs, but I opted for the self-service elevator to the fourth floor. Even without the industrial decor of pipes left exposed and painted in bright primary colors, à la Paris's Centre Pompidou, it would have been obvious that the building was occupied by nonstandard tenants. Most of the individual doors had been decorated by their respective artists. The level of detail ranged from a trompe l'oeil rear view of a person entering the apartment to the minimalism of a matte-black paint job with a series of red slashes in the lower left corner.

Carlos had glued a mirror to the center of his door and surrounded it with a collage of vines and flowers, so that I saw myself as if I were emerging from a jungle. I didn't make an altogether flattering picture. Before I knocked, I tucked up the stray strands of hair that had escaped from my bun. I wished I had some lipstick to apply.

Not that I was in the least interested in a fling with Carlos, or anyone else for that matter; I just wanted to look my best for him. I was struck by the contradiction—Grant, who came on to me, made me uncomfortable. Carlos, who didn't make overt approaches, provoked me to flirt with him.

I was still peering into the mirror when the door opened.

"You're gorgeous, Anita," Carlos said. "Even without primping."

I blushed, and got a wide grin in response.

"It's a two-way mirror. A photographer on the second floor is going to help me wire a Polaroid with a light-trigger mechanism that goes off automatically if something darkens the field."

It seemed pretty passive-aggressive to me, an underhanded way to greet one's visitors. I wouldn't have wanted to be photographed unawares. I struggled to find something polite to say.

"Come on in." Carlos, shirtless in black jeans, ran a hand through his tangled hair.

I found his half-naked body more discomfiting in the flesh than when covered. For one thing, he had no chest hair. For another—well, there was the unmade futon on the floor, its black and tan striped sheets in lascivious disarray. With Carlos right next to me, I couldn't avoid breathing in the musky body aroma of a man who'd just woken up. I'm accustomed to the way my husband smells, but this stranger scent was doing something not altogether unpleasant to the pit of my stomach.

I'm of the school that believes it's okay to flirt as long as there's no chance of either party taking it seriously. I walked over to the tall windows and looked across the street to the newly painted space where I'd just been. Breathe, Anita. Nothing is going to happen here.

"Coffee?" Carlos asked. There was the whirr of a grinder from the kitchen area.

"No thanks, I've already had more than my quota for the day."

When I turned around, Carlos had put on a gray T-shirt and was folding the futon in half to get it out of the way. I will say I was more relieved than disappointed.

"I ran into Grant Farrell in "D" Space this morning," I said, by way of a conversational opener. "Did you know he's made friends with one of the Jehovahs who hangs around the neighborhood?"

Carlos looked at me like I'd kept on walking after stepping merrily into a pile of dogshit and he was trying to figure out how to tell me about it.

"What?" I was embarrassed all over again.

He took a mug from the dish drainer, moved the pot away from the coffeemaker, and held the mug right under the drip. When it was half full, he switched the pot back into its rightful place. After adding a hefty shot of half-and-half, he took several sips before looking at me.

"What?" I asked again. "The kid's name is Richard. They were having breakfast together. I think Grant's trying to unconvert him."

"That would be the pot rubbing soot off the kettle."

Whatever the analogy meant, I didn't get it. "Grant said he likes to get him wound up by citing Bible verses."

"Anita, your innocence is charming. Those two have interests in common more earthly than quoting Scripture at each other."

"Like what?" I didn't care for his condescending tone.

"Did you come here to tell me about Grant and his new friend, or was there some other reason for you to wake me up today?"

"Actually, there was. Have you signed the lease for the studio already?"

"Tuesday."

"That was two days ago, but you didn't—"

"I know, Anita. I promised I would call the detective, and I will. Inez Collazo, isn't that her name?"

"Great memory." I said it sarcastically.

"I have had other things to take care of."

"Was one of them getting the air and the walls tested for toxic residue?"

"What do you mean?"

"Like you don't know."

"No, I don't." He frowned at the view of his future studio from the window.

"Do you know who rented it during the summer, while you were busy buying Ecstasy over there?"

"What difference does it make?"

Not exactly an answer, I noticed. I said what I'd come to say anyway. "Whoever sold you that Ecstasy was also operating a clandestine lab to make methamphetamine. You know, crystal meth, workhorse of champions?"

Carlos snorted into his coffee mug. I plowed on. How much more of an idiot could I sound?

"Okay, so you knew. Do you realize how toxic one of those labs is? The paint job should go a long way to sealing in the contaminants, but you should really have the place tested before you move in."

"I appreciate your concern for my welfare, but it's not necessary. What went on there—it wasn't much, and as you said, the paint will take care of any residue."

"Were you in on it with them?" My stomach did not have a good feeling about where this conversation was going. "Is that why you didn't want to go to the police?"

"You think I was cooking meth?" Carlos's expressive eyebrows went up in the middle. "Why would I do that? Tweaking holds no appeal for me."

Tweaking. I didn't repeat the word; its meaning was all too clear. "You know who did, though, don't you?"

"What if I do? The operation has been shut down."

"Since when? Before Simon was murdered, or after?"

"I really don't know, Anita. Please excuse me. I have an appointment at noon and I need to shower. If you don't mind—?" He gestured toward the door, inviting me to leave.

I did mind, very much.

"The key you took from on top of the fuse box opened both doors. I think the people who killed Simon stashed his body in the vacuum press so they'd have time to clean up the meth lab and get out of there before he was found."

I moved nearer to the door, ready to bolt. "A person doesn't have to use the stuff to make it. You knew where the key was hidden, and how the vacuum press worked. You already told me you bought Ecstasy from Simon, so you knew him too."

Carlos grabbed my wrist. His fingers felt like a too-tight bracelet. "I was in France when the boy died."

So you say, I thought. But it wasn't for me to disprove. "If you weren't involved, then why haven't you contacted the detective yet?"

Right on cue, Carlos's cell phone played the first notes of "Round Midnight."

Thirty-seven

I DON'T KNOW WHAT IT IS ABOUT THOSE THINGS—THEY RING, and their owners answer them. No matter where or what they're in the middle of, that summons takes precedent. Janis has done it to me in the middle of a lunch date, carrying on a conversation as if I weren't sitting two feet away.

"I'm not alone," Carlos was saying. "It will take me at least half an hour. I'm not dressed—no, it's only Anita. She's about to leave, and then I'll—"

Only Anita? I should've walked out right then, but I was curious who he was talking to.

"It's all right. I said I would. I have to go out to— Yes, I told you I could do that much. —No. Calm down. You know that's the paranoia talking. There is no reason to—" Carlos held the phone away from his ear and looked at it like he couldn't believe the person on the other end had hung up on him.

"Who was that?" I asked.

"No one you know." Carlos lied as if I hadn't heard him refer to me by name. "I'm sorry, I really have to get going now."

"Fine. But you should know that there's a new detective on the case, Michael Dougherty, and I already told him what you said about the Ecstasy dealing. I'm sure you'll hear from him soon."

"*Hija de puta*," Carlos swore. "What are you doing to me, Anita?"

"To you?" I was furious. "You tell me! Because Simon's

grandmother was murdered, too. Beaten up, her fingers broken. She was an incredibly talented artist—Helen Baum, maybe you've heard of her?"

Carlos frowned slightly, as if Helen's name meant something to him.

"The police found a lot more of that Ecstasy you bought, in her apartment. Whoever killed her was probably looking for it. So yeah, I told the detective. If you had any decency, you'd have done it yourself."

I put my hand on the doorknob.

Carlos stretched his arm out, holding the door so I couldn't open it.

"You have no idea what you're doing. You act like this is a game, stirring things up. Why couldn't you leave it alone?"

"Because two people were murdered, and I think whoever's responsible should be brought to justice." It sounded pompous even to my ears. "Simon died in my space. I worked right beside his dead body for a week and I didn't even realize he was there. His grandmother was a remarkable woman. Doesn't any of this mean anything to you?"

We stared at each other. There was a hostility I'd never seen before in his eyes.

Carlos lowered his arm and opened the door for me. "What I care about is my work. What other people do is their business and I'm trying like hell to stay out of it."

"Yeah, sure, whatever." I stepped into the hall. "If by some miracle you wake up and decide to rejoin the human race— you know, the one where people actually care about each other?—here's Detective Dougherty's number."

Carlos accepted the card I held out. Feeling encouraged, I hesitated, about to press my point.

"Go on now." Carlos swatted me on the backside as if I were a recalcitrant cow. "Go back to your husband before he finds out what you came here for."

I whirled around and hit him, an openhanded smack across the face. I did it without thought, before his words even registered. When they did, I was even more furious.

Carlos caught my hand before I could slap him again, and actually grinned at me. There was a vivid red blotch on his left cheek. "You know we can't keep on like this, *ANITA*."

"Why don't you—" speak a little louder so the whole building can hear, I was about to say, when I realized that that was exactly what he was doing.

Carlos was creating a scene, the romancer of married women shedding yet another of his lovers. Great, just great. I felt as betrayed as if I had been.

"I thought we were friends," I whispered, meaning it.

For a moment, I saw the Carlos I'd trusted. Then he went back inside, leaving me like a fool in the echoey hallway.

I was too humiliated to wait there for the elevator. I pushed through the fire door to the stairwell and sat on the top step to settle my battered nerves.

What on earth was that all about? Okay, so I was "only Anita," someone to pass the time with at lunch. No more to him than he was to me. So why the staged show of brushing me off? I was leaving anyway.

If this was how charm worked, it made Grant Farrell and his open passes look good. At least with the direct approach, you knew what you were dealing with. I was an idiot.

Carlos, Grant—I wasn't interested in them, and yet I'd been flirting like a horny teenager. I thought about heading for the luncheonette, but there was another one: Arsenio, always with a compliment to make me blush. Maybe I'd been married too long, spent too much time working with other women—I had no idea of how to relate to a man who wasn't my husband other than by engaging in that juvenile kind of sexual jousting.

Even with Michael, there was an edge to our friendship. I'd thought it was safe to carry on that way since I was married and had no intention of following through, but now it just seemed silly. Lighting matches, letting them burn until my fingers got singed, flicking them to the floor.

I pushed myself away from the wall and took the stairs down. By the second landing, I was over the outrageousness of Carlos's behavior enough to remember the phone call.

What was Carlos up to? Meeting someone somewhere. Probably a woman. Certainly none of my business.

I hesitated inside the stairwell, thinking I'd wait until he left the building and follow him.

Right, Anita, like he won't see you. And what if he goes out the side door again? I fished in my bag for a cigarette. Stall and think, always a good tactic. I had at least as long as it would take Carlos to shower.

The garbage truck parked across the street would provide perfect cover. From behind the big bumpers, I could see both exits and give him at least a block lead before I started walking. Real smart, me.

I pushed through the door to the street and smack into Grant Farrell's broad chest.

"Hey, Anita, leaving already? I was just hoping to catch you."

I thought fast. "Sorry, Grant, I'm meeting Benno at Papis and I'm late."

"No you're not." He wrapped an arm around my shoulders.

"I just saw Benno, and he's kind of tied up at the shop right now."

I didn't like the tone in his voice. When I looked at his face, I liked his expression even less. "What's wrong, Grant?"

"Nothing, now. I'm on my way to see Carlos. C'mon up with me."

"No, I can't. We didn't part on good terms, and if I never see Carlos again, it will be too soon." I still thought I was talking to a rational person, that I could joke my way out of the situation.

"Yeah, well, you'll have to get over that." Grant steered me toward the elevator. I decided not to resist until I knew what it was all about.

It was a mistake not to run while I had a shot at making it out of the building.

Thirty-eight

IN THE ELEVATOR, I NOTICED THAT GRANT HAD SOMETHING heavy in the right-hand pocket of his leather jacket. There was something about the shape of it that made me glad I hadn't tried to get away from him in the lobby. I didn't allow myself to name what I thought it was.

Grant tightened his grip on me while he pounded on Carlos's door. I thought about yelling, creating another scene in the hallway—not that anyone had noticed Carlos giving me the bum's rush ten minutes ago.

"Don't even think about it." Grant read my intentions reflected in the door mirror. He emphasized his words with a jab from his pocketed right hand. I kept still. A lifetime of training in not making waves doesn't get overthrown in a minute, and besides, I couldn't have gotten away without a struggle.

"Just a moment," Carlos called. "Who's there?"

As if he couldn't tell from his side of the two-way mirror—what was going on?

"It's me! Open the damn door." Grant kicked it.

"He was just getting in the shower when I left," I explained.

Grant crushed me against his chest with his elbow and put a hand over my mouth. "Shut the hell up and knock again," he told me.

I did. It felt as if I were being held in a vise. I tried to pat his arm, meaning to convey that he could relax the pressure, I wasn't going to run. Grant's response was to force my arm down by digging his elbow into my ribs and pushing me in front of him.

"I'll be right there," Carlos said.

That got another booted foot against the bottom of the door. "Right now, man!"

I figured Carlos was stalling—he had a clear view of Grant holding me captive. The question was, what would he do about it? Call the cops, I thought. Please, Carlos, call the cops. This isn't the time to play coy.

There was the sound of three locks clicking open, then the door swung wide. Grant let go of my mouth and shoved me hard into Carlos. The momentum propelled us toward the folded futon, which broke our fall. Grant slammed the door with a backward kick.

"Sit up," he ordered.

We did.

I know from nothing about guns. What Grant had pointed at us was shaped like a miniature skull with a single round eye and a square jaw. It looked like the devil, ready to send me right to hell. I realized my lips were moving in a Hail Mary. There are no atheists on the wrong end of a gun.

"Hey, take it easy." Carlos rose in a single graceful motion and took a step toward Grant.

Grant pointed the gun at Carlos's chest. I drew in a breath.

There was no shot, just Carlos falling backward onto the futon.

I started breathing again.

Carlos scrambled back to a sitting position. "I thought you needed money, Grant. I was just on my way out to the bank."

Grant scratched his forehead with the back of the hand holding the gun.

I found there was something very focusing about the presence of a firearm. I knew exactly where it was at all times. My thoughts were concentrated in the moment, and yet there was a whole other back channel of disbelief that kept up a running commentary.

Of course, I've thought about getting shot. I mean, I've lived in New York for more than ten years; I know people who've been victims of gun violence both random and personal. I always believed that if it happened to me, it would be as unpredictable as a car accident—a matter of wrong place, wrong moment in time. If a gun were ever aimed at me, I assumed I'd do what Benno had the one time he was mugged: hand over the money.

I operated under the assumption that whoever had the gun would know that firing it would lead to certain capture. In other words, I figured that even a lawbreaker would exercise common sense and not carry through with a losing plan of action. Now that the hypothetical had become actual, I had no such faith in Grant's rationality. Would a sane person have gone as far down a self-defeating path as this?

The evil eye was watching me again. More than anything, I didn't want it to blink.

Grant was rocking on his heels, for all the world like he was *davening* in prayer. His head bobbed up and down, nodding to himself. Tweaking, Carlos's word came back to me.

Grant was looking like a sure bet for a meth user. That would up the chances of him being in on the clandestine lab— along with his friend Richard, who'd bought all that cough medicine loaded with pseudoephedrine, and maybe Simon and the Hasidic man Carlos had sketched.

Unless Carlos was involved himself, and he'd made up the Hasidic partner to throw me off. Because why else wouldn't he have gone to the police? Whether he used the stuff or not, Carlos was acting like he and Grant were in cahoots.

Which meant what we had here was a falling out between drug users.

All this occurred to me in a matter of seconds. My brain felt as if it were on a contact high from Grant. He'd taken a few steps backward so he was standing against the door. Although he had the gun aimed in our direction, he kept looking around the room, as if he was hoping to locate the answer to an intractable problem.

I figured he probably had no more idea what to do next than I did.

I glanced over at Carlos. He didn't look back at me, but he moved his hand slightly to cover mine, and squeezed reassuringly.

Okay, I thought, if you've got a plan, count me in. I sure wasn't coming up with a way to talk us out of here. I squeezed back.

"Grant. Do you want the money or not?"

"Yeah, we'll get to that. Shut up a minute and let me think."

"Would you like to wait here while I get it?"

What about me? I wanted to wail, but I had the sense to keep my mouth shut.

Grant flipped his wrist back and forth, so the gun wavered between me and Carlos, Carlos and me.

"Okay, here's the plan. You got some duct tape or rope or something around here?"

"There is a roll of masking tape on the table," Carlos said helpfully.

Gee, thanks.

"Tape her up."

Grant allowed Carlos to fetch the tape. He knelt in front of me. I held my hands out, wrists together, the obedient captive.

"Behind her back, idiot," Grant kicked out at Carlos.

I moved my arms. Carlos came around behind me, so my body was between him and the gun. I felt him place something small and sharp in the palm of my right hand. I ran my thumb around the edge and identified it as the pointed blade from an X-Acto knife. I held it carefully while the tape went around and around and around.

"That enough?"

Grant walked over to examine the mitts Carlos had made of my hands. "Yeah. Do her ankles, too. You got a belt?"

"In the closet."

"What are you going to do with me, Grant?" I didn't intend to be trussed like a chicken without knowing why.

The gun whirled on me. "Shut your damn mouth."

I did. Absolutely.

"How long have you been up, Grant?" Carlos asked.

"Monday, Tuesday, what's today?" Grant shrugged. "I'm fine. Never been better. Okay, get the belt. I want her strapped to the chair. Yeah, around the waist."

When Carlos helped me up, I could tell that a few hard jerks with my legs would rip through the masking tape around my ankles. If you ever have to be bound, get a friend to do the tying up.

Belted to the chair, I started to feel better about my chances for survival. Why go to the trouble of having Carlos immobilize me if he was going to shoot me? I thought about Helen Baum's broken fingers. Whatever Grant wanted from me, he could have.

"You both have cards that work in the ATM at "D" Space, right?"

We did.

"Where's yours?" Grant asked me.

"In my wallet."

"Get it," Grant ordered Carlos. "What's your PIN?"

"Four-two-four-two-four-two."

Carlos wrote it down without being told to.

Grant took a cell phone out of his pocket and used his thumb to punch in a number. "Get your butt up here. Four B, yeah, Four B."

"The most we can get from the ATM is five hundred each," Carlos said. "Will a thousand be enough?"

Very obliging, that Carlos. Pandering to Grant, providing me with the means to set myself free. What was his part in all this?

"Thanks for your concern, bro. With what I got from Benno, I've got enough to get set up again."

"Benno? What did you do to Benno?"

"Do?" Grant nodded, up and down, up and down. "Do? Not a whole lot. Can you believe your husband thought I didn't know he kept cash in the shop? Some people. Twenty-four hundred in that chess table. Pretty smart, right?"

I started to work the blade into a usable position.

"Did you hurt him?" Now I knew what truly scared felt like.

Grant grinned at me, still nodding his head. "He was all wound up in duct tape the last time I saw him."

I had an image of Benno as a silver-wrapped Egyptian mummy. If only he could breathe!

"I don't know what you think you're doing, Grant. You'll

never get away with this. The police already know about the meth lab, and Simon selling Ecstasy, and Jacob—"

Carlos jabbed me in the back, hard.

Grant stopped nodding and steadied the gun so it was aimed at Carlos again.

Thirty-nine

"YOU WENT TO THE COPS?"

"No." Carlos stood very still. "She's just making wild guesses."

I knew Carlos was on my side, really, I did. I knew Carlos knew more about what this was all about than I did. I knew I should leave it to Carlos to finesse the situation and get us out unharmed.

I knew all that. I clamped my lips together so I wouldn't blow it.

"Why don't we go out for the money so you can get on the road?"

"We? You think I'm a dumb hick from the sticks, right? No, no, no, Señor Sanchez, I'm a man with a plan, and you are not part of it."

"Tell us about your plan, Grant," I chipped in.

Now that wicked round eye was staring at me. Yeah, I closed my mouth.

"For Christ sake, shut your trap."

Carlos gripped my shoulder. He couldn't have said it better himself.

"Tape her mouth, Carlos. Stupid New York women, they always have to put their two cents' worth in. This isn't about anyone getting hurt, so don't piss me off!"

Carlos slapped a strip of tape across my cheeks. He didn't look too happy with me, but he had the presence of mind to wrap the tape around the back of my head, where it didn't stick very well to my hair. I could tell I'd be able to slide it off by rubbing my cheek against my shoulder.

If Grant would just get the hell out of here and leave us alone—I was ready to start sawing at the tape. One step at a time. Benno—Clea—don't go there, Anita. You're going to survive this, that's the only option.

I was looking at the door when Richard's face appeared in the hallway outside. He checked out his reflection, exactly the way I had. He straightened the collar of the letter jacket and shrugged his shoulders to settle it more comfortably.

I prayed Grant wouldn't turn around, see Richard, and realize that Carlos hadn't been taken by surprise earlier. Because I was really, really hoping Carlos had used the minute he'd stalled to call for help.

I grunted and rocked forward just as Richard knocked.

Grant put the muzzle of the gun in my right ear. "Open the door! Right now, or Anita gets it."

I froze, just literally froze. The ocean roared in my head. Men were talking, and I couldn't understand a word.

A lifetime later, Grant stepped back. He took the gun with him. My heart slowed down.

"Okay, tear up that sheet," Grant told Richard. "You, in the bathroom." He herded Carlos along with the gun.

Unpredictable, erratic behavior. Four days into a meth binge. I couldn't believe Grant had seemed so normal a few short hours ago.

Now that I was breathing again, I was actually glad my mouth was taped closed. No chance I'd blurt out anything else to set him off. Or Richard, who was going at Carlos's striped top sheet with remarkable energy.

He took two long strips along with him into the bathroom.

From the sound of it, Grant was making Carlos lie facedown in the tub so Richard could tie his hands and feet together behind his back. "Good job, Dickie. Trust a farm boy to know how to hog-tie a man."

Richard laughed. Could have been wishful thinking on my part, but it seemed to me he sounded more nervous than pleased by the compliment. He stepped back into the studio and we both listened to Grant taking a leak.

I tried to get Richard to look at me, hoping even then to influence his better nature. Not only wouldn't he glance my way, but he was doing the same kind of impatient, balls-of-the-foot bounce as Grant had. Tweakers on a binge. I offered up another Hail Mary.

"Okay, eventually one of you will get loose." Grant came out zipping up his jeans. "No harm done and no hard feelings, right?"

Yeah, right.

Grant walked over to me and bent down to whisper in my ear. "Simon dying was his own damn fault. I'm not a bad guy, I just cleaned up the mess."

Gee, thanks for telling me that.

Grant patted me on the head. "Sit tight and this'll be over soon."

He slid the gun back in his pocket. Richard already had the door open, and they were gone.

Damn if I didn't have to pee myself.

Forty

I FIGURED OUT RIGHT AWAY THAT I COULD NOT MANEUVER THE X-Acto blade at the same time I was trying to rub the tape away from my mouth and kicking my feet to break them free. First things first, Anita. It took an agonizingly long time to apply enough pressure to cut through the tape around my wrists.

By the time I succeeded, my hands were damp with blood from dozens of tiny slashes.

I unbuckled the belt, ripped my ankles free, and dealt with my mouth on the way to the bathroom for Carlos.

Hog-tied. It was an ugly thing. There was a sock stuffed in Carlos's mouth, and I got that out first.

"I'm sorry, Anita, I am really sorry. I never thought Grant—"

"Shut up or I'll leave you here." I was frantic to get across the street to Benno; fury at Carlos could wait.

When I saw how the strips of sheet were knotted, I went to retrieve the blade that had freed me. It took three slices to cut him loose. The Gordian knot solution, still effective after all these years.

"You call 911. I'm going to Benno," I told him.

I took the blade with me and ran for the door.

And straight into Michael Dougherty, who stopped me with an arm no less imprisoning than Grant's had been.

"Let me go!" I pounded on his chest and scraped the back of my hand on the butt of a gun in a shoulder holster.

"Benno's fine." Michael held me by the elbows. "Benno's fine, Anita. Come on, I'll show you."

I stopped fighting and Michael opened the door to the stairwell for me. I ran, not waiting for him, bouncing off the wall as I turned the corners of the landings.

"Hey, Social Worker, hold up! Rate you're going, you'll be in worse shape than your husband!" Michael was right behind me.

I burst into the lobby. There were at least four uniforms and a pair of paramedics. No Benno among them.

Michael had me by the arm again. I tried to jerk away.

"Slow down, he's right outside. A little duct tape residue and a bruised shoulder, that's all."

There were two ambulances parked on the street, one with its back doors open. Benno was sitting on the bumper with his chin up so someone could dab at it with an alcohol swab. Not that that would do anything to remove the adhesive, I thought inconsequentially.

I stood on the sidewalk, so full of joy at the sight of my husband that I didn't even need to touch him just yet.

As soon as Benno saw me, though, I was in his arms. We stayed like that while the sun set and rose, set and rose, and people in all sorts of uniforms swarmed around on the street.

When I started shaking, a female paramedic peeled me away from Benno and into the ambulance where she wrapped me in a blanket and made me lie down.

Benno held my hand while she did the blood pressure thing.

"I need to pee." I sat up.

"She'll live, Brenda," Benno said. "Can I take her to the bathroom in the shop?"

Paramedic Brenda pretended she didn't like it much. "You oughta stay lying down for a little longer, but—just come right back, okay?"

We promised.

They had Carlos in the back of the other ambulance, Michael standing over him.

The freight door to our building was up, so we took the elevator. I don't know if I could have climbed the four flights. I kept an arm around Benno's waist, my thumb tucked into a belt loop. No way I was letting go.

Well, except when I got to the toilet.

Once one floodgate opened, they all seemed to. Benno heard me sobbing and opened the door. He perched on the magazine rack and held me until I realized my pants were around my ankles and my butt was getting cold.

I pushed him away and tried to regain my dignity by pulling up my britches from a sitting position. It was so ludicrous, we both started laughing.

"Anybody in here?" Michael's voice, who the hell else?

Benno warded him off so I could get decent.

"We're having a little statement party over at the Eighty-fourth Precinct, and you're all invited."

"That's all right," Benno said, trying to make it casual. "No need to put yourself out on our account, we'll just head on home."

Michael wasn't amused. "Actually, invited was just a figure of speech. Your friend Carlos is already on his way over there. I figured you'd rather ride with me than in a squad."

"Did you get Grant and Richard?" It didn't occur to me until that minute to ask the more obvious question. "What are you even doing here? How did you know—?"

"Forget about home, Benno," Michael advised. "The missus here won't rest until she's had the whole story."

"You got that right," Benno agreed. He ushered us into the freight elevator and took it down. "There's a few things I wouldn't mind knowing myself."

It was me he was looking at when he said it. Honestly, I didn't think I'd held anything back from him this time.

"So how did you know to come?" Just in case, I changed the subject.

"That artist fellow, Carlos, got me on my cell. The cavalry woulda been here sooner except all he told me was to see Benno so I could have a look across into his place from over here. Nice show you folks put on."

"How did you get into the building?" Benno asked.

Michael grinned. "Same way everybody does. Pushed all the buzzers and someone came down and let me in." We stepped into the sunlit street and stopped to let our eyes adjust. "Good thing for you the guy didn't lock the shop when he left."

"What did Grant do to you?" I moved out from Benno's arm so I could see all of him. The skin on his cheeks was already red from where the adhesive duct tape had been pulled away. One arm of his black T-shirt had been cut so to reveal a well-muscled shoulder. My husband the hunk.

"Got me to give him all the cash I had on hand, then ducttaped me to a chair." Benno shrugged. "I looked like one of Clea's art projects."

"Your shoulder?" I touched it gently.

"I was trying to reach a chisel to cut through the tape on my wrists, and I fell. It's just a bruise."

A light breeze blew across from the river. I shivered. Just a bruise. Tied up and staring into a gun. It was nothing, really, nothing at all.

Forty-one

ALL POLICE STATIONS MAY NOT BE THE SAME ON THE OUTSIDE—
Brooklyn's Eighty-fourth Precinct was a modern mocha
brick—but the interior had the same indestructible ivory tile
walls and blue-painted doors as the Twenty-sixth Precinct in
Manhattan. The front entrance, however, was swagged in
black bunting above photographs of the two dozen officers
missing since September 11. A tide of flowers, candles, flags,
and stuffed animals had washed up alongside the adjacent fire-
house.

We civilians were put in a less-than-nondescript room on the
second floor where a skinny cop with Ingala on his name tag
brought us cups of coffee. Benno took a sip of his, black, then
laced mine with sugar and nondairy whitener. Ingala hauled a
chair away from the table, sat himself off to the side of the
room, and tried to pretend he wasn't there to keep an eye on us.

Not that we had anything to say to each other at that point.
No one had bothered to pull the shade over the window in the
door and we could see clusters of people, both uniforms and
not, in the hallway. There was no way to sort out who was in
charge or what was happening.

Presumably Grant and Richard were locked up somewhere
in the building. Presumably Michael would come talk to us as
soon as he could. Presumably we'd get to leave in time to be
home for Clea. I checked my watch. Not even two o'clock in
the afternoon. If nothing had happened by three, I decided I'd

raise sand with Ingala over there, sitting with his chair tipped
back on two legs.

Benno made me drink the coffee. "It's hot and sweet, Anita,
you need to get some liquid into you."

I swallowed a mouthful. "Battery acid with sugar is still battery acid," I told him.

That got me a smile. I glanced over at Ingala. No sign he'd
heard.

Benno shrugged. "What's going on?" he asked the cop.

"Detective said to sit with you folks. Coffee was my idea."
He brought the front legs of the chair down to the floor. "If it's
too strong, I could get youse sodas instead."

"No, it's fine," Benno answered for us both. "But maybe
you could find out how long we'll be here?"

"We've got a twelve-year-old who gets home from school at
four," I chimed in.

Ingala nodded and stood up. It was like watching one of those
folding wooden tape measures open, a matter of segments
aligning themselves. He had to be six-five at least. "Yeah, okay.
Lemme see if they got anything to say."

Alone at last, and what were the first words out of Benno's
mouth?

"What were you doing at Carlos's?"

Now that we were safe, the jealous male lurking in even the
most trusting of husbands had to ask.

Tempted as I was to snap back with something about afternoon delight, I'm not entirely stupid. "I did some Internet research on crystal meth. It's easy to make, but it leaves a lot of
chemical waste. I thought the space next to the spray room
might have been used as a clandestine lab. It's the perfect
setup—isolated, industrial, big sink, electricity. So I went over

to Carlos's to warn him that he should have the walls tested for toxic residue."

"What are you talking about, a meth factory? And we didn't notice?"

"Why would we? They worked mostly at night, and it wasn't going on for very long."

"And you think Carlos—"

The door opened. There was the man in question, Michael right behind him. Ingala followed with a chair. He set it down by the table and Michael gestured for Carlos to sit.

"What's going on, Michael?" I asked.

"I'll be back in a few minutes."

"No." Benno stood up. "We haven't broken any laws, and we don't have to be here right now. We came as a favor to you, and unless you tell us what's up, we're going home."

"I'm sorry, Benno." Michael raked a hand over his hair. "I don't exactly know myself. We got six different jurisdictions wanting to hear what you have to say, and I'm waiting for someone to locate a tape recorder so you only have to say it once. Bear with me a little longer, okay?"

Benno sat down.

"Clea's due home in a couple hours," I said. "Do you think you'll be done with us before then?"

"I'll try my best."

In the silence after he left the room, Benno and I looked at Carlos. He kept his head down, watching his long fingers drum on the table.

"So, Carlos, Anita tells me you were making methamphetamines in our building," Benno said.

Ingala didn't move, but there was a change in the quality of his alertness, as if the hairs on his arms stood at attention.

I nudged Benno and nodded in his direction. Carlos followed my gaze.

"No, I wasn't," he said, his voice shaky. "As I told your wife, uppers don't interest me."

"But you knew Grant was," I said. "And Richard, too, right?"

Carlos shook his head. "I'm very sorry about what happened, Anita. I know I hurt your feelings. I wanted you to leave before Grant came." He looked directly at me. "When he brought you back—I did call the detective."

So that's what the lovers' quarrel scene was all about. I supposed Carlos had done his best; it was my fault I'd gotten involved, asking questions and jumping to conclusions without knowing all the facts.

"Thanks for using masking tape," I said. "And the X-Acto." I turned to Benno, intending to explain how Carlos had provided me with the means to cut myself loose. The look on his face shut me right up.

My husband was pissed. Not without reason, either. It wasn't the first or even the second time I'd been in a police station for questioning in a criminal matter after a narrow escape from danger, and I'd just confirmed that this occasion wasn't any more accidental than the others had been.

"Save it for the tape, Anita," he said. "I don't even want to hear it."

I almost heard Ingala's antennae lower themselves. He glanced at the large mirror on the far wall. We'd all been ignoring it, acting like we weren't guppies in a fishbowl.

We sat in silence until Michael reappeared, tape recorder under his arm. He nodded at Ingala, who unfolded himself and said, "Gentlemen, if you'll just come with me, please."

Carlos stood.

Benno didn't. "I'm not going anywhere."

Ingala looked to Michael for instructions.

"Outside the holding pen is the only place there's room to sit. Don't let them talk to anyone." Then to Benno, gently, "You all have to be interviewed separately. I'll get you as soon as I'm done with Anita." And to Carlos, "You say a word to anyone in the cells, I'll have you locked up. There's not going to be any getting stories straight in advance, you hear me?"

Carlos shrugged a shoulder.

"No," Benno repeated. "Either I stay or Anita's not talking to you without a lawyer."

"I want him to be here," I said, trying to make nice. "I don't have anything to hide."

"That's not the point." Michael stared at the mirror as if it would tell him what to do. "Ah, hell. Tell you what, Benno, I'll take your statement first. When we're done, you can stay while Anita does hers. That's the best I can do."

Benno and I nodded in unison.

"Okay. Ingala, get Mr. Sanchez out of here. And send someone for Ms. Servi, would you?"

Two people came in before the door closed behind Carlos. One was your standard-issue plainclothes cop: male, white, middle-aged, muscular but starting a paunch, short hair going gray, expressionless face. Wearing a navy-blue zippered jacket with a big white NYPD on the back, which he shed and draped over the back of the chair Ingala had been sitting on. Michael didn't introduce him.

The other was a young black woman in uniform, who nodded for me to follow her out of the room. Brown was the name on her tag.

What can Brown do for you, I thought. Nice. All this going

on and I had ad slogans on the brain. Show me to the women's room turned out to be what she did for me. Then the locker room, where we sat on a narrow bench and she squelched my feeble attempt at conversation.

"Were you there when they—"

"I don't mean to be rude, ma'am, but I really can't say anything."

Sir, ma'am. They must teach them to talk like that in cop school. Manners used as a show of deference to put you in your place while making it clear who's really in charge.

I used the time to go over the events of the past weeks and try to put them in some sort of logical order. Simon using, selling, smuggling drugs. Diamonds, art, teenage lovers. Orthodox Jews and Jehovah's Witnesses. Grant, Jacob, Dovid Fine, Richard, Leah. I had more questions than answers. Why Simon and Helen were killed, that was the biggest.

Michael elicited my story by the book, calling me Ms. Servi sprinkled with plenty of ma'ams as he took me through the day in chronological order. I began with shopping at the green market on 116th Street, my subway ride to Brooklyn and what I read about clandestine meth labs on the way, then coffee at "D" Space, seeing Grant and Richard together, what Grant and I talked about—that we went over twice—then the shop, my failure at sanding shelves, my discovery that the same key opened both spaces on the third floor.

At that point, I glanced over at Benno. He was looking at me as if I were certifiable. Michael's expression wasn't much better, but after the second time I repeated that I'd gone downstairs out of habit and tried the keys on impulse, he moved on.

I'd been through this kind of statement before, and I knew enough to be abjectly apologetic about not calling him the

instant it occurred to me that the space had been used to manufacture crystal meth. Michael waved my admissions of criminal stupidity aside. Benno had his eyes closed and was visibly
counting to ten.

Then we got to the scene at Carlos's place. I didn't realize I'd
reached for Benno's hand until I came to the part where Grant
had forced me to go back upstairs. Benno squeezed my fingers,
all his attention now on helping me tell what happened. I took
a deep breath and described the gun, Carlos slipping me the
X-Acto blade while he bound my wrists with masking tape.
Might as well put in a good word for him; I had a feeling he'd
need it.

The whole time, I was braced for Michael to ask about the
sequence of events that had led me to the baths, the conversation with Irina and what she'd revealed about Jacob and Ecstasy. I'd told Benno none of that. He'd be counting up into the
thousands to keep his cool when it came out.

But Michael didn't go there. He made me repeat what Carlos and Grant had said to each other three times, each rendi-
tion virtually the same, until Benno put a stop to it.

"That's enough, Detective." Two could play at formal. "I'm
taking my wife home now."

My hero, I thought. Home was where I wanted to be.

I SPENT THE NEXT TWO DAYS ON THE COUCH READING MYSTER-
ies, historicals set in ancient Rome, in a world before airplanes
and towers and vacuum presses. They kept the present at bay
until Sunday afternoon when Benno decided that we should
do as the mayor urged and spend money in the city.

"That's a new one, you agreeing with Giuliani," I said.

"Actually, there are two things the mayor and I are in ac-
cord on."

I waited for the punch line.

"Term limits. I grant you Giuliani rose to the occasion after
the eleventh, but he showed his true colors with the whole
waffle routine about changing the law so he could run for a
third term. Eight years of Rudy and his comb-over is enough."

Benno made a few phone calls and found that tickets were
available for *The Fantasticks*. It being my favorite day of the
year, the one when they give back the hour of daylight saving
time they steal from us in the spring, I put on a good face and
went along with my family. What better way to be cheered up
than by the oldest story in the world—boy meets girl, boy
loses girl, boy gets girl?

But the tears started with the first words of *"Try to remember, the kind of September, when life was . . ."* In fairness, it
wasn't just me. The words had a resonance that hadn't been
there in the show's forty-plus-year run until this particular
September. The audience seemed to stop breathing for a moment while the cast sang with a catch in their collective
throats. It got better from there; Clea and Benno laughed out
loud at some of it, but my eyes stayed damp.

Young love seemed so impossibly hopeful.

Forty-two

MONDAY MORNING, I MUSTERED THE STRENGTH TO MAKE A shiva call on Helen's behalf. I forced myself to put on clothes and get out in the world, away from murder mysteries and soap operas. Navigating the intricate subway route was just what I needed. By the time I hit Lee Avenue, I was back to feeling like a competent adult. I stopped at the bakery and bought a chocolate *babka* to take to the house.

A woman I didn't know opened the door and accepted the pink box. This time there were no men smoking on the front stoop, no coat rack in the hall. The dining room was as it had been before, though, the table laden with coffee and sweets. Ruth sat on a low bench in the center of the room with Zehava beside her. Several young women clustered in a corner, talking quietly together. I knelt to offer my condolences.

"Thank you," Ruth replied. "It was good of you to come."

I'd been dreading Esther Swersky, and was relieved that neither she nor Leah was present. I didn't recognize any of the other women, and none of them spoke to me other than to offer coffee and a slice of cake. I accepted both.

My presence seemed to have drained all sound from the room. I didn't stay long. Ruth herself saw me to the door.

"I know it's too soon for you to think about your mother's affairs. I'm going to start with what I have to do—will you let me know when you're ready?" I took both Ruth's hands in mine.

She returned my grip for a brief second before withdrawing hers. "Yes, thank you. I will call."

And I was on the street again, looking both ways to see if a young Jehovah's Witness was lurking in the neighborhood.

But no, Richard Linden was currently residing at Rikers Island. I trekked over to Swersky's Drug. Leah was behind the counter. I wanted to shake her, to demand: What did you know and when did you know it? Why didn't you *tell* someone?

I waited at the counter until she looked up. The misery and remorse in her expression were so evident that I didn't have the heart to confront her.

"Were you really in love with Richard?" I asked.

She nodded. "I didn't know about the drugs he made. Shimon—Richard came here with him, the first time. Shimon helped us to see each other. When I took the Ecstasy, everything was so clear. I knew what to do. Here." She pressed a hand to her heart and looked up at me. "I was going to go with Richard. Then Shimon . . ."

Leah's already pale skin went whiter. She gripped the edge of the counter and bowed her head. "*Hashem* forgive me, I didn't know."

Maybe she did, maybe she didn't.

The police had been through her cell phone records as well as Richard's. The young lovers had spoken daily for the past two months, with a spike in frequency that corresponded to the day Simon died and ended completely when his body was identified.

Michael, of course, had interviewed Leah—at her home, in the presence of her father and an extremely competent attorney. According to what he told me, Leah had admitted to a relationship with Richard, albeit one that went no further than the cell phone conversations and an occasional meeting in the drugstore while she was working.

"Oh, yeah, and once a soda at someplace just outside the neighborhood," Michael had snorted. "An innocent little miss, my left toe. But I couldn't get to her without the father, and no way she was going to cop to anything having to do with drugs in front of him. Richard didn't give me anything to go on, either, so that's the end of it for little Leah Swersky."

Well, she'd just admitted to taking Ecstasy. Either way, I felt sorry for her.

"Do you know what will happen to him?"

Did she really care? I searched her face and found genuine remorse—whether it was for Simon, or Richard, or the way life had closed in around her again, I couldn't tell. Leah was a young woman from a strict background who had tested the waters of a wider world and found herself in over her head. It looked to me like she'd opted for the safe harbor of community and custom. I figured I'd help her to stay there.

"He'll spend some time in prison, but they don't know how much yet. Detective Dougherty said Richard is making a deal with the district attorney's office. He admitted to manufacturing and selling methamphetamine, and to covering up Shimon's death." I hesitated, then decided why not give it all to her. Whatever Leah's role was, she could at least answer to her conscience and her own God for not speaking up soon enough to maybe have prevented Helen's death.

"Richard claimed Shimon was dead before they hid his body, but according to the autopsy that wasn't true. If they'd taken him to the hospital—but they had the meth lab to protect, so they got Shimon out of the way and went on cooking up their drugs. Do you know what happened to Shimon? What a vacuum press does?"

I was suddenly angry with this sheltered young woman. I wanted Leah to see Simon's body as I had.

"The press is like a flat tabletop inside a plastic bag that gets sealed at both ends. There's a motor that sucks all the air out, so the bag presses down on whatever's inside of it. Your sweetheart Richard and his buddy Grant Farrell took Shimon's clothes off, everything but the tzitzis, and stuffed him into the bag. They turned the motor on, and after all the air was gone it sucked the fluids out of Shimon's body, sucked until blood was running out of his nose, his mouth, his ears, even his eyes were . . ."

Leah sank back onto the stool behind the counter, her hands pressed over her ears, and started to cry.

Good, you suffer too, I thought. Then the anger drained out of me. I bore a measure of responsibility for Helen's death myself, and there was no excuse for me to lash out at Leah like that.

A cup of coffee, a *profiterole*—it happened in all innocence, but my big mouth had provided Grant with the crucial link between Simon and his grandmother. Once he knew Helen Baum's name, Grant was able to get her address. He passed the information on to Jacob, providing him with place to look for Simon's supply of Ecstasy.

I walked behind the cash register, put my arms around Leah, and patted her back until she quieted. I had a daughter of my own, and I prayed she'd have more sense than to get tangled up with trouble the way Leah had.

What hope was there? You raise a girl in an insular community, away from television and movies and navel rings, and still the world reaches in for her. Richard, Simon—on the surface, clean-cut polite young men. Drugs and danger were everywhere in this world.

"I'm sure you'll find your real *bashert* soon," I told her. "Everything's going to be all right."

A pregnant woman no older than Leah entered the store, and I left the young woman to wait on her future.

I rode the subway back to Manhattan, thinking that Leah would be married with half a dozen children before Richard got out of prison.

Grant wouldn't get off as lightly as Richard but he'd be out well before he qualified for Social Security. He'd also been allowed to plea bargain—to the manufacture and sale of crystal meth, and to manslaughter for his role in Simon Edelman's death. In exchange for which he'd agreed to testify against Jacob Stern for drug smuggling, distribution, and torturing Helen Baum.

Her death had evidently been due to a heart attack precipitated by being beaten and having her fingers broken. Michael didn't know yet exactly what degree of murder they'd be charging Jacob with, but it was unlikely to be first degree.

As closure, it wasn't very satisfying.

"Yeah, it sucks," Michael had agreed. "Nobody, me included, has much patience for dealers right now, but hey, crime goes on. Proving either death was intentional—the D.A. didn't want to risk it. At least we cleaned up one pocket of illegal drugs."

A drop in the bucket. Jacob's arrest had resulted in the arrests of ten Orthodox boys—his retail distributors. "A minyan of dealers," Benno had joked. "Pushers who pray together pay together?"

.   .   .

IT WAS DEEP IN DECEMBER BEFORE I SAW RUTH BAUM EDELMAN again. We met at her mother's brownstone so she could go through Helen's personal effects with me.

"There are charities I would like to donate her things to, if that would be all right with the estate," Ruth said when she finally called me.

I had some idea of how Helen would feel about Orthodox women wearing her clothes and eating off her dishes, but it was a decision for the living to make. "Help would be nice," I told Ruth.

We met on a Tuesday after lunch and began in the bedroom. We sorted everything into piles: rags, charity, and a few things Ruth chose for a memorial quilt. Our talk was all about decisions, filling bags. Ruth wanted none of the costume jewelry, so I put aside several necklaces I thought Janis would like to take apart for the beads. We worked like that until four, when I suggested tea.

The kitchen table and chairs were gone—to the gallery that was restoring the Martha Wolfes, where they'd be exhibited and sold. Ruth faced the sink, counted out the steps to the hidden compartment, and lifted up the removable section of flooring. It was empty. Ruth looked a question a me.

"The jewelry is in a bank safe deposit box," I said. "Is chamomile tea okay?"

"That's fine." She replaced the floorboards. "There were thirty of my grandfather's stones left, you know. My mother gave them to my husband so he could buy that building and have his own business. I didn't know until after she died."

"Your husband didn't tell you?"

"No." Ruth shook her head. "No, he didn't."

I didn't press her for a reason, but there was something else I was curious about. "Whose jewelry was it, the rings and earrings?"

Ruth frowned. "It must have been my grandmother's. I don't know, I only saw it once, years ago, when my mother showed me the hiding place."

Another mystery, I thought. Lost to the past, along with the family left behind in Russia when Helen's father financed his new life with stolen diamonds. The kettle chirped like a bird. I picked it up and poured.

"Would you show me her studio?" Ruth asked.

"Of course."

We carried our mugs of tea up the stairs and I unlocked the door.

The ambient glow from the street filled the large north windows and illuminated the studio. It was a beautiful light, like being inside an empty gray pearl. Ruth stood in the doorway.

Helen's paintings had all been crated and taken away. The easel with Simon's work-in-progress was still there, draped with the dark cloth.

"Would you like to see your son's work?"

"My son's—?" She followed my gaze to the shrouded easel and shook her head. "Not now."

She walked the perimeter of the room, pausing at both front and rear windows.

"Does the building have to be sold?"

The question put both of us in our places. No longer two women packing up the belongings of someone who'd passed away, we were executor and heir.

"That's really up to you."

"Me?" Ruth looked as if she had no idea what I meant.

"Yes. Your mother didn't specify who would inherit if Shimon died before she did, so as her next of kin, what would have gone to him is yours. Didn't Grace Davis, your mother's attorney, explain it to you?"

"I—I'm sure she did, but—I didn't realize . . ." Ruth looked dazed. "Are you saying that the house will be mine?"

"The renters have lifetime tenancy, but yes, the building is yours." I could see it already, the rooms occupied by Orthodox Jews, Helen rolling over in her grave.

"What will you do with it?" I asked. From the smile on Ruth's face, I surmised she was thinking the same thing: finally, a chance to stick it to her mother. I was wrong.

"I'd like to establish a quilting workshop." She gestured around the room. "Good north light for the cutting table. Three machines and the ironing boards on this side, and still plenty of room for quilting frames. In front of the south windows, comfortable chairs for the hand sewing. I know several women who will work with me."

So Helen's studio would remain a place where art was made. In a city bereft of happy endings, it was a start.

JUN -- 2004